THE TALK SHOW

HARRY VERITY

Print ISBN 978-1-913942-30-4

'There's the granddad who pawned his wife's jewellery to fund his crack habit and has been disowned by the rest of the family...'

Edward could hear a discussion taking place behind the production gallery door. They were female voices. He knocked.

'No, we've had enough old bags on the show... next.'

No response.

'There's a man with an addiction to dog food, wife left him...'

'Imagine. We'd save a fortune putting him up in doggy daycare rather than a hotel...'

Edward could wait no longer. He prized open the door and slid in.

There were indeed two women inside the cramped room, both sat around a rickety-looking desk. One was white-haired, short and casually smoking a cigarette. The other was taller and a lot younger, sporting pink jeans and a white cardigan; she wouldn't have looked out of place in a fashion catalogue.

'Hello,' Edward said. 'Is this the *Michael O'Shea Show*? I'm the new junior researcher...'

But before he could proceed any further with his introduction, the elder woman's phone rang. She picked it up straight away.

'What! Oh, fucking hell!' She marched to the back of the small room and turned on a desktop computer. She tapped the mouse impatiently as she waited for it to load up and then scrolled straight to the home page of *The Lion* newspaper.

The younger woman – who could only have been in her early twenties, Edward's age – picked up her moleskin notebook and followed the elder woman to the computer monitor. Edward huddled in too, trying to get a glimpse of the headline that had been posted just minutes ago:

TV MICHAEL IN FAMILY PAEDO ARREST

-O'Shea 'on the rocks' after brother 'bang to rights' for sex crimes
-Family yet to make statement
-Fears O'Shea will return to the bottle

There were shocking scenes today as the brother of controversial talk show host and celebrity judge Michael O'Shea was sensationally arrested and charged with viewing indecent images of children on the web and sexually abusing his neighbour's son. Phillip O'Shea, 36, the younger brother of the embattled presenter, is a regular guest on the show. He was taken from his home at dawn to a police station where he was allegedly questioned for just twenty minutes before he was charged with being in possession of over five hundred indecent images of children and three counts of indecent assault against a minor, aged nine.

'Yes. Yes, it's Mags.' The elder woman, Mags, was still on the phone. 'Yeah, get over here ASAP. We'll get on this.'

She ended the phone call and turned to Edward. 'Here's a job for you. We've been shat on, sort it out.'

Edward had expected many things when he'd applied to work on *The Michael O'Shea Show* as a junior researcher but not this.

'I was planning a holiday. I was supposed to be on a beach. A beach! And instead I'm dealing with the fact our star guest is a fucking kiddy fiddler.'

Edward read on, as Mags scrolled through the various photos of Michael O'Shea with his arms around his younger brother. Edward knew enough about *The Michael O'Shea Show* to understand why this story had gotten so big.

Phillip O'Shea had appeared on the show no less than twenty times in the past year. He was the flagship example of Michael's self-help mantra. Disabled and living on benefits and family handouts, Michael had cut off his funds, forcing him into getting a job. With each episode, viewers had seen him make progress – from refusing to turn up to interviews Michael had arranged for him, to volunteering at a local shop. By the time of the latest segment Phillip had become an ambassador for a homeless charity and was about to start writing an autobiography.

'This is what you're going to do. At this very moment Michael is on his way over. He is a busy man and he's got no time, no time whatsoever, to be dealing with this bullshit. I don't want a single pap of him on the way in. So you're going to distract the press. Violet,' Mags, the woman with a penchant for cigarettes, pointed to her younger colleague on her left, 'is going to dress up in a driver's uniform, go down to the garages and sneak out the back, you will be in the passenger seat with a towel over your head. She'll drive around for a bit in a blacked-out car and then come in through the front. When you're in position, about to enter, text me and Michael will come in round the back.'

'Right,' Edward said, though he was still struggling to take in everything Mags had told him.

'Once you've done that, you will spend the rest of the day putting together a show to go out tonight! You will ring round every paper, putting a good spin on this and if any of these shitty rags have got the tenacity to suggest that this bullshit might have even an ounce of truth, you tell them straight: the old boys in blue have got fuck all on Michael's brother. They've barely spoken off-camera the last year and if he's found guilty, Michael will disown the little bastard. Got it?'

Edward, fairly speechless at this point, could do little more than nod as Mags hurried them out of the gallery.

'Didn't know this job involved PR,' Edward joked to Violet as they headed to the garages.

She didn't smile. 'There's a lot you don't know about this job.'

'Really?'

'One guy, long before you, couldn't hack it. After two weeks tried to kill himself.'

'He did?'

'Yep.' It didn't seem as if she wanted to elaborate.

'I reckon I'll last longer than two weeks.'

They made their way through an underpass to a set of garages – a gated compound – on the other side of the road. Inside the end garage was a black BMW with tinted windows.

'Get in,' she murmured, opening the passenger door. Edward climbed in while Violet went to use the driver's door and Edward, his heart already racing, recoiled as she reached behind her for a drivers' uniform and a towel on the back seat and then started to undress in front of him. She unbuttoned her cardigan but then grabbed the towel and tossed it squarely over Edward's head.

He smirked under the towel as he waited for Violet to finish getting dressed into the uniform and for the engines to rev up. He felt the car jolt forward and plod towards the gates of the compound.

They drove around the side roads a few times, then Violet pulled over, texting the producer. This was it. They were going in. And suddenly Edward's towel was ablaze with light. Cameras flashed in his face and he could hear questions repeated over and over.

'Michael, Michael, what do you have to say about your brother? Is Phillip a paedo, Michael? Will you disown him?' Edward didn't flinch as the questions continued. 'Are you a paedo too? Have you been helping your brother with his crimes?' It was hard to keep a straight face. Edward imagined his own sarcastic response *Yes*, he thought, *Yes, you got me. I'm guilty of it all*. He felt the motors rev forward and then come to a sudden stop.

'Wait,' Violet whispered. It was a good call. Even after the main front gates had completely closed behind them, he could still hear a helicopter hovering above.

'This towel doesn't come off until we're back in the studio,' she whispered, again. He heard a door shut and felt a breeze as Violet opened his car door and grabbed hold of his hand, dragging him inside.

~

'Looks like phase one of the operation didn't go too badly!' Edward joked. They were back in the studio and the real Michael O'Shea, suited and even more slick in real life, had made it in, unscathed. Edward and Michael were around the same height and of similar build, though there were twenty years between them.

'Phase one?' Mags, who Edward now knew was the producer, said, puffing away.

Michael took over. 'This is not a game, son, there are no phases, no strategy. You have one task and one task only, to cover my arse.'

'We've stopped *The Lion*, for now...' Mags said. 'No guilty-as-fuck shot of you in the back of the car.'

'Good.' Michael brushed through his hair with his hands. 'They're absolute pricks at that paper. Now,' he clasped his hands together, 'this is what we're going to do. We're going to put out a show tonight. A one-off special. Upstairs will clear whatever bollocks is on this evening and give us our usual five thirty slot. Victims of press abuse, how the tabloids ruined my life. We're going to track down anyone that paper has trashed and we're going to give them a platform to shit on those bastards. Don't believe everything you read.'

Mags licked her lips. 'We could start a campaign, a national day of action, boycott *The Lion*, burn the rag live on stage.'

Michael smirked but said nothing and the meeting seemed to be at an end.

'Do we have an office?' Edward asked Violet, as Mags and Michael wandered out of the production gallery.

Violet tilted her head towards the back of the room.

Edward was confused. He saw a small battered-looking desk at the back of the gallery, covered in rubbish. There was one telephone and a dated desktop computer. It seemed quite unreasonable to Edward that a huge television network like *People* had cramped him into a small corner of a basement.

'Rather an odd way to meet someone isn't it, driving round London with a towel over your head?' Edward said.

She shrugged. 'We need to get moving if we're going to put out a show tonight. Here…' She handed him a huge file.

'This is a list of people who've rung the show. We're looking for anyone who's been a victim of press intrusion, anything we can spin. Failing that, get on Google. Look for any high-profile cases… people wrongly accused of murder, oddballs that the press has trashed, low-list celebs looking to make a comeback who want to rant about being caught cheating by the papers.'

'But no one is going to be available at such short notice…'

'You really know nothing about television, do you? How on earth did you manage to get a job here?'

2

The breathy saxes of the theme tune reached their coda and the cameras panned to Michael O'Shea as he bounded onto the stage, his stage, shaking hands with as many members of the audience as he could before their applause fell away.

'Every day this show gets taken apart in the press. Last week I'm a cokehead who's out every night and this week my wife is about to leave me for a younger man because I'm too dull! Too dull, folks?'

There was a faint murmur of laughter that didn't seem to satisfy him.

'Today, we're looking at victims of the press. That's right, we're turning the tables...'

The lights in the audience dimmed and a montage began to play of various newspaper stories and a dramatic strapline:

'Don't Believe All that You Read. The Truth Behind the Headlines'

From the gallery above Edward looked on. His 'office' was now a hive of activity. A host of techies huddled around the gallery control desk, talking between themselves, with Mags at the centre. Edward was wearing a headset so he could talk to Violet who was backstage with the guests…

Suddenly Michael O'Shea was sombre as he introduced his first guest.

'Some of you may have followed his career since he was dramatically forced to quit the second series of *Make Me a Star* after false allegations emerged that he lied and cheated his way to the final. Here's just a snippet of what he had to put up with…'

Michael's voice narrated another montage of newspaper headlines and clips.

'On the cusp of stardom, singer Charlie Heaton was just twenty when, days before the final of the country's biggest talent television contest, *Make Me a Star*, allegations emerged in certain newspapers that he'd tried to bribe one of the judges, had taken professional singing lessons – strictly against the rules – and had a secret cocaine addiction. From national sweetheart to enemy number one, the press turned on Charlie. He was forced to leave the show and endure a month-long police investigation for bribery. All the while he was subjected to a tirade of abuse from newspaper columnists and branded Britain's biggest liar…'

The sequence panned onto a particularly furious column from the gossip pages of *The Lion*.

'Nearly six months later it turned out that the allegations were false. The newspapers had not checked their sources and a vital tape of him discussing bribing the judge was found to be fake. Many believe the newspaper deliberately doctored the tape. But the damage was done.'

The cameras panned away from the montage and back to the stage.

'Following his abrupt exit from *Make Me a Star* he's recently been doing the rounds to set the record straight… and relaunch his career, Charlie's on the show, everyone.'

A taller and visibly older looking man with a trimmed beard

and a low-cut V-neck made his way out on the stage, his hands in his pockets.

In the gallery, Mags was puffing away, apparently enjoying herself.

'Doing the rounds? Cheating Charlie's been on every show going for the last two years, bleating out the same sob story over and over. He's probably made more money from appearance fees than if he'd actually got the record deal; abuse, my arse.'

She was clearly talking to the techies at the control desk who snickered.

'On fine form, as always boss,' one of them guffed.

Edward remained straight-faced.

'So, Charlie, first of all thanks so much for coming on the show, mate, really appreciate it,' Michael said, down in the studio below. 'Cast your mind back to the day that story was published, to the day you realised what had happened. What was going through your head?'

'At first I laughed it off. I thought that's ridiculous, tabloid papers always do that. You know what I mean?'

Michael laughed and so did the audience. 'Yeah, mate, I know exactly what you mean! There's a lot of that about lately.'

Charlie continued. 'I thought all press is good press... but then it seemed like everyone believed the papers. After the initial story about the cheating, the next day *Make Me a Star* called me into the studio to tell me they were dropping me, and I was mobbed on my way out. That's when it hit me. It didn't feel real, I'd lost everything but up until then I'd been living in this bubble, this media frenzy. The day after that the police came and raided my house and interviewed me. I felt sick. I didn't know what to do.'

'Tell me what it was like living through all of that.'

'It wasn't the police investigation that took its toll on me. I knew they had a job to do, it was the press, the media. They mobbed not only me, my family as well. It was non-stop, day in, day out. They wouldn't leave me alone. I couldn't even go out to the supermarket to get a loaf of bread without a photographer waiting for me. But then it got proper frightening.'

'You started getting death threats, didn't you. Tell the audience at home all about it.'

'I never use social media. I was never one of them ones who went on, courting attention.'

'No, course you weren't!' said Mags to the gallery.

'But one day, one of my mates she came up to me and she said, "Charlie, I reckon you need to see this," and even though I wasn't on it, she'd managed to bring up all these people.'

'I actually think we've got a screenshot of some of the vile abuse you were sent, it's absolutely disgusting, isn't it?' Michael said.

'This is what I didn't understand. I knew the police had a job to do and I knew that people on the internet say stupid things but the press. I thought they were supposed to have some standards. They started joining in as well.'

'Do you think certain newspapers were encouraging the death threats?'

'Definitely. Just look at that piece by–'

Michael interjected. 'We take the moral high ground on this show, we don't name names but we all know exactly *which* newspapers you're talking about.'

The segment continued as Michael turned to questioning Charlie about his future plans and his hope to return to stardom soon.

Next up, Violet had arranged for a man wrongly accused of abducting a university student to give his version of events of how the papers had burgled his home looking for information.

For much of the recording of the episode and the latter half of the afternoon, Edward had found himself with little to do. With no idea of any of the procedures, he felt that by saying, let alone doing anything at all he might well disrupt the recording. He was glad when the day came to an end.

'I felt pretty useless today,' Edward said, as the hands on his watch approached half past five and he made his way towards the gallery steps.

'Then don't,' Violet said, following him down.

'Don't what?'

Violet turned out the lights. 'Feel useless.'

3

M ichael Matthew O'Shea MBE had built his career on rising from the ashes. It had been his alcoholism and his sobering up that had led to him securing his first job as an agony uncle on local radio and the termination of that contract for accidentally swearing live on air that had brought him to the attention of two executives looking for a fiery host to front a new TV show. But Michael knew that there were some things that it was impossible to come back from and paedophilia was the ultimate nail in the coffin.

Yes, his stupid incompetent brother had been caught looking at all manner of filth on his computer. In many ways Michael was partly responsible. Practising what you preach had always been an important facet of what he did, so right from the start Michael had brought Phillip on to his show. His brother had seen no real need to get a job or to do anything other than sit in his house all day.

So Michael had confronted him on stage, got him to get a proper job, helping out at a soup kitchen. Off the back of that and with his newly found fame, Michael had lobbied hard for

Phillip to become an ambassador for a homeless charity. For a while he'd been slightly proud of him, turning his life around. But after all Michael had done, Phillip had soon slacked off – as he always did – complaining that he was too ill to do any work for the charity and now this. This utter mess. It wouldn't be a story at all if Michael hadn't turned Phillip into some half-arsed celebrity.

As Michael drove to a rundown hotel room on the edges of town – away from the prying eyes of the reporters who would undoubtedly be camping outside of Phillip's house, scouting for a good headline – Michael O'Shea contemplated what he would say to his brother. He had thought long and hard about how best to handle this crisis during the drive north from London and he had rapidly come to the conclusion that he was screwed either way. He could throw money at the problem, hire the best lawyers to get him off, do a deal with his accuser but that was only the half of it. If his dim-witted brother did indeed have a dirty hard drive, he failed to see how even the most expensive lawyer could exonerate him.

On the other hand, if his brother was guilty, *he*, Michael, would be done over by the papers for helping him. The other option was to have it out with him, tell him he'd have nothing to do with him and leave him to rot. It was his own fault after all, why should he help him? Of course, the press might run a few stories if, by some miracle, Phillip got off and Michael hadn't lent his support but a few pieces about his disloyalty was surely a far better option? The only other solution was to denounce Phillip publicly and fund his court costs in secret, though this was bound to get out eventually. Michael wasn't exactly ecstatic about the prospect of spending his hard-earned cash on a lawyer either.

When Michael pulled into the hotel car park, he carried out his usual routine of turning off his headlights and surveying the area. Journalists had a habit of surpassing all expectations when it came to surveillance. It was, of course, reasonable in this day and age to expect a reporter to sit outside your house during the middle of the day and he knew colleagues – the vain, stupid ones who cared more about their relations with the media than their own dignity – who had actually gone outside and chatted to them, brought them tea and even posed for the photos they wanted. But Michael had, in the past, made the mistake of thinking that after a week or so the hacks would give up and that he would be okay to go about his normal business without it appearing on page five of *The Lion*. This couldn't be further from the truth.

Michael hated journalists more than anything. They would go to extreme lengths to print lies and propaganda for their masters like obedient dogs.

Michael, on the other hand, was a true storyteller. He would ground people in the truth, expose them for what they really were; he was a mirror to them. It was only when they caught a glimpse of their own reflection that they could make amends for their behaviour.

If the press did cotton on to what Michael was really doing tonight, they wouldn't allow him to explain himself or give him the opportunity to understand his dilemma, they wanted to hang him out to dry, no matter what, and he wasn't going to allow that to happen.

So Michael waited until he had seen every occupied car vacate the tarmac before he slipped out into the rain. He didn't bother hanging around and headed straight for room forty-five of the hotel. The door had been left slightly ajar so that Phillip didn't have to get up from his bed; he was disabled, the result of being run over by a car when he was fifteen. The accident hadn't left him anywhere near as crippled as he liked to make out. He certainly didn't need the crutches he insisted on taking with him everywhere or the generous disability allowance he was afforded by the government.

Michael closed the door and stared at him for several moments. 'You really are an idiot, aren't you?'

Phillip said nothing.

'So…' Michael could already see the sweat seeping from his brother's forehead. 'Did you do it?'

Michael had observed enough liars on his stage to know that what he was about to hear would hardly be the pinnacle of wholesale truth and integrity.

But although Phillip O'Shea opened his mouth, no doubt wanting to reel off a pack of lies, Michael's brother looked like he was overcome with such paralysis that he couldn't actually bring himself to utter any words.

'You're sick, you know that?' Michael screamed, moving towards the bed. Phillip winced as Michael went to grab him but he withdrew at the final moment.

'I've met all sorts of people on my show: drug dealers, alcoholics, wife-beaters but NEVER a paedophile and yet here I am confronted by the fact my own brother has been touching up the boy down the road and looking up disgusting filth online.'

'So what are we–'

'What are WE GOING TO DO? I'll tell you what WE are going to do: absolutely fuck all. YOU are going to tell me what exactly was on your computer and then you're going to stay in this hotel and you are not to leave it without my express permission. You are not to talk to the press, you are not to ring anyone and if I find out you've so much as stepped foot in an internet café, your life won't be worth living. One thing's for sure: I'm not funding the costs of a paedo, believe me.'

Phillip whimpered.

'Save the pathetic helpless act for your trial. I need to speak to the police,' he spat, 'so, for now, brother, it looks as if this is goodbye.'

'G-goodbye?'

'Go and fuck yourself,' Michael said one last time before he stepped out of the hotel room, closing the door behind him as if nothing had happened.

Everything he had said was true. He would speak to the police to find out what exactly they had on dear Phillip but hell would freeze over before he intervened and got him off the hook: it could be done, oh no doubt it could be done, for the right price, but the chances of his intervention staying hidden forever were… well, he didn't fancy his chances. No, this was just a case of finding out what exactly they had on Phillip, how likely they were to pursue a conviction and whether there was any point even bothering with a solicitor. The police loved Michael: there would be no question of him being able to set up a sly coffee, maybe even a quick backhander to say thanks, if it came to it.

He sighed. This whole business was such a mess. Not since he had given it up seven years ago had he felt the pull of the bottle so intensely. It was like an itch he couldn't scratch. And what was worse was that the night wasn't over. Before he could relax he had one final journey to make but nobody could know about this one. He had assured his wife Karen that this business with his brother would take some time to sort out and that he would need to stay overnight in a hotel. Michael was taking advantage of the situation. And not a soul was to ever find out. For if they did, he knew he'd lose everything. No, that couldn't happen.

So, he waited inside his car again to check that there were no journalists on his tail before he set off. He drove to the multi-storey car park he'd looked up on the internet and paid the overnight fee; to many a costly excursion, but £25 to Michael O'Shea was nothing.

Then he changed his coat and headed out into the cold, walking for little over a mile before he reached the rundown lockup, his secret. And there, inside it, was a car: a rundown red KA that no member of the press would suspect belonged to him. You see that was the difference between Michael and Phillip, that was the reason he was superior: he would never be stupid enough to get caught, he would always take precautions, above and beyond what was necessary. He opened the driver's door and then started the engine to begin the journey to pick up his most precious cargo…

4

The press, who'd remained stationed outside the *People* studios where *The Michael O'Shea Show* was filmed, had all but abandoned their temporary campsite by the time Edward had walked out of work that evening and they had not bothered to return the following morning. So, without so much as a whisper in his ear, Edward was waved through security and headed back to the basement studio for what he hoped would be a far more productive second day. He didn't see how he could carry out his job effectively if he didn't at least understand how the show was put together.

This time neither Michael nor Mags were anywhere to be seen. Only Violet and a serious, intellectual man with greying hair had made it in. As they both busied themselves with something at the back desk, Edward wandered to the other side of the small room, to the gallery deck itself with its many buttons and monitors, all eerily dead, and then to the giant window which looked down upon the set itself. The man who had been chatting to Violet was the Director of Guest Rehabilitation.

'Hello,' he said as Edward approached the back desk, getting up to shake his hand. 'Dr Bernard Braithwaite, nice to meet you.

Now, as I was just telling Violet, it is not surprising I suppose – as so many people want to be on television these days – but we do get rather a lot of requests from people ringing in, wanting to be on the show. We have a backlog that the last researcher recorded.'

'Oh I see,' said Edward.

'So–'

'Ultimately it is up to Michael, Mags, and the new co-host when she gets on board, to make the final decision about who is on the show but they have given us some specifications about the sort of stories they want.'

'They'll want something explosive for the first show of the new format,' Violet said.

'Quite,' Braithwaite replied.

'Have a look through the database and make a few inquiries. If there is nothing that you think is suitable then that's fine. I have to have a conversation with potential guests after you've inter-viewed them to make sure they are stable. Any questions?'

Edward said nothing.

'Right, I'll leave you to it. We can regroup after lunch.' Braith-waite departed the gallery leaving Violet and Edward alone once again.

'Who is the new co-host?' Edward said.

'Olivia Dessington-Brown, Liv.'

Edward had heard of her. She was, if he remembered correctly, a fairly famous reality TV star, a regular fixture in many shows after nine at night, no less. Violet did not seem interested in elaborating.

'How are we going to do this?' Edward asked instead, turning his attention to the computer.

It took an age to load and when the screen finally did come to life, the database programme Violet wanted to use took a further five minutes to open. Edward watched her select print with the mouse. He searched around the cramped gallery for any sign of the printer but couldn't find one.

She pulled out an ID card from her pocket that looked a lot more worn out than Edward's.

'Take this to the printers in the station newsroom. I was friends with one of the assistants there and he hooked my card up to their system. My password is mildredthecat, no spaces, all lowercase. Swipe in, enter the password and press the green button? Got it?'

'But I don't know where the newsroom is...'

Violet pointed to the gallery door.

'All the more reason for you to go.'

In fact, the newsroom was quite hard to miss. Backtracking along the corridor from which he'd come, up the stairs and past the reception desk, Edward soon found himself in the central lobby with the glass lifts. The buttons for each floor were helpfully labelled: the newsroom was on the fifth floor.

The newsroom was completely different from the O'Shea studios. Not only was the space itself about three times as big, it was plush, open plan and not at all dark. There were rows of desks with Apple computers but every four or so rows there'd be a small space for comfy-looking sofas and a coffee table. The printers were in the corner in a separate booth of their own.

When Edward returned, with all one hundred and seven pages of the database, Violet was sifting through the newspapers.

'What's the coverage like today?' he asked, wondering whether their work the previous day had paid off.

Violet folded over page seventeen of *The Lion* and pushed it in his direction.

He had to scan for several seconds before he noticed the small nib in the corner.

'Troubled' O'Shea To Launch New Format

Troubled talk show host Michael O'Shea is to launch a revamped version of his show in a bid to quash allegations that his brother is a paedophile. Sources close to the teatime show, fronted by the former alcoholic, say Michael wants to draw attention away from the arrest of Phillip O'Shea, his brother, and further speculation that he has hit the bottle again, by pushing the show to sensational new boundaries and introducing a new co-host. The Michael O'Shea Show returns to our screens at 5.30pm on People next week.

Edward recognised the byline.

'Sources close to the show...' Violet said. 'Me, they mean.'

'Was that the only coverage we got?'

She pushed the stack of newspapers to one side. 'Never mind about them.' She reached forward to grab the paper copy of the database from under Edward's arms.

'Anything remotely unusual or exciting, circle it. You heard yesterday. They want real juice for this week and, in my experience, if you want juice it doesn't just land on your lap, you have to go and find it so I doubt there'll be anything in here...but it's worth a look.' She split the pile into two and pulled out her headphones, plugged in, and got to work.

Contrary to what Violet had said, Edward seemed to have found a strong story on the first page of his stack. Identical twins, working for precious little money as dancers and adult movie stars had fallen out of love with each other after one of them had a baby whilst the other had started seeing a controlling boyfriend. Their USP, so to speak, was in jeopardy and they wanted help resolving their differences so they could start working together again. This was three months earlier though. By now they might have sorted out their problems and given up on the dancing. Edward circled it, nevertheless, and carried on.

Other stories were more recent but far less interesting. There was the daughter who hoped to reconcile with her abusive father and the drug addicted husband driving his family into debt and despair, or in a more bizarre vein, the woman who elected to leave her husband in order to identify as a three year old child. She refused to speak in anything but sobs or eat anything more substantial than baby food. All of these stories, however, seemed to lack that 'juice'.

'There isn't enough conflict,' Violet said, as Edward whittled off his circled stories.

'Okay,' Edward said, turning to the front of his stack to reveal his trump card, which he'd saved until last: the identical twins' story.

'It's a start... it's not perfect. Their reason for contacting the show is to resolve their differences and it's in their interests to come carrying a white flag, seeing as they've both been pretty much unemployed since they fell out. But maybe if we can plant the idea this guy they've been seeing has been playing them off against each other, bring him out as well, turn them both against him, I guess that could work.'

'Right,' said Edward, tentatively, 'that's all I've got. So shall I go and call Bernard?'

'Top tip,' she snipped, curtly, 'Bernard Braithwaite stays out of everything.'

'Oh?'

'He thinks about the guests, we think about what makes great TV. We fend him off until we have a strong line-up and then it's too late for him to do anything.'

Violet reached inside her pocket, pulled out her wallet and handed Edward a ten-pound note. 'Go and fetch me today's local papers, a cheese sandwich and a packet of crisps, please.'

'The local papers?' Edward said.

'As many as you can find. *The Brixdale Gazette*'s a good one.'

Edward didn't want to question Violet any further, but she could still see the confused look in his eyes.

'For the court reports,' she said, but he still didn't fully understand.

Edward did as he was told and returned little more than twenty minutes later. With the database exhausted, they were turning to a new source of inspiration for stories...

'We can't prejudice ongoing cases so anything we use is all dependent on the verdict and whether the trial will be over by the time the show airs.'

'I see...'

It was clear to Edward that Violet sensed his hesitation. He couldn't help but feel a little shame at approaching people to appear on the show at one of the worst periods in their lives.

'What did you expect? You're working for *The Michael O'Shea Show*.'

'But I thought we'd at least...'

'Morality,' Violet clipped, 'is not our department. That is what Braithwaite is for. We just make great TV.'

Edward said no more and continued with his work.

This time, the two of them dissected the back pages of the papers together. Edward suspected this was because Violet thought he might ignore some of the most show-worthy cases as he worried for the safety of potential guests, though she needn't have bothered. He'd been told once and wasn't going to make the same mistake again. So, up and down they searched until by the end of the afternoon they'd got what Violet thought was a good strong set of cases for the following week.

'That's ten stories. I think that's enough to go on.' Violet swept the newspapers into a pile, picked up her handbag and headed towards the gallery steps. 'Tomorrow we'll investigate further.'

'Right.' Edward wondered whether to catch up with her.

'Goodbye.' She waved as Edward turned out the lights in the gallery and in the end he made his way out of the building at his own pace.

5

Violet had never been one for sticking around. This job, however, was the longest she'd stayed at any job. Not out of any loyalty for Michael. She wanted a promotion and she had a strong feeling one would be coming her way. Producer of one of the highest rated shows on television would perk up her CV no end and the extra pay would not go amiss. Then she'd make a name for herself for a few years and jump ship.

Even if this paedo affair did not derail her boss, Violet knew it would only be a matter of time before Mags was shown the door. True, she was Michael's pet project, but someone that unhinged would not last long, particularly if the management interfered – like they eventually did on all the other shows – and that was surely inevitable given the amount of press they were getting. Biding her time, that was what Violet was doing. Riding the wave.

Outside the *People* studios, she crossed the road and walked further up The Strand until she was safely away from prying eyes. Then she hopped into a taxi and asked the driver to drop her at her favourite bar.

Everything about *The Albatross* suited her purpose. The tall ceilings and endless alcoves and columns meant Violet could easily hide away in one of the smaller booths and nobody would disrupt her. And, what was more, there were no windows. Everything was permanently dim, draped in a kind of fake candlelight to give it a prohibition, jazz-age feel. All in all, she could get as drunk or as high as she wanted and nobody would even notice, whatever time of day it was, not that any of the bartenders would have called her out on it. The drinks were so expensive: in this bar, you paid for discretion.

By the front door was a steep, narrow staircase. Violet stalked off down the steps as quickly as she could. Nobody appeared to notice her, as she preferred. The toilets were just as opulent as the bar. There was a small sofa and chandeliers above, glistening in the circular mirrors. They looked real enough not to appear tacky but of course, they were fakes.

Violet was in no mood to admire the decor. She rushed straight for the cubicle and locked the door. Without even a moment of hesitation, she reached inside her handbag and rummaged around for the small plastic packet she so craved.

Cocaine was a necessity in this job. How could she function without it? With crisis after crisis, this was all that kept her from burning out. At least she was buying it with her own hard-earned cash. *The Lion* let their reporters claim it on expenses, though the pressures of *that* job didn't bear thinking about. She had it easy...

But tonight, the cocaine had another purpose: she could drink herself under the table but still feel in control. Although she could still function after a couple of drinks following a hard day's work alcohol had a tendency to send her straight to sleep. Combined with the cocaine, however, two or three drinks gave her just the right buzz. Though drugs would not be the only source of her adrenaline tonight...

Violet snorted back the white powder and let it wash over her whole body, giving her a fresh sense of purpose. She was careful to wipe her nose of any residue, before she proceeded to change into a sleek pink outfit, brushed back her hair and re-did her make-up. Her phone pinged and she looked down at the face of the stranger she was about to meet, wondering if they would look as handsome as the picture on their profile made out.

6

The weather the following day was unfortunate. It had been fairly bleak since the beginning of the week but now, as Edward and Violet made their way across the road to Blackfriars Tube station, it seemed to take particular umbrage with them: the rain lashed down onto the tarmac at an almost frightening speed and at one point the gaps between the thunder and the lightning grew so short, Edward felt genuinely concerned that they would be struck down.

'I hope it hasn't affected any of the trains,' Violet said. Edward wasn't particularly enthusiastic about where they were heading. Yes, they were off to go and meet potential guests, to a council estate no less. The two of them had spent the morning doing some light research about each of the families. Double-checking or, in Violet's words, 'making sure they got the full picture', plugging the gaps in the guests' version of events with bank details, birth certificates, criminal records.

'And then we confront them with the truth during the show,' Violet said, as they awaited their train, 'and…maybe let slip to other family members what they've been up to beforehand.'

'What! That's…' Edward protested.

'That's television,' Violet said, barely lifting an eyelid.

As it happened, the train to their first stop: Graysmead Park – the council estate home to the identical twins they had discussed the previous day – was neither late nor disrupted because of the weather.

Violet said almost nothing for the entire journey, so Edward had first taken to his phone, until the signal had inevitably faded. He instead took solace in the broadsheet newspaper that had been discarded on the opposite seat. Michael O'Shea's family drama had finally been overshadowed by the failure of the coalition government to pass their budget and speculation about the inevitable general election that was to follow.

Edward had never really taken much of an interest in politics, despite the encouragement of his parents, or the fact that he had already been eligible to vote in three general elections; and this particular paper with its commentary about the various in-fighting and deal breaking only served to confuse him further. In the end, he gave up and stared out of the window. The greenery was fading and in the far distance he could see the outlines of tall buildings, the council estate could not be far off.

Indeed, Edward felt himself slumping into a small depression as he caught glimpses of Graysmead for the first time and saw for himself the abandoned factories and the enormous council flats, towering above him like giant concrete pillars. It was a terrible sight.

They pulled into the station and the sun broke through the sky, casting an ugly shadow over the rows and rows of council flats, all of which looked a visibly darker shade of grey in the aftermath of the storm. Violet put on her sunglasses nevertheless and they stepped out onto the single platform. There was no ticket office and the only shelter was a burnt-out wreck; it was as if they had arrived in the middle of nowhere.

'The twins live on the tenth floor, in the east tower of Deacon

Court,' Violet said, looking at her phone once again. 'It's about a fifteen-minute walk.'

'Right,' Edward replied, realising she probably hadn't been texting earlier but checking for directions.

This was a journey that Edward was dreading. They both looked out of place but Edward more so than Violet. He was cleanly shaven, his black hair was combed over his forehead neatly and, though the overcoat he was wearing was long, it had a tendency to flap open, revealing his suit and tie. Violet, on the other hand, had been a little more tactful with the way she had dressed, perhaps to help her gain the trust of the people they were about to interview. Instead of her usual colourful cardigans, she had donned a white tank top and jeans, her hair was tied back tightly and even the bag she was clutching was a lot less ostentatious.

When the two of them finally did reach the east tower, they pressed the buzzer for the flat they wanted but, worryingly, there was no reply. Edward and Violet hesitated for a few seconds before deciding that, since there were so many people walking in and out of the building freely, it probably wasn't too much of a crime to sneak in through the front door and make their own way up. They took the lift rather than tackling the stairs and instantly regretted it. The distinctive and putrid stench of cheap cannabis did little to ease the awkward and cramped few seconds as Edward and Violet ascended to the top floor.

When the lift doors finally creaked open, they made their way to flat fifty-two. The front door was already ajar.

'Hello?' Violet called, tentatively, pushing the red door even further open.

There were gentle sobs from within.

'Hello?' she said again. The sobs grew louder.

There were smashed ornaments and broken plates scattered across the carpet.

'We're here from *The Michael O'Shea Show*,' Violet explained, making her way through the corridor and into the living room. Edward followed shortly behind. The girl within looked a mess. Her hair, which had been cropped into a bob, was frayed and quite obviously dyed, her make-up had run down her face, flowing like a river.

'We spoke on the phone this morning, didn't we, Tiffany isn't it?' Violet said. She had adopted her telephone voice. 'You did say it would be okay to pop by for a little chat. Can we sit down?'

''Course!' Tiffany had a vaguely cockney accent. 'Jayden's in bed, surprised he wasn't woken up…'

She was clearly talking about her child, a little over one year old.

There was silence for several seconds. Violet took off her sunglasses and smiled.

'My twin sister,' the girl began, breaking down, 'she's left!' She tried to mask her tears by burying her face into a nearby pillow.

'I'm sorry, we could come back another day?' said Violet.

As much as Edward sympathised with the girl and was glad to be temporarily free of the office, he couldn't help but hope that they didn't have to return to this place.

'No, no. It's fine. I'm, I'll be okay,' the girl said.

'And, sorry to have to bring it up, but your sister is Annabel? That's all correct?'

'Yes, that's right. My twinnie. We used to do everything together.'

'Why don't you tell me all about it?'

Edward noticed Violet discreetly taking out a notebook and a pen.

'Annabel used to work at a club, dancing. She earned a bomb; I went to go and see her and she suggested I do it. 'Course I gotta do everything with my sister and the manager liked us dancing together. So that's how it started and then, I dunno, one thing led to another. Then we made videos, posting them on the internet.

We got loads of views and were offered a proper contract for a professional site but…'

'That was when you got pregnant, with Jayden?'

'Yeah, I didn't plan it, but I had to stop everything. We were out of work. Then my sister started seeing…'

'And this man your sister is seeing…?'

'Yes, he's the manager of the club. He's really controlling.'

'Tell me about him.'

'He won't let me see my sister and he doesn't want her to leave the house or to work anymore. He wants to keep her all to himself.'

'Do you think he's abusing her?'

'Yes,' Tiffany said, though it looked to Edward that she was saying what she thought Violet wanted to hear.

'And talk to me about your childhood.'

'It was all right.'

'Where were you brought up, around here?'

'Yes…'

'Do your parents live here?'

Edward wondered why Violet was even bothering to ask these questions. It wasn't as if she didn't know the answers, as did he. They'd already searched for the death certificates. And it wasn't as if Tiffany was lying, just naturally tentative about discussing the nature of her parents' death. When Violet pressed her again, however, she seemed to liven up.

'Never knew my dad. Probably someone my mum got with when she was high. My mum… well, she was a good mum. It was just her drug problems. She died of an overdose when I was seventeen. It was my sister that found her, sitting there, all still on the sofa. Guess we always knew it was coming.'

'Have you ever taken drugs?'

'No! Never. Not after Mum. Always been clean.'

'Not even weed?'

31

No doubt you'd get high by osmosis if you spent long enough in Graysmead, Edward thought.

'Once!' she protested. 'But that was before Mum died.'

'And what about your sister?'

The silence seemed to say it all.

'Does her boyfriend give her drugs?'

'Maybe…'

'Maybe?'

'I don't know.'

'So, have you seen her on drugs?'

'He has such a hold on her, he's stopped her doing any more work and now she's moved out. She spent most of her time round his anyway.'

'So you think this boyfriend has been giving her drugs and that's why she's with him?'

'Yeah.'

'And tell me,' Edward knew Violet was going in for the kill, asking the question – or at least attempting to elicit a vaguely sympathetic answer – from which the entire show would hinge, 'tell me, Tiffany, have you ever slept with your sister's boyfriend?'

Tiffany's cheeks lit up and, although she kept perfectly cool, Edward knew Violet was clocking all of this.

'What's with all these QUESTIONS?'

Edward started to sweat. He'd never liked confrontation and here he was, bearing witness to Violet poking a poor girl with a giant wooden stick. Violet, however, seemed to realise she had gone too far. She put down her notepad and crossed the room, gently placing her arm on Tiffany's shoulder.

'It's all right,' she said, 'we have to ask these questions for the show. It's just so we can get a good picture of what's going on.'

Tiffany seemed consoled enough and was quite content to take out a cigarette and start smoking. Violet moved away and returned to her seat.

'Am I really going to be on TV?' Tiffany said.

Violet smiled.

'Of course.' The ease with which Violet lied had impressed and sickened Edward with equal measure. Nothing had yet been agreed. There could quite easily be a problem with some of the information Tiffany had told them. Equally, Braithwaite, Michael or Liv could veto the story. Nevertheless, Violet moved the conversation on.

'Do you know where we might find your sister and her boyfriend?'

The front door, which Edward had made sure to close behind him, burst open to loud voices.

'Speak of the devil,' Tiffany said.

In walked a girl almost identical to her. Almost, that was, apart from the colour of her top and her face, which was substantially less made up than her sister's. Beside her, a gruff-looking man of about thirty. He was tall but by no means handsome: he had a large belly on him and ugly crossbow tattoos on his arms that had long since faded.

Tiffany rose to her feet as soon as he walked into the room.

'What do you want?' she spat.

The man smirked. 'Who are they?'

Edward wanted to go. He didn't like to pre-judge people, but this man could be dangerous. Weren't they best to let the police deal with him? They could just leave a card. What did it matter anyway? They could forget the whole story…

'Hello, we're from *The Michael O'Shea Show*.'

The situation could not get any worse. How could they have been so foolish to come here alone?

But the man seemed to cool off. In fact, it was Tiffany who really seemed to lose it.

'GET HIM OUT OF MY FLAT!' she screamed. 'GET OUT.'

Edward could see the man's cheekbones retracting as if he was about to smirk, but he managed to restrain himself and it was the other twin, Annabel, who responded to her sister.

33

'Oh shut up, will you,' she spat, 'we've come to collect our stuff.'

'Our stuff?' Tiffany questioned. 'But... but sis. Why can't you see he's an idiot? Why can't you just...'

'The only reason you want me to stay is for the sake of your stupid career. I ain't staying a moment longer. Here.' She threw her key into the air and Tiffany didn't quite know what to do.

Violet, thinking tactically, interrupted.

'Would you be able to leave me your new address and a phone number? We're sorry about what's happened but we would like to ask you a few questions, for the show.'

'You mean we're going to be on telly?' Annabel exclaimed.

The man's expression, however, soured. Violet saw it too and Edward knew she would already be making a mental note to research just what was making the man reluctant to appear on television.

'And what if I don't think all this is a good idea? 'Ey?'

'I can assure you it's worth it. I will send you pictures of the aftershow resort where we send all our guests and you will get to meet Michael himself of course and the new co-host who is also a big star.'

Edward could tell that Annabel was convinced by what Violet was saying but her boyfriend was most certainly not. So here layeth the problem. For, if the boyfriend really was as controlling of his sister as Tiffany had indicated, and his behaviour, even in these few short seconds, was certainly evidence of that, then the key to getting the show to go ahead was smooth talking him.

'Here's my phone number.' Violet had already written it down. The man placed it into his pocket. 'I think now is a bad time. I'll ring you to arrange a more convenient date for us to come down or maybe we can pay for you to come to us, buy you dinner, a drink.' She slipped it in, coyly, like it was the most casual thing in all the world and Annabel's eyes lit up. 'Because it really would be great to feature you in one of our shows.'

Edward and Violet made their way back out of the red door. Edward half expected to hear the shouting begin again but Violet clearly had more confidence in the bombshell she had dropped.

'That should get them on board. A meal out at a fancy restaurant usually works. If they're still itching, we'll put them up in a hotel and make sure it's five-star.'

'But isn't all this… bribery?'

'Yep.'

'Well… it's just–'

'Just, what?'

'That man doesn't seem like he wants to go on the show, even with everything you promised him. He probably has a criminal record, something he wants to hide. He's not going to come on if he knows we're going to use that against him.'

'We're not going to use anything against him. We're going to get to the bottom of whatever he's been up to. We'll give him whatever protection he wants, blur his face or use a voice actor if he's on the run from something.'

'I see.'

'Not everything is designed to screw people over. Here,' she handed Edward a brochure as they waited for the lift, 'every single guest and their families get a two-week stay at our clinic in Florida after the show. Free tickets to *Disney World*, one-to-one therapy sessions, group counselling and then, when they are back home, a dedicated therapist and a twenty-four-hour phone line for as long as they need it.'

The lift arrived and Edward scanned the brochure: residential clinic was the wrong word. It was a mansion, high up on the hills, surrounded by palm trees and complete with roof terraces, jacuzzis and rooms to rival *The Ritz*.

'It must cost a fortune.'

Violet nodded, taking back the brochure and returning it into her bag.

'It's what most of the show's budget goes on and why I

constantly feel overworked. In an ideal world, there would be a team of junior researchers beneath me.'

Edward scoffed at the thought; even the mere suggestion of not only having to navigate Violet, Mags and Michael but also to compete with some hungry TV type for the most head-grabbing stories filled him with dread.

As they headed away from the twins' apartment, Edward hoped their next stop would at least be a bit more cheerful.

7

The estate that greeted Edward and Violet next was certainly slightly more affluent than Graysmead but not by a wide margin. Rather than rows of council towers, there was street after street of terraced houses. But there were still no shops or supermarkets in sight and the factories and the industrial estate they saw in the distance had all long been closed, left to vandals and thieves.

It took Edward and Violet a while to find Thurlow Road and when they did someone had spray-painted over the sign. 'Never-leave Street' said the blackened graffiti. Edward shuddered slightly. Whether the words were a dark reference to the notoriety of the street or mere cynicism about the lack of prospects in the area, Edward could only speculate but he knew he did not want to hang around here for too long.

The story of the woman and the daughter they were on their way to meet was tragic. The daughter: Millicent or Minnie, a rather cruel nickname for any fifteen-year-old girl Edward felt, had already run away from home at least ten times. After a little investigative work, they'd realised that Minnie's stepfather Stan was addicted to crack cocaine and had, allegedly – a word that would no doubt pepper that day's show – been violent to his wife and probably Minnie too. But that wasn't why Jo, the mother, had called the show. All she was bothered about was whether this vile man had cheated on her. Her plan for the show, if she got her own way, was to mount an extensive undercover investigation, stalking her husband's every move until they had photographic evidence that he was playing away. Minnie would barely come into it.

Violet had taken the lead with Jo's story the previous days so he only knew a little about it but he was sure she wasn't going to let it run as Jo wanted.

Violet knocked on the door of number 33.

A wrinkled woman with a cigarette in her hand opened the door, almost immediately.

'You must be Jo. Hello, we're from the Michael O'–'

'I know who you are.'

As Edward and Violet headed inside, past the half-empty paint cans, the black and uneven skirting boards, the stained carpets and the broken camp beds, they soon realised that the woman was not alone. But the half a dozen or so men occupying the room did not seem like the sort of people about to hold out their hand and say hello. All of them were tall and well-built, sporting ripped leather jackets and thunderous expressions.

'Is there somewhere quiet we can go to?' Violet asked tactfully, hoping Jo would ask the men to leave. But there was no such luck.

'Up here,' she said, leading them up a narrow staircase. As they crossed the room, the men scowled them up and down. Violet clearly knew better than to ask Jo who they were or what they were doing in the house within earshot.

It was only as they reached the top of the stairs and entered a bare bedroom with little furniture to cover up the mouldy carpet or the damp that had crept up the walls, that Edward realised how dark the house was. Downstairs he'd put it down to the closed curtains but it was only up here that he realised it had more to do with how many buildings had been cramped onto each plot of land; they were just metres from next door's bathroom.

'Have you started the surveillance yet? Caught 'im in the act? 'Ey? Is that what this is all about?' Jo asked.

There was a pause.

'Before we can start planning for the show we need to ask you a few questions and we'll also need to speak to Minnie and your husband.'

'Soon to be ex-husband if I find out he's been playing away. You can't speak to Minnie...'

'Oh really, how come?'

'Because the little bitch has run away again.'

Edward could do little to disguise how repulsed he was at her use of such language to describe her daughter. Violet, on the other hand, remained unfazed. She had no doubt become accustomed to such vulgarity, hearing it on a daily basis.

'Right. Well, Jo,' Violet said, 'we'd like to ask you some questions, to help us with the show.'

'And it's definitely going ahead?'

Again, Edward observed Violet's reaction with interest. Would she tell Jo an outright lie to pacify her? No, it seemed, she was quite blunt.

'Only if your daughter and your husband will agree to come on the show too.'

Jo looked horrified. 'Maybe I don't want to answer any QUESTIONS!'

Violet reached inside her bag and pulled out the aftercare brochure. It would be naïve of Jo to expect to come away unscathed from a show featuring her husband and her daughter, even if it was proven without a doubt that her husband had been cheating. Jo was banking on the fact that her daughter would be missing, and her husband would be too high to know what day of the week it was, let alone agree to come on the show. But Violet had just killed that idea dead in the water. She needed a new bargaining tool.

'You don't have to answer anything you don't want to but if you and your family were to come on the show there are a lot of perks...' Violet sped through the details of the hotel, barely needing to exaggerate the details, and Edward could see Jo struggling to keep a neutral expression. She was weighing up whether airing her own dirty laundry to millions of people was a price worth paying for the promise of a week in paradise.

'I guess I can answer some questions...' she conceded, finally.

'Great. Perhaps you could start by telling me about Minnie's father.'

Edward listened intently as Jo told Violet her entire life story, albeit a heavily editorialised version. How she'd entered into a relationship with Minnie's 'scumbag' of a father when she was working at the checkouts at a local shop, long since closed, her heartbreak when he abandoned her shortly after Minnie's birth for a better job and a prettier girl, then her re-marriage to her current partner Stan, her outrage at being 'unfairly' dismissed from her job and finally her despair at her daughter's disappearance; all of it so tragic, yet so obviously exaggerated.

Jo was so volatile that confronting her with almost anything would ensure she fizzed up like a shaken can of cola. Edward could see Violet building up to her next question, the one which may well result in them both being lynched by the men sat downstairs.

'Can we arrange a better time to come back and speak to your husband and your daughter?'

Edward supposed what she said could rather be construed as blackmail; for if Jo did not get her husband and daughter on board and let them tell their side of the story, there would be no show, no exposé into her husband's cheating and, therefore, definitely no trip to Florida. 'Thank you for all your help,' Violet said, heading to the door. The woman did not show them out and Edward worried about walking through the living room unaccompanied, but the men appeared to have decamped to the overgrown garden.

Back on the street, Violet seemed content.

'Do you think Minnie and Stan can be persuaded to come on the show?' Edward asked.

'We'll see.'

After a quick break for lunch at an over-priced café on Fleet Street when they had returned to central London, Edward helped Violet go over the notes she'd made and strengthened her case against her stories. By four in the afternoon they were ready for their meeting with Braithwaite.

'Right, what have you got for me then, guys?' he said, clutching an espresso and a thick red book as he crossed the gallery to the makeshift desk.

Violet flicked through her notebook and put forward her cases. Braithwaite wobbled slightly over the twins' story, given it potentially involved violence on the part of Annabel's boyfriend, but he eventually conceded, indicating that if worst came to worst they could simply interview them both separately. Braithwaite reluctantly agreed to a show involving Jo, Minnie and 'cheating' Stan but Edward didn't like the idea of putting surveillance on Stan. Braithwaite threw a wobbly about a few of the cases they'd found in the courts and took particular umbrage about a case involving an elderly single man who'd fallen into depression since his dog had died and now spent his days eating nothing but dog food.

'We could overrule him if we really wanted,' Violet admitted as they packed up their things.

'Have you done that a lot?' Edward asked.

'A few times.'

'But it's best to keep him sweet?'

'No, it's just protocol,' she sneered.

It was approaching six. Edward was exhausted, all he wanted was his bed, but Violet had one more task for him as she prepared to switch off the lights and leave the building. She wanted him to oversee a television interview that Liv was doing.

'Jim Cartwright is a good guy. There shouldn't be any trouble.'

Edward had seen his show a few times, on the odd occasion he watched television on a Saturday night. Cartwright was an American who'd come to Britain to make it and his show usually involved twenty minutes of his stand-up routine followed by a fifteen-minute interview before he got his guests to do something slightly embarrassing, related to whatever they were trying to plug.

'Under no circumstances do you let him mention Phillip, the trial, Michael's alcoholism or Liv's ex-husband. I've already emailed a list of no-go topics, so they know the deal. They don't want you sitting in the gallery and having access to her earpiece so if anything comes up, you need to walk onto the set and physically drag Liv off. It's more important that we get her off than saving face with the show. But that won't happen.'

It was agreed that the embarrassing act that Liv would partake in was a simulated version of *The O'Shea Show*. Cartwright was going to don a wig and pick on a member of the audience. They'd throw insults at each other and Liv had to sit in judgement and tell them how to sort it out.

When she arrived, Liv was not in a good mood at all.

'I'll be looking after you,' Edward had said, thinking he should introduce himself to the woman who was effectively his boss.

'Let's get a few things straight, little man. You won't be looking after anyone today. I look after myself.'

Nevertheless as soon as the cameras began to roll the sourness faded. But by the time the producer called the show a wrap, Edward wanted to cry he was so exhausted. It was late into the evening and he still had over an hour on the Tube to get himself home.

How easily a trap can be set, how predictable the world can be. You can be famous, they say, the world's your oyster, a car, a holiday, your greed and vanity need know no bounds. And higher and higher they jump, like a lamb to the slaughter, a turkey at Christmas, a junkie on crack.

But today the game would play out differently. As the sun set over the estate and the car made its way around the roads, the first victim was in sight. The real show was about to begin.

'Here,' Violet said, handing Edward a copy of *Spice* magazine. It was already open on a double page spread with Michael O'Shea's face and stills from the show. Beside it was a low angle shot of Liv leaning against a lamppost on a rundown industrial estate.

EXCLUSIVE LOOK ON SET OF NEW REBOOTED SHOW. HAS O'SHEA MET HIS MATCH?

It's not often that one of our most talked about reality TV stars takes up the mantle of such a well-loved institution but last week the new co-host of The Michael O'Shea Show *was finally revealed. Yes, very shortly Liv Dessington-Brown, best known for her crushing put-downs to contestants on* Help, I Need to be Famous, *will be serving up plates of wisdom and drawing on her remarkable life story to solve the nation's problems alongside reformed alcoholic O'Shea...*

A week had passed since Edward and Violet had started putting together the first set of shows of the new season. Edward put down the magazine.

'I don't know what's worse, when they really go to town trying to rubbish us or when they indulge in this ridiculous hyperbole.'

Violet gave a rare smirk.

At last, they were recording the first couple of shows to go out later in the week. Over the weekend the set designers had been working flat out to transform the studio. The old tiered seating had been thrown out and replaced by rows of permanent leather chairs and the stage itself had been decked out in green. There was also a host of new technology which had been installed: projectors soon to be lit up with the show's logo and a giant screen which, with the flick of a button, became a see-through sheet of glass into a pod where guests waited to come onto the stage.

The gallery was also no longer the preserve of Edward and Violet, it was awash with people. The techies had taken up seats on the complicated-looking deck and the studio below was all lit up.

'Here, put these on and sit down,' Violet said, handing Edward a chunky headset. 'I'll be backstage, tending to the guests. Your job is to sit up here and make sure everything's going smoothly. Press the red button and you'll get through to me.' Edward noticed there were a series of buttons down the side of his microphone. 'If it looks like it's getting out of hand then you give me a shout and I'll try to cool them down, off stage.'

'Right. Thanks, Violet.'

From above, Edward could see the audience filing in, awe-struck at what they saw before them: O'Shea in an open-necked blue shirt and Liv in a cream cardigan, awaiting instructions.

'Twenty minutes till we start the recording,' said the technician next to Edward. They were both observing a screen that was split into four. One for every camera.

At five minutes to, Braithwaite – complete with a clipboard

and his own set of notes – took up the seat in the corner. Edward noticed he didn't have a headset and so would be unable to hear what was happening below. Edward acknowledged him and Braithwaite gave him a small flicker of a smile back.

The chattering in the audience died away and the techies surrounding O'Shea and Dessington-Brown crept off the stage. The lights dimmed and then, when the countdown had concluded, the projector screens lit up with the new title sequence. Michael O'Shea walks down a rundown street where he bumps into a busking saxophonist who is blaring out the opening riffs of the theme tune. As he continues in his stride, he bumps into Liv and a montage of them both, gesticulating and lecturing guests, intercuts with them shaking the hands of the neighbours on the street, before they both come to rest on the same lamppost used in the *Spice* article.

The audience rose like puppets, right on cue, and their applause drowned out the coda of the theme tune as Michael O'Shea leapt onto the stage arm in arm with Liv.

'Thank you, thank you. Welcome! And we're starting off our new series with a bang. Not only do I have a new set, but I also have a new co-host. Yes, I will be joined by none other than Olivia Dessington-Brown. With no shortage of life experience that I'm sure you've all no doubt read about, Liv is the perfect host to help me untangle the crazy lives that come before me.'

'Yes, that's right. I'll be here every day with Michael, getting to the heart of our guests, really trying to understand what makes them tick and then telling them how I see it.'

'So,' Michael said, rubbing his hands together, his eyes flickering in the studio lights, 'shall I bring my first guest out?'

There was silence.

'Well, shall I? Come on!' He wanted the audience to play along but they weren't really interested in a pantomime and only a few of them shouted back.

The techie next to Edward seemed to be panicking.

'Roll the tape before you introduce the guest. Roll the tape.' He was clearly speaking to Michael over his earpiece.

Michael did not react but remained straight-faced as he spoke to the audience.

'Not good enough I'm afraid, folks, going to have to try harder than that. Guess we'll have to watch this clip instead. Here is a little bit about my first guest.'

And a montage of backstage footage, a short interview with Minnie, Jo and Stan and the occasional image of Dessington-Brown laying into them both, intercut with tabloid-style captions, flashed onto the screens built into the back of the set.

Then out came the three of them, accompanied by a shorter, more menacing arrangement of the show's theme tune. Jo, already wound up and determined to play up to the audience, sluggish Stan, with his hands in his pockets and small, timid Minnie, unable to hide her worn-out expression; she clearly wished she was somewhere else, as did Edward…

'Shush!' O'Shea said, pathetically, only properly trying to silence the room after a good few minutes of booing and unashamed retaliation from Jo.

'Oi!' he said, as Jo continued to wag her fingers and use language that would no doubt give the editors upstairs a field day. 'Be quiet and let's get to the bottom of this.'

'You're here to get the results of our surveillance aren't you, Jo?' Liv probed, calmly. *Was this good cop, bad cop?* Edward thought, though he soon realised it was more like bad cop, bad cop.

'Yeah,' Jo started 'because that PRICK…' this time she was given a warning by Dessington-Brown who promptly told her to wash her mouth out, 'has been cheating on me.'

'Cheating on you? Bit of a hypocrite aren't you, love?' Michael said.

There were pantomimic gasps from the audience and Edward

too could not help admitting to himself that he too found the accusation curious: they had found evidence of Jo cheating.

'We asked some of your friends and they didn't paint you as a paragon of virtue, love, believe me,' Michael continued.

Violet, who had remained silent up to then, watching the show from backstage, clearly felt she had to step in; her voice appeared in Edward's ear.

'This could explode if we're not careful...'

'Do you want me to speak to Liv?'

Unlike Edward, Violet could not contact Michael or Liv through her own earpiece, only Edward could do that. The procedure was supposed to safeguard the authority of those in the gallery, who had a better picture of what was going on.

'Keep an eye on it. Tell her to pull back if it goes further. If worst comes to worst tell the cameramen to cut away at any sign of a punch up.'

But although Violet sounded fairly calm about the situation, Braithwaite seemed to be having a fit of hysterics.

'No- no- she can't say that.'

Edward looked at him and caught his glance.

'I do hope you've told them to pull the plug, Ed.' Edward winced. A few close friends from college called him Eddie but nobody ever called him Ed. 'I'm responsible for the well-being of the guests and I won't have it.'

'Er...'

'I'm going to speak to Mags.'

The gallery door opened and in walked Mags.

'Seems my ears are burning again.'

Braithwaite went silent, his tongue clenched firmly between his front two teeth, his forehead wrinkled with rage.

'Fuck off, fuck off, fuck off,' Mags shouted.

'B- but surely you understand, with all due respect, I do have a duty of–'

'Yeah, you have a duty all right, a duty to FUCK OFF!' Mags

49

spat.

Edward turned his attention back to the show. They were about to film the cliffhanger where the ad break would go when the show was edited. Violet jogged briefly onto the stage to pass O'Shea an envelope.

'And so here it is,' he said, 'the results of our surveillance. This is what you wanted, 'ey, Jo, justice?'

'Don't forget, everyone,' Liv added, 'she said if he hasn't been cheating she'll let this waste of space walk right back into her house. Hardly great for her daughter, is it?'

The audience claps.

'Yeah, hang on a minute, Liv. What does Minnie think?'

O'Shea made his way to Minnie. 'Do you think your stepdad's going to pass the test, honey?'

'Dunno,' came the reply, 'guess so.'

'And standby to pause so there's space for the ad break,' said the techie next to Edward.

'Let's find out'! O'Shea opened the envelope.

'Well, well, well,' O'Shea smirked. 'Time for an ad break.' The audience groaned and he relished in their disappointment, appearing to lick his lips. 'You better not go anywhere!'

Edward opened a packet of Worcester Sauce flavoured crisps from his bag. As the show was recorded, the ad break would be added in later but everyone took a two-minute breather anyway. The tech guys remained where they were, using the interval to speak to the cameramen. The first half had been nowhere near as bad as Edward thought it might be but it was still incredibly strenuous to watch. Violet had explained that much of his task was to keep Braithwaite quiet and make sure he didn't disrupt the show. So far he'd hardly needed to do anything. Since Mags had put him firmly in his place, Braithwaite seemed to have shrunk into his chair like a naughty schoolboy. Not that Edward didn't sympathise with him, somewhat. He was, after all, trying to moderate and stop the guests being exploited, a noble cause. In fact, in some ways Braithwaite made Edward feel guilty for not exerting himself more forcefully, though whether anybody would have taken any notice of a word he'd said, he highly doubted.

In no time at all, they were back.

O'Shea manoeuvred himself so that he was in much the same position as he was before, at the front of the set, with his card close to his chest.

'The results of our surveillance...show that Stan HAS been cheating.'

There were gasps from the audience and a sudden fit of swearing from the stage.

But there was more...

'Our surveillance also showed Stan regularly visiting women's houses, even on several occasions meeting with them behind the bushes in a park. And to top it all off, ladies and gentlemen, our good friend was also caught buying drugs.'

The audience erupted into boos and Jo stood up.

'I KNEW IT! You lying cheating bastard. Got ya, haven't I?'

Sluggish Stan seemed to have life in him yet: he got up from his chair and fought back, throwing all manner of insults and accusations at Jo and then at O'Shea himself. It was chaos. In fact, the only person in the entire room who did not seem to be shout-ing, gloating or indeed trying to pick a fight was Minnie. The poor girl looked frightened. At one point she placed her hands over her ears and closed her eyes. But nobody seemed to have noticed her. Liv was busy pointing her fingers at Jo and trying to explain to her that she was no better than her husband and that it was absurd that they were here for a show about cheating when Stan's drug taking, alcoholism and lack of income had destroyed her relationship with him and her daughter long ago. She was, according to Liv, 'a worthless, feckless, lazy and irresponsible mother who should be ashamed of herself...'

Edward could see Braithwaite wiggling once again. He was tempted to side with him. He didn't understand why Minnie had to be on stage for the results, in fact, now he thought about it, Edward didn't understand why Minnie had even been included in the show in the first place.

Eventually, Stan saw fit to walk off the stage... surely the sensible option, though not according to O'Shea who taunted him for being a coward.

Now it was two-on-one. Liv and Michael levelled on Jo.

'So, what's it going to be then? Are you going to go home to him? Bet you are, aren't you? Just going to carry on playing happy families. Go on then... you've had your fifteen minutes of fame, taught him a lesson on national telly, punished him, so why don't you head back home and carry on fighting?'

She looked resigned, as if it was her only choice; despite the bravado, there was little fight in her now.

'...or,' Liv piped up. *So, this really was bad cop, bad cop*, Edward thought. '...or you can take the hard option, you can leave him. Come on. You know he's not worth it. You need our help, and we can give it to you. We can make sure he leaves, get you a proper job, build you a life again.'

The grand mansion in Florida, the peace, the tranquillity, the birds, the palm trees, it fluttered to the forefront of Edward's mind and he knew Jo was thinking the same. Liv was subtly reminding Jo that for all the abuse she'd been forced to face on stage, there would be a reward: it would definitely be worth it.

'Now, do you want our help? We have the best people. Don't worry about him,' Liv said, referring to Michael.

'Come on, give her a big round of applause, ladies and gentlemen...' Edward had to hand it to them. Somehow, in the space of a couple of minutes, Michael and Liv had transformed the entire show and managed to make the audience forget about Jo's misjudgments, turning her into a victim.

'Right, I do hope Jo and Stan sort out their differences. Now, my next guests, Annabel and Tiffany are twins and exotic dancers and adult movie stars.' Michael pulled a strange expression with his face, clearly trying to overemphasise his displeasure. 'But since Tiffany got pregnant and had her first baby and Annabel began dating the man who coaxed them into these X-rated shenanigans, the two have been at loggerheads. Now Annabel is accusing Tiffany of cheating with her boyfriend, can they resolve their differences and get back together or have they let their lust for men destroy their relationship? Let's bring them on.'

The twins were brought out together. Clearly enraged, Edward could only guess at what had been said to them back-stage, though from everything he had seen from that day at Deacon Court, they needed little encouragement. Of course, nothing was to get resolved during the show. The surveillance that had been placed on Tiffany had proved inconclusive, there was no evidence either way that she had been cheating with Annabel's boyfriend, who incidentally walked onto the stage only to be showered with abuse by O'Shea. When he went to lunge at him, O'Shea retreated quicker than Edward had ever seen him move before, though all the cameras cut away. Security carted him off and he never got to have his say.

'He acts the big man, but men like him are scum and you can never trust him, you understand that, right? Liv, help me out here.'

'You have to think logically. Here are the facts: you met him in a rundown nightclub and he has encouraged you to enter this seedy, dirty world. So why would he give that all up for you? He's stringing you all along. He probably has half a dozen girls on the go that he is seeing.'

'No he hasn't!' Annabel said. 'And if he did cheat on me… why didn't the detective see him?'

Liv took hold of her hand whilst Michael shook his head.

'Sweetheart, he probably suspected we were tailing him if he knew he was coming on the show and our expert says it was inconclusive.' She did not seem happy with the explanation, so Michael jumped in and did something that made everyone, including the techies in the gallery, gasp.

'Tiffany, I've got a question for you. I want you to answer it, honestly. Did you sleep with him? Did you have it off with your sister's boyfriend? You've told us you haven't before but here's your chance. If you want your sister back, away from that man for good...'

Annabel went pale and looked into her sister's eyes but Tiffany hesitated.

Liv got down beside Tiffany and grabbed her hand as well.

'The truth is important, girls, don't you think? How can you have any sort of meaningful relationship going forward if you don't tell each other the truth? She needs to know, Tiffany, she needs to know...'

Michael asked her again.

This time Tiffany's response was definitive.

'Yes!'

The studio erupted in shock and Annabel walked off stage.

Tiffany sat quite still, unmoving but it didn't matter. The show was at an end.

Annabel, apparently locked in one of the toilet cubicles, told Violet – who had chased after her with a camera crew – that she never wanted to speak to her sister ever again.

'Sometimes people just want to go their separate ways,' Michael said, 'we can try to help but I still believe the truth is the most important feature in all our stories. You can't hide from the truth. It will all come out one day. And the truth is we've run out of time, it's the end of the show. Join me tomorrow, same time, same place...'

Braithwaite, shaking his head and muttering to himself, left the gallery.

'What's the matter?' Mags shouted, as the door to the gallery blew shut. 'Cat got your tongue?'

He didn't reply.

'Fucking strange, that one,' Mags said to the remaining members of the gallery. 'Bloody red tape, forcing us to employ nutters like him.'

'Our contestants tonight all have one question for our judges, "will you make me a star?" But what does it take to make it on this show? What are our star judges looking for?'

'Looking at what the rest of the panel put through last week, seems all you need to do is dress up in a costume and blurt out a good sob story and you're in.'

The audience in the stadium burst into laughter and some began to clap.

Michael was being his blunt self but that was what people paid him to do, that was why people liked him. He was in the middle of a live recording for *Make Me a Star*. The talent show contest on which he was a judge – a gig his agents had lobbied hard to get him for years – was beginning its eighth series. The premise of *Make Me a Star* was simple. Anyone of any age could come from anywhere in the world and perform, present or persuade the judges to invest in them or their project. The investment could take the form of money or sponsorship, setting up a meeting with the right people or signing them up to a record deal. There was even a pot of money supplied by the channel to fly people out who could not afford to get to London. The most common contestants were singers or members of a band but people had also come on the stage and pitched charities they felt needed funding. On one notable occasion an amateur theatre troupe had asked for permission to put on their play: producers had worked overnight to completely transform the stage into their set.

They were currently at the audition stage. The contestants would come in and make their pitch usually in the way of a performance and then Michael and the others would have three options: make them a small offer there, which the contestants had the choice of accepting or trading in to go forward to the next round – though they might be sent home at a later stage with nothing – send them straight through to the next round or send them packing.

Just like his work on *The Michael O'Shea Show*, he found himself frequently in a room with people full of delusions of grandeur, their appetite for fame unquenchable, their desire for a quick fix to their sorry lives, unrelenting. It was his job – his moral and national civic duty – to put these people out of their misery.

'So come on, who's up first?'

Last time Michael had sat through two female singers with the stage presence of a sloth and a man asking for money to fund a brewery business, though Michael's suggestion that perhaps the money would be better spent on sending him to an Alcoholics Anonymous detox course, hardly curried favour with the audience who appeared to feel sorry for the drunken brute.

As it happened the boy band who performed first were actually quite good. Not mind-blowing but decent. Michael's offer to set up a meeting with a record producer, however, was overruled by the other three judges who decided they deserved to proceed further into the competition.

All in all, it turned out to be a more productive session than

Michael had anticipated. But, if truth be told, his mind had been on other things.

Sure, his brother's crimes seemed to have faded into obscurity – throwing the book at him, isolating him, had been a good decision – but it had been a stressful couple of days. He was glad he had a release, something mouth-wateringly exciting to look forward to.

Now all he wanted was to speed through things. He would usually have stayed for longer: the audience were screaming his name and flashing their camera phones. He knew he couldn't sneak out straight away, whilst the other judges did their bit, grinning like hyenas. Some bright spark would make a deal of it in tomorrow's papers. So he made sure to sign at least two dozen signatures and waved before heading off.

Of course, the press were waiting for him outside, as they always did. There was a car ready to whisk him away from the Palace Theatre and, predictably, a group on motorbikes.

'Would you like me to try to lose them?' Michael's driver said. Of course, he knew there was no point.

'The motorbikes never give up until they've got what they want. No, slow down, let them catch us...'

'Very well...' the driver said.

Michael combed his hands through his hair as the motorbikes pulled up alongside them and he tried not to blink when the inevitable flashes of camera light flooded through the windows.

'They shouldn't disturb you for the rest of the evening...' Michael's driver said.

No, Michael thought, *they better not. Not tonight, of all nights.*

Of course, Michael's driver was accustomed to this lifestyle. He had driven many celebrities before Michael had taken him on full time and had been trained in how to get rid of these pests.

But not even Michael's driver, as discreet as he was, could know anything about Michael's little escapade.

As the car pulled up outside his plush Chelsea home, he

surveyed the area and then waved goodbye to his driver, waiting for several moments before he proceeded to head out. He wasn't going home to his wife. There were other places he wanted to be. Driving the KA back from Manchester and then hiding it had been an extremely wise move. In the boot was a change of clothes – a hoodie, some dark glasses, and even a fake moustache – to make doubly sure he wouldn't be spotted.

All he had to do was hope and pray the car was still in the same place he'd left it.

In one afternoon, they had recorded a week's worth of shows, the first of which involving Minnie and the twins was to be broadcast first thing on Monday evening, the show's usual teatime slot. Violet seemed assured that the bar was always high for the first week and that there wouldn't be half as much pressure to find good stories moving forward.

Monday morning, as they prepared for the show's debut later on that evening, was, therefore, supposed to be a fairly laid back affair. With virtually no one in the office and Violet not needing his immediate attention, Edward was even able to have a coffee break, almost losing himself in the hustle and bustle of Fleet Street as he searched for his favourite café chain.

When he returned with an espresso for himself and a cup of tea for Violet, Edward noticed a freshly delivered stack of newspapers.

'Thanks,' Violet said, as Edward handed over her tea. She barely took her eyes away from the computer.

'I didn't realise we had to look through the papers every day. Is there not a PR team?'

'No. Besides, if you want a job doing...'

'Get me to do it!' Edward joked, though Violet did not respond as he pulled the papers from under her nose.

'I suppose it shouldn't take so long.'

Indeed, there was scarcely anything in the tabloids, just the occasional fleeting reference in an article:

'...*he looked like the sort of man who'd be caught with his pants down on Michael O'Shea.*'

Other than that there was precious little else. Edward flicked through the broadsheets, knowing that it would have had to have been a very slow news day for any self-respecting reporter or columnist to even mention the show. Indeed, the headlines of most of the broadsheets that day centred around when, not if, the prime minister would call an election. Beneath the national papers, there were also a few local ones. Though Edward assumed they were primarily to search for new stories, he checked them anyway, half out of wanting to do the job properly and half wanting to avoid doing something more taxing.

It was what he found on the back pages that made him recoil in horror. It was only a small article, but he instantly felt overwhelmed with guilt. Minnie, the same girl who had been sat just a few metres below him had run away again only this time she had not returned.

'*The girl's mother Jo is anxious for her to return in time for their all-expenses trip to Florida, following their appearance on The Michael O'Shea Show, due to air...*'

'Violet,' Edward said, 'look.' He showed her the article. But she did not seem moved. 'How did they even find out about it if it's not been broadcast?'

'It's a local paper. No one will read it.'

'She went missing after she appeared on the show.' Edward, distressed, buried his face in his hands. 'We pushed her over the edge!'

Violet seemed confused. 'The girl had a history of running away. It was the stepdad and the mum who are responsible.'

'But we...'

'Our job is to source and research the show and to make good television. If you've got a problem with that, well I guess you've broken the record and not even lasted two weeks.'

'But we caused the girl to run away, she could be in serious trouble.'

Violet seemed genuinely agitated. 'Looking after the guests is Braithwaite's job.'

'So I can go and tell him?'

'Yeah, if it makes you feel any better. He probably already knows. It's his job. Yours is to get back on with reading those papers.'

Edward reclined into his chair. The two said almost nothing to each other for the rest of the day. On reflection, he didn't know why he'd gotten so upset and supposed Violet was right. He didn't want to make the same mistake as his predecessors. He tried to make things less awkward with Violet the following morning. Catching the Tube earlier so that he could stop off at a coffee shop, even buying her a cake as well.

'Cheers,' she said, 'but I'm on a diet.'

He resigned to eating the cake himself.

'We need to start sorting the shows for this week,' Violet said.

'More trips to council estates, then?'

'You'd be surprised. We sometimes get very respectable people calling up the show.'

'Really?'

'That's what I wanted to talk to you about, actually. Someone phoned Braithwaite – he'd been recommended – but they wanted his help. Two retired solicitors. They think their daughter's developing an eating disorder, that or drugs maybe. She's seventeen. They've tried to get her into a clinic before. They think the Michael O'Shea treatment might work for her, she watches the show apparently, plus she wouldn't turn down the chance to appear on TV. She wants to be famous...'

Edward sighed. Another child. This time the parents at least sounded responsible. 'I see. Are we going to interview them?'

'Already scheduled in for the afternoon. The daughter has agreed to speak to us as well.'

'We're going to speak to the girl separately?'

'It's the best idea. Her parents have agreed to it and she wants to. They live in a quiet village, it's about an hour from here. We'll leave about two.'

'Right.'

~

The train journey was quiet as usual. Knowing Violet's proclivity for ignoring him, Edward had bought a novel by PD James to read as Violet, right on cue, once again took out her phone.

'I mentioned Minnie to Braithwaite,' Violet said, rather suddenly, 'he already knew what was going on.'

'I'm sorry,' Edward said, 'I didn't mean to lose it, I wasn't... it's just I–'

'Bernard Braithwaite, for all the hassle he causes us during the filming, has an important role to play. He talks to the families, makes sure they are coping. He'll coax Minnie back. But you should know if you start worrying about all the stories we work on you won't sleep at night.'

Edward thanked her for the advice and tried to smile at her, but she remained straight-faced and returned to her phone.

As they pulled into the station, Edward immediately felt that this was a town he would feel comfortable in. Even if he had somehow not spotted the ancient stone church, the cobbled streets or the gated mansions from the window of the train as they came gently to rest at the platform, Edward could not have avoided the grand three-storey bookstore which stood before him as he left the railway station. With its iron gates and ornate stone gargoyles, it reminded Edward of a saying his father had once shared with him, that you should judge a place not by how friendly its people are or how green its parks are, but on the size of its book shop.

It was quite a walk to the small private road where Mr and Mrs Butler lived. Barrington-Stoke was so rural that virtually every road was separated by at least one field. The Butlers' house was not quite as big as some of the properties they had passed but it still boasted a tall black gate and a wide sweeping driveway to match.

Violet pressed the buzzer and they were promptly let in by an elderly well-dressed man.

'Thank you so much for coming. My wife is just about to make tea,' he said, and Edward instinctively took off his shoes.

'So you think we can help your daughter?' Edward took the lead, as his greying wife joined them. They were led into a plush pink suite in the corner of a large room filled with books and a grand piano.

'Yes,' Mr Butler replied. 'Jessica. Bless her. We don't know what's up with her. At first, we thought it might be drugs but we simply don't know. We think she might have an eating disorder.'

'Why do you think that?' Violet asked, taking a notebook from her bag.

'She keeps disappearing all the time,' Mr Butler said. 'She fell out with her friends a while ago and ever since then she's been hanging around with... well, with people who want the same thing as she does.'

'And that is?'

'She wants to be famous. At first, when she was fifteen, she said she wanted to be a model. We tried to tell her to do well at school and then she could decide what she wanted to do later, that she'd have loads of options but she was quite adamant that she wanted to become a model and be on the telly. She told us that next year, when she turns eighteen, she wants to apply on that show. What is it? The one where they send ordinary people and celebrities to an exotic country, and film them to see how they get on?'

He was obviously relaying what his daughter had told him, verbatim.

'*Celebrity Holiday Home*,' Violet said, and when she said it Edward remembered that Liv had once been a contestant.

'But you wouldn't have to be particularly thin to go on that show?' Edward asked, sipping his tea. It was too weak for his liking.

'Yes, precisely,' Mr Butler said. '...and she's worried that these magazines, the newspapers, that they'd take photos of her and point out what she perceives as her flaws. She keeps talking about working on herself before she goes on the show. But whatever the newspapers wrote about her when she's on that show would only make her situation worse, she reads negative things into everything.'

'I see,' Edward said.

Violet took another sip of her tea.

'I'm afraid I'm going to have to ask you quite a lot of personal questions. We need them for the show,' she said.

'Oh, I see,' Mrs Butler said. Mr Butler, however, did not look impressed. He said nothing.

'And we'll also need to talk to Jessica as we agreed.'

'Okay.'

Edward smiled at them and tried to make them feel comfortable.

'Right,' Violet said, 'how long have you been married?'

'Er... thirty years.'

'And just to confirm Jessica is your own daughter?'

'Yes. We tried to have children for a very long time. It took us years but eventually, we had beautiful Jessica.'

'And have either of you ever had an affair?'

Mr Butler stood up. 'Good God! I shan't be asked that.'

Mrs Butler gently pulled him back down.

'I'm sorry, these are questions we have to ask. We have to know the full picture.'

'It's okay,' Mrs Butler said.

And for the next twenty minutes they answered Violet's questions with not a hint of hesitation. No, neither of them had ever taken drugs, nor suffered from depression. They had never mistreated their daughter and couldn't even remember the last time they'd raised their voices at her. Everything, it seemed, was whiter than white. There was only one thing that Violet needed to ask before Edward followed her upstairs to Jessica's bedroom. 'Would you give us permission to have your daughter followed, to find out what she's up to?'

Both Mr and Mrs Butler looked incredibly uncomfortable.

'But she trusts us,' Mrs Butler said, 'she'd be horrified if she knew we were spying on her, what if she never speaks to us again?'

Edward wondered if Jessica actually watched the show. For if she did then she must have realised that it was at least a possibility that they would make use of a private detective: 'research', so to speak.

'I believe you've spoken to Dr Braithwaite, he is very qualified,' Violet added, appealing to Mr Butler's rationality. Why would a qualified psychiatrist allow a private detective to follow his daughter if he thought it would seriously damage her?

There was silence until finally, Violet got up.

'Have a think, perhaps we can discuss it on the phone tomorrow or later in the week.'

'Yes,' Mr Butler said, getting up as well. 'Yes, I do think that is a better idea.'

'Brilliant,' Violet said as Mr Butler moved to shake her hand.

'Would it be possible to see your daughter, Mr Butler?'

'Certainly, she should be in her bedroom,' and Mr Butler led Edward and Violet out of the living room and to a plush pink staircase with brass handrails. Up they went until they reached the third floor and a plain white door with a fluffy pink sign that read: 'Jessica'. Inside was a sitting room complete with beanbags, sofas and a television, the other was a small study with a pink desk and a bookcase but it was in the final room, the bedroom, that the girl was sitting, upright on her double bed, surfing the internet on her laptop.

'Jessica, sweetie, these are the people from *The Michael O'Shea Show*, they want to ask you a few questions,' Mr Butler said.

She beamed and leaped off the bed.

'Now, darling,' her father said, 'if they ask you anything you feel uncomfortable with, if there's anything you don't want to answer, then remember you don't have to, you can come downstairs and get us. You know that, don't you?'

'Yeah, yeah, I know, Dad.'

'Okay, well, we're going to leave you now.'

Mr Butler closed his daughter's bedroom door behind them and Mrs Butler followed him out. Violet waited for a few minutes until he could be sure they had started their descent back down to the living room.

Jessica was only seventeen and yet Edward couldn't help feeling that she was trying too hard to fit into the stereotype that usually graced reality television; lots of make-up and far too much perfume. The meeting wasn't supposed to be an audition. Or at least that wasn't how Edward saw it.

'Do you have a boyfriend?' Violet said, bluntly.

Jessica blushed.

'Why? Is your friend trying to chat me up?' She pointed at Edward.

He went bright red as well.

'No.' Violet laughed. 'We need to know for the show.'

'No,' she said.

'Have you ever had boyfriends?'

'No, nothing serious...'

Violet moved on quickly.

Next, her alleged eating disorder. Violet asked her directly and studied her reaction intently. She fidgeted and seemed particularly edgy at the prospect of being probed on the subject during the show; there was undoubtedly something going on.

'What about drugs?' Violet said.

'I've tried them,' Jessica said. 'Cannabis a few times and cocaine at a party once but I'm not addicted... my parents don't know.'

'And what about your home life? Are your parents mean, abusive?'

'They can be rather annoying, sometimes, but they're wonderful and give me everything I want. I do feel bad for keeping secrets from them.'

She knew they'd be ashamed at her drug use, but she was careful to point out that she definitely DID NOT have an eating disorder. She wanted to go on *O'Shea* because she wanted to get noticed and to help put her parents' minds at rest, to show them that she was capable of getting the career in the media she wanted.

'Will I get a chance to meet Michael after the show, maybe he can give me some advice? Help me boost my profile. Please?'

'Of course,' Violet said, 'thanks so much for your time, Jessica.' And with that she and Edward bid goodbye to the Butlers and headed back towards the railway station.

'I feel sorry for her parents,' said Edward.

'Yes, the girl definitely has a problem.'

'But Braithwaite can help.'

'If we proceed.'

'If? I thought the Butlers were a dead cert.'

'There's no conflict. I was having doubts anyway but when we asked her point blank about her parents she said they were wonderful. We might have been in with half a chance if she'd slagged them off.'

'So we're just going to leave her?'

'Yep.'

'But she's got a problem. We're the only people who can help. Surely we can run it? It'll pull at heartstrings, it would make a good show.'

'You've changed your tune.'

Edward went red. He'd seen the girl. She was so thin. The trade-off that Violet had talked so much of, was, he had to admit, a sensible approach here. Jessica wouldn't admit she had a problem, she wanted to be famous. By allowing her on the show and 'exposing' her behaviour to her parents and the world, she would get the help she needed and perhaps Michael's straight talking would make her see reality.

'What about Braithwaite, he'll be on board with it all, won't he?'

Violet took a deep breath.

'If you want to come back here and see what can be done for Jessica Butler, fine, good shout. But in your own time. We turn up to work in the morning, we make good television and then we go home. You need to accept we're not social workers or you need to leave, Edward.'

Edward opened his mouth to speak but no words came out. He remained silent for much of the journey back to the studio.

'It's a no,' Violet said. Braithwaite flapped. They were back in the gallery.

'But, but, that girl needs specialist attention, it's the only way to get through to–'

'Not happening,' Violet said definitively, 'take it up with Michael.'

'This is preposterous, you can't expect me to sit back and–'

'Even if,' said Violet, 'we went ahead it's far too early in the run for anything soppy. We've got some celebrity specials lined up in three weeks, *if* we're going to run it then it will be sandwiched in between. That's the only way we can guarantee viewers.'

Braithwaite stormed off and Violet set about finding a suitable replacement story, with Edward's help.

~

The following day Violet was already at the desk and as Edward climbed up the gallery stairs, he could already hear Mags.

'What the FUCK is this shit?'

She was clutching a newspaper and holding it up.

'I don't make a habit of reading what these people churn out but on the one day, the one fucking day I have the sodding *Lion* shoved in my face on the way out of the Tube and it's full of this.'

Edward said nothing and read the paper over Violet's shoulder as fast as he could.

EXCLUSIVE: O'SHEA CUTS TIES AS 'PAEDO' BROTHER IN COURT

- Michael won't fund court costs

- Insiders: Michael is pushing for a guilty plea to avoid embarrassment

The story was self-explanatory.

'It's a miracle that's on page seven, would have been front-page material if those fucking clowns across the road weren't throwing their toys out of the pram.'

Liv had walked in. She was, of course, referring to parliament and the impending election.

'Hang on...' Violet's mobile was ringing.

'A miracle!' Mags protested, as Violet stepped out to take the call. 'I tell you what would be a miracle, if someone went round there and put the kiddy fiddler out of his misery.'

'Right, well...'

Several moments later Violet stepped in with a worried look on her face.

'We might have a problem.'

'For fuck's sake...' Mags said.

'It's Minnie. She's run away. Jo's rung reception, ranting. She's saying that we pushed her over the edge. She was screaming down the phone, apparently, said she's going to go to the police and sue us.'

'Sue us! The spoilt little shit. We're about to pay for her to go to Florida,' Mags snapped, 'and this is how she repays us? Get on this!'

'We will sort it,' Violet said.

'But I don't understand,' Edward protested, as the meeting disbanded, and he and Violet proceeded to their desks at the back of the studio. 'What are we supposed to do? If her daughter has run away, what can we do about it? Surely it's a matter for the police.'

He was, of course, subtly referring to her comments yesterday.

'No, Edward. We don't want to get the police involved if we can help it.'

'What? You're expecting us to find her on our own? She could have been abducted. Anything.'

So much for not being social workers.

'Doubt it. She's run off dozens of times before and always comes back. It's not about the police, it's about guest rehabilitation. Looking like we–'

'Actually give a shit about people?' Edward snapped, losing control.

Violet quelled him a sharp look and he regretted being so blunt.

'I just don't want her to go telling tales.'

'Okay… okay…' Edward breathed. 'So we're going to go down there and talk to her?'

'Sorry, Edward, you're going to have to do this one on your own. I'm needed here. I need to firm up the rest of the week's shows and get next week's sorted.'

'You want me to go, on my own?'

'Take Braithwaite with you if you really must but…' Violet paused for a moment.

'What?'

'I don't want you getting carried away.'

'What do you mean?'

'If we go to the police it will make the situation ten times worse, attract attention.'

Edward went down the gallery steps and to Braithwaite's office.

As it happened, he was not that helpful. He seemed agitated by the fact Edward was getting involved in his area of expertise.

'This really isn't necessary,' he started. 'I can work with the family to try to resolve their issues on my own.'

'Do you know where Minnie is?' Edward asked, politely.

'No,' Braithwaite said, fidgeting with his glasses, 'but we have procedures. I don't want you going round to the house and bulldozing everything I am trying to do. It's not for some junior researcher to jeopardise the authority of the director of guest rehabilitation.'

Edward didn't know what to say.

'I'm sorry,' Braithwaite said, seeing Edward's sunken expression. 'The family is fragile, volatile. I'm trying to help them put their lives back together...'

'Then maybe I can help...'

Braithwaite changed tack. 'All right,' he said, 'all right, but I'm coming with you. We can help find her together.'

'Right, there's a train that leaves in twenty minutes.'

'I've got a car,' Braithwaite explained, and they headed out of the studio, through the underpass and to the garages.

'I presume you're under instructions to keep the police out of this.'

'Er, yes,' Edward said, opening the passenger door to Braithwaite's BMW.

'It's ridiculous. If we could put out an appeal. Minnie's family is so...' He stuttered slightly. 'They're hurting and that manifests itself in their shouting, bickering and arguing. Knowing the police were investigating would help put their minds at rest. I want to help them get through it, you know?'

'Right.'

Thankfully, there was little traffic in London but Edward got the impression that was because Braithwaite knew all the side roads and back passages that only an experienced commuter would. When they finally reached the council estate, Braithwaite insisted on parking the car a few streets away.

'I don't want to draw attention to the fact we're here,' he explained. 'I don't think Jo gets on too well with her neighbours. They already resent the fact she has been on television and they haven't. If we're seen to be giving her even more attention it could cause more conflict.'

They walked down the streets and knocked at Jo's door. Hearing no response, they pushed open the door and headed inside. The house was more of a mess than it had been before. The living room was piled with clothes and unwashed bed sheets.

'Jo!' Braithwaite shouted. 'Jo, it's Dr Braithwaite from *The Michael O'Shea Show*.'

They went to climb the stairs. Jo was lying stooped over them, a bottle in hand, her eyes glazed over. When she tried to speak, her words were so slurred Edward couldn't work out even remotely what she was trying to say.

'Come on,' Braithwaite said, grabbing hold of her arm, 'let's get her into the living room.'

Edward obliged but Jo resisted.

'No,' she screamed.

'We're just trying to help,' Edward said. She didn't seem impressed, but her grip seemed to soften nonetheless and Edward and Braithwaite were able to lift her onto the battered sofa in the living room.

Braithwaite went straight to the kitchen and poured her a glass of water, almost having to force Jo to drink it. She reached for the bottle of wine. Edward took it away from her and she halfheartedly tried to grab it back.

Braithwaite forced more water down her and they sat with her for fifteen minutes. Eventually, she seemed to calm down.

'Jo,' Braithwaite said, and she at least seemed able to actually understand what they were saying, 'I do need you to think, right now, where could Minnie be? Could she be staying with her friends?'

'B-better- better off without me,' she said.

'That's not true!' Edward protested.

'Edward's right, tell us where she might be so we can go and find her.'

'Factory...' she said, 'the factory.'

'What was that?' Braithwaite said.

'I saw it on the train when we first came here,' said Edward. 'There's an abandoned industrial estate on the outskirts of town. She must be talking about one of the derelict buildings.'

'Right.'

'You stay here,' Edward said. 'I should only be about forty minutes. If I'm longer than an hour, call me.'

And with that, Edward headed out of the door. He had a vague idea where the factory was but he still felt slightly uneasy about heading out into the town.

Edward climbed over the shards of broken glass that littered the floor and onto the concrete. There were warehouses and smaller buildings that had once been shops but Edward knew that the building Jo had been talking about was more likely to be the giant three-storey complex that dwarfed the rest of the site. A little more care had been taken to lock this building down, it seemed, but that hadn't stopped the intruders.

Though there might have been padlocks and giant wooden boards sealing off the ground floor, the windowpanes on the third storey had been left uncovered and somebody had climbed up, making sure to graffiti their tag on the walls as they went. Edward checked around the back of the building. It was as he thought. Once the initial break-in had been completed, somebody had knocked one of the ground floor boards through from the inside creating a small gap to squeeze into.

'Hello!' Edward called out. He wished he'd brought a torch with him. It was dark. He pulled out his phone, turned up the brightness and stopped to shine it around. He walked forward. He was in the centre of the building, where manufacturers had once sat; cramped, sweaty and overworked, the sound of machinery and foremen shouting their orders intolerable. Now all he could hear was his own foot splashing in the puddles in front of him and what seemed like faint voices in the far distance.

'Hello,' he said again but that only made him feel more afraid.

Then a thud and a huge splash.

He screamed out and scanned the room with his phone. There were two teenage girls standing a few metres in front of him. They had jumped down from the landing above.

'Are you friends with Minnie?' he asked instinctively.

'What's it to you?' one of them sneered.

'She's gone missing. I've come to find her.'

'Maybe she doesn't want to be found.'

So that was it, Edward thought, *she was safe, just hiding.* 'What do you mean? Have you seen her? Her family is worried.'

'Oh please,' said the other girl. In the light from the cigarette she was smoking, Edward could see that she had a nose piercing and a pale complexion. 'Her mum couldn't give a fuck about her. She's the reason she's run away.'

'So you know where she is?'

'I don't have to tell you anything. Who are you anyway?'

Edward hesitated to tell them. 'I work on a television show,' he said, vaguely.

Their interests seemed momentarily pricked.

'And what's someone like you doing around here? Making a documentary about us, are you? The council estate freaks?'

Edward tried to remain calm.

'No. Please,' he said, as the girls turned their backs on him and returned to whatever it was they were doing. 'I'm trying to find your friend. It's in her best interests.'

'I'm telling you nothing,' they spat and Edward knew the battle was lost. He started to make his way to the tiny hole where he'd entered. 'You're lucky we didn't have your phone and knock your teeth out,' they said. He shuddered at the thought.

Back at the house, he told Braithwaite what he knew. Jo was lying on the sofa, asleep, covered by a tatty old throw. Edward might not have found Minnie but it certainly sounded as if her friends knew where she was.

'I don't think she's been forcibly taken…'

Braithwaite though was not convinced.

'She's fifteen. It doesn't matter whether she's voluntarily absconded or if her friends have knowledge of her whereabouts, she's still missing. And those girls didn't admit to anything anyway. You don't know for sure that they were covering for her.'

In an ideal world, Edward agreed with Braithwaite. They needed to find the girl, she could be in danger, she was better off at home under careful supervision or indeed under the care of social services. That was perhaps where they should have referred the girl when she had first been booked onto the show. But the voices in his head told him he had what he'd come for, confirmation from Minnie's friends that they knew where she was. It didn't matter about their source, it was enough to kill the story and get the press off the case. He was needed back in the office.

'Bernard,' Edward said, he knew Braithwaite hated it when

people referred to him only by his surname, 'can you, can you help find her? Maybe you can stay here, talk to Jo until she tells you something.'

'Look,' he said, agitated, 'tracing missing girls is a job for the police.'

Jo was still asleep. She had been so inebriated that Edward and Braithwaite had no doubt that she'd not heard a word of their conversation. Edward thought about what to do. If he told the police – as he knew he really should – then he would almost certainly lose his job, if not directly, then he knew that Mags, Liv, and Michael would ensure that his life was made very difficult. He was deliberately creating a scandal and bringing unwanted attention to the show at a time when they were already feeling the pressure.

'Jo,' Edward said, waking her.

She came round. 'Have you found her?'

'I spoke to her friends, they–'

'What did they say?'

'They said they knew where she was…' he lied.

'Then where is she?'

'She doesn't want to come home, yet. They wouldn't tell me where she was. But you know she's alive, she hasn't been kidnapped.'

'She's my daughter. What if they were lying? They're the wrong sort, them lot. I want her home.' Jo got up. 'I'm going to ring the police. I should have rung 'em straight away, yesterday!'

'I don't think that's a good idea…' Edward said.

Braithwaite's eyes narrowed, his brows furrowed. 'I want to speak to you–'

Edward held up his hands in protest and ignored him.

'Argh,' Jo screamed in a drunken rage. 'What's the point! I've lost her. She doesn't want me.'

'If she hasn't come home by the end of the week then call them but I think she's out there, she just needs time to cool off.'

Before they left, they ensured that Jo's door was firmly locked and that her remaining bottles of alcohol were discreetly disposed of while she slept.

Neither Edward nor Braithwaite said a word to each other on the journey back. In fact, all Braithwaite offered Edward as he left his car was a small flicker of his hand in farewell. Edward imagined that Braithwaite, for all his staunch protection of the guests he counselled, was just as glad to be away from that house as Edward. He was evidently not a man who took well to chaos and disorder.

~

Violet was snowed under when Edward arrived back in the office. He explained what Minnie's friends had said and Violet seemed grateful.

Thankfully, the stories Violet had lined up to run were not nearly as controversial as the previous week. There were two men in a relationship who both thought they were cheating: that one was pretty much a go. Violet instructed Edward to liaise with the private detective agency. A drug addict had also agreed to come on the show so long as he was offered help. Violet had promised that he would be packed off to the best private clinic for six months and that they would delay the paid-for-trip to Florida until he had recovered so that he had something to look forward to. All in all, it was set to be a fairly typical week in the life of *The Michael O'Shea Show*.

~

The Friday recording came and the drug-addicted man went off to the clinic without a hitch, even after a gruelling session on stage, in which O'Shea called him a waste of space and a pathetic excuse for a human being, amongst many other things. And, as it turned out, neither man who had come for the results of the surveillance had been cheating: the private detectives had gone to extreme lengths to try to prove that they were, but it turned out both of them were simply paranoid.

'I'm off,' Violet announced, almost as soon as the recording came to an end. Edward couldn't blame her. It had been a long week. As she marched off towards the gallery door, Edward wondered momentarily if he should ask her something. *Would it have been such a crime to see if she wanted to come for a drink with him?* In the end, he ran out of time.

But he wasn't planning on going straight home. He texted one of the only people he knew in the capital, outside of work: his friend Cate. She was two years older than him and had secured a job as a social media engagement officer for a prestigious city business. The two of them had been at sixth form college together, but he rarely got a chance to see her so he had rather hoped that they might get to see more of each other now that he was living in the City. Sadly, however, he was wrong. His phone vibrated and he knew that a response that quickly meant only one thing:

Really sorry, Eddie, it said, *snowed under here. Another time?*

Edward sighed, heading for the Tube, intending to reply when he got back to his flat. Predictably, the Tubes were packed and nobody so much as smiled at him; London was a lonely place, far more so than he'd ever anticipated. Back at his small one-bedroomed flat on the outskirts of the city, he got in, dumped his stuff and laid on his bed. He'd spent so little time here, that he still hadn't figured out how to use half the appliances in his kitchen and he couldn't be bothered with cooking anyway. So he lay in the darkness, falling asleep almost instantly, trying desperately to retain the optimism with which he had first come to the City and hoping that the weekend and the week that followed would not be quite as stressful.

13

Unfortunately, Edward's life did not get any easier the following week, despite a relaxed weekend spent largely in bed. The only topic of discussion on Monday morning was Minnie. She had still not returned home.

'Jo wants to hold a press conference and get the police involved,' Violet said, closing her eyes momentarily and running her hands through her hair. 'Braithwaite's idea,' she muttered, breaking the news of a heated conversation that she'd had with him.

What on earth were they to do? Violet couldn't seriously be suggesting they ignore Jo's wishes and attempt to block a police investigation, just to uphold the reputation of the show?

'She's a missing girl, we were never going to be able to suppress this forever.'

'That's not how Michael or Mags will see it.'

'So what do we do then?' As he spoke, Edward knew Braithwaite was on his way over.

Violet looked as if she was about to start tearing strips out of her own hair. 'Minnie should be low on our list of priorities. We've got this week's show to do and I've still got to book the resort for last week's guests. I can't deal with the press and Michael laying into me as well. If the police start an investigation it will be all over the front pages and if the show is found to have pushed Minnie too much, we'll be hounded. You weren't here before...'

No, that was true, Edward hadn't been at the show the last time but he'd sure read about it... Michael had allegedly wound up a guest so much that when it was revealed his brother had been having an affair with his wife, he flipped out, destroying the set, threatening the guests and breaking the brother's nose. The police were waiting in the wings to charge the man at the end of the show and at the trial, Michael himself was called as a witness. Summing up, the judge condemned the show as a 'morally bankrupt playground' with a 'producer who cared only for salacious gossip, titillation and public humiliation'. If the show didn't change and start looking after its guests, the judge said, he'd have no hesitation in suggesting the police charge the channel's executives with corporate negligence...

'I'm sure there won't be a court case,' Edward said, though deep down he wasn't quite so sure. 'I mean, you can't prove that the girl ran away as a direct result of the show. For all we know she could have gone home and fought with her mother or maybe she has a secret boyfriend she's run off with.'

Violet rolled her eyes.

'You're far too naïve for this business. It doesn't matter what the courts think, if Minnie's disappearance gets into the press they'll savage the show. The channel will close it down, we'll all be out of jobs.'

Edward didn't have time to respond. Braithwaite had just entered the room.

'I've been to Minnie's house again. Her mother is distraught. We still can't find her.'

'So you think involving the police is inevitable?' Violet said.

At that moment the gallery doors flew open. It was Mags.

'DON'T TREAT ME LIKE A FUCKING IDIOT, BRAITHWAITE.'

For a few moments Edward seriously thought she was going to deck Braithwaite. He crumpled, instantly, his head curving into his spine and his hands retracting inwards as if he was hugging himself.

'I- I- I-' Poor Braithwaite could barely get his words out.

'I've just got off the phone to Chief Constable Gardner and do you know what he said? There's a woman saying her daughter's been missing for over a WEEK, a FUCKING WEEK, and do you know the last time she was seen? The day she went on this fucking show. WHAT THE FUCK do you think you are FUCKING playing at?'

Edward and Violet could only look on in horror.

'Now we know where the hell you've been all week, you were trying to stop her from going to the police weren't you? Do you know how guilty that makes us look? Do you have any idea of the amount of shit we're in? It looks as if the brat ran away because we didn't do our job properly and then we tried to cover it up! And remind me who is responsible for aftercare?'

'We were… trying to limit the damage.'

Mags took no notice and pulled out her phone.

'What are you…' Braithwaite started.

'It'll be none of your fucking business what I'm doing when I have security march you out that door, along with all the shit you keep in that garage of yours.'

His already pale face lost even more colour.

'We're going to need you in as soon as you can, looks like there's a bit of a situation…'

There was a pause: she was clearly on the phone to Michael O'Shea.

'Yeah well… it's got nothing to do with me I can assure you. Yeah, okay. Yes, see you soon.'

'Michael's on his way over: emergency meeting as soon as he gets here…'

'But I thought you said I was…' Braithwaite stumbled, having regained at least enough colour in his face to be able to speak.

'Fuck off, Braithwaite,' Mags said.

Edward, with no idea how he'd gotten off so lightly, didn't say a word to Violet who was also clearly expecting some verbal turbulence from Mags.

Just twenty minutes later they were cramped into the gallery with Michael, Liv, Mags, and even two techies.

'So… is someone going to tell me what's going on?' Michael snapped. Liv nodded. Violet, who had made a few phone calls of her own and gathered the facts in the twenty-minute gap, filled them in.

'The police have been called. They are suggesting that Jo do an appeal for the press and that she makes as many TV appearances as she can, it's scheduled for tomorrow at four. The newspapers will know by now.'

Michael banged his fists on the table. 'This is a joke, you know that, an absolute joke. If you'd been doing your job properly, we would not be in half as much shit.'

Edward was outraged. Violet, however, remained cool, diplomatic and even apologetic.

'I understand that,' she said, 'however, we do think there is a solution.' Edward had not heard her mention anything before. *Was she making it up on the hoof?*

'Go on.'

'You wouldn't deny that the show was at fault and you'd make sure you went to go and see the family, to join the campaign for Minnie to come home safely.'

'Admit we screwed up? We'd get slaughtered…'

Violet seemed to have got through to Liv. 'Being honest, admitting your mistakes, it's in your philosophy. This could be a bold move, Michael, you could show the people you don't just talk-the-talk, you practise exactly what you preach.'

Michael nodded.

'But how can I fit in all those interviews, my judging for *Make Me a Star*, my book signings and record the shows for next week?' he asked.

'We could scrap what we've got and run follow-ups,' Violet said, 'with just a voice-over and straight reruns or maybe tape something at the weekend when the furore has died down.'

They decided that recording follow-ups that could be put together with an extra twenty minutes of Michael's voice-over was the best way forward. It was a quick way of highlighting the shows successes; they would do a few features returning to previous guests. The idea of having Jessica Butler, the girl with the eating disorder, on had also been mooted. Getting an entire week's worth of shows researched and recorded as well as trying to hold the press at bay would have been far too much of a challenge, even for Edward and Violet. This week would be manic as it was. And sure enough before the meeting in the gallery was even over, the phone rang.

It was *The Lion* no less... they'd already caught wind of the press conference and were busy putting accusations about negligence to Edward. Edward knew how to respond even without asking: 'Michael will be right over for a face-to-face interview,' he assured the reporter though didn't sound convinced and continued her line of questioning for another ten minutes. When she finally hung up, Edward leaped down the gallery stairs and to Michael's dressing room. The door was already ajar. Braithwaite was inside poring over some notes with him, much to Michael's delight.

'*The Lion* want an interview, I said you'd be right over.'

Michael looked vexed. 'Fine,' he said, 'I swear I get more shit off these journalists than the nutters who send me messages on the internet.' He pulled out his smartphone.

Edward knew better than to engage with Michael when he was like this, other than to nod vaguely in sympathy with him. He waited for him to finish his coffee and then headed back to the gallery.

None of the other papers or TV stations had caught up with what was happening but they would in time. So Edward and Violet leaped into action, organising the follow-up shows. The two of them barely even thought about what might make the best line-up: they simply scrolled down the list of previous guests, circling drug addicts that had been through intensive rehab, abusive relationships that the show had helped to defuse and cheaters who had reformed and managed to fix their relationship. They were going to take the time to highlight what a force for good the show could be.

'They'll jump at a chance to be on again,' Violet explained, 'and they won't mind doing it at short notice. Most of them don't have much going on in their lives and we'll be providing the transport.'

And, sure enough, as Violet rang round, nearly every guest responded with enthusiasm.

'So I'm guessing we don't really need to do research for these, if they've been on the show before.'

All we need is an introduction from Michael and a voice-over explaining what has happened since last time, the rest is just archive footage from the previous shows. Anyway, I need you to book their train tickets and go and pick them up.'

'Right.'

'Here's a list of what we need, all to arrive at Blackfriars station.' Violet handed Edward a list of guests' hometowns, none of them more than forty miles away. He bid her goodbye and headed out across the road to the station armed with the company debit card. When he finished he walked straight back but not to the studios. Asking at reception, he got directions to the mail room: a huge hub with a labyrinth of small cubby holes for various executives and presenters, and stacks of stationery, packages and envelopes for all occasions. Edward grabbed one of the smallest envelopes he could and began writing on the addresses of the guests.

A tired-looking old man sat by the franking machine, surrounded by red postbags. Edward asked him to send the tickets by special delivery. He grunted, mumbling something about budget cuts, before telling Edward they'd be in the post by the end of the day.

When he returned to the gallery it was to Braithwaite arguing with Violet.

'If you think I've got time to go fact-checking, interviewing all of their family again then you're sorely mistaken, Braithwaite. These are catch-up shows.'

'But but– look, surely you realise that half the reason we're in this situation is because we failed to do the proper checks. If we carry on–'

'We're in this situation because a girl, with a *history* of running away, has gone missing again. I haven't got time for... ah, Edward, the tickets are in the post?'

'Yeah, they should be with them tomorrow.'

'Look, slow down, slow down, this is all too–'

'Bernard,' Violet said, calmly, 'please can you leave us to it?'

His enthusiasm suddenly evaporated and he stalked off down the gallery stairs.

'That man,' Violet whispered. 'That bloody man.'

The following day Violet left for Minnie's school where the press conference was being held. She was going to coach Michael and Liv on what – or rather what not – to say to the reporters. Edward had been left at the studio to take charge of tracking down the footage from previous recordings. The editors had to order the tapes themselves and manually incorporate them into each episode. Violet had made a list of ten memorable guests she wanted to watch back before forming a shortlist. The trouble was, without an exact date Edward was having to sift through hours of footage.

He sat back, slumped in his chair, pondering over his problem before he had an idea and loaded up the computer. He tapped the general premise of some of the episodes he was looking for into YouTube and smiled to himself. Somebody had helpfully uploaded every single recording as far back as three years earlier and in the description box had offered up as much information as they could, including airing dates. *Some people really had too much time on their hands…*

As half ten approached – the time the press conference was due to air – Mags, Braithwaite and a few of the techies gathered into the empty studio below and Edward felt he should join them. The projector above the stage had been set up with a livestream to Michael's press conference.

'Who's going to bring us some popcorn then, 'ey?' said Mags.

Edward did not find her at all amusing.

Sure enough, at half past ten, the local news broadcaster cut away from his interview with a local MP and to the inside of an assembly hall. A table had been put up where Jo, two police officers and Michael himself sat. As the cameras panned around the audience, Edward noticed Violet at the corner, notepad in hand.

Nearly every single seat in the room was filled.

'We'd like to start by thanking you all for coming,' one of the police officers said. 'As you all know, we have arranged a press conference to discuss the disappearance of fifteen-year-old Minnie Jenkins. Minnie has a history of running away and at this stage we do not believe there is anything suspicious. We do not believe Minnie was abducted. We believe Minnie could be staying with friends; however, for obvious reasons, we would like her to return safely as soon as possible. We must stress to anyone watching who might have any information regarding her whereabouts, friends or otherwise, that neither yourselves nor Minnie will be in any trouble if she is returned. Even a phone call would be greatly appreciated to let us know that she's okay. Thank you.'

Now it was Jo's turn to speak. She had composed herself quite well, considering the circumstances, though, of course, it was not the first time her daughter had run away.

'I wanna say...' As she spoke, Edward could tell that she'd had at least a couple of drinks. 'I want my girl home, I want her home. Just me and her. I know I ain't been the best mum but at the end of the day, I'm sorry. Please, Min, come home, please.'

She stopped and Michael saw fit to intervene.

'Guys, what's happened really is terrible. Anyone who saw the show the other week will know that Minnie's had a pretty tough time of it recently. Her mum, you know, she's made some bad decisions. She married the wrong guy and she'll be the first to admit that she's got a bit of a drink problem. But we've been working with her to try to solve her issues and I think it's really important that we say this – because of all the stuff you might read in the press about "oh she's an unfit mother, we're not surprised she ran away" and that we're exploiting her – Jo loves that kid and she wants her back, as do we. No mother deserves to wake up every morning and have that feeling of uncertainty, of always wondering if their kid is dead or alive, so, please, if anyone knows anything about where she might be or if you're watching, Minnie, please, love, give us a call. Even if it's just to say you don't want to have any contact with your mum anymore, we can help you with that but at least we'll all know you're safe. Thanks, guys.'

'I think he's single-handily saved us!' Mags shouted. 'Someone buy that man a drink!'

The second of the police officers concluded the conference.

'I would reiterate that anyone who knows anything about Minnie's whereabouts should phone the number on the screen or head to the nearest police station. You can call anonymously. We do want to ensure that Minnie is safe.'

As the conference came to an end, the words of the policeman struck a chord with Edward. He'd almost forgotten that he did indeed have some information about Minnie that may be of interest to the police; the conversation that he'd had with those girls in the ruined factory. They had implied that they knew where she was, that she was safe and simply didn't want to be found. He needed to speak to the police, they might be able to track her down.

Back in the studio, Violet gave her assessment.

'There's no denying it was a slick performance, but this wasn't.' She pulled out the morning's copy of *The Lion*. The interview Michael had given was not in any way sympathetic. More to the point, it wasn't an interview at all, they'd simply extracted two sentences as a quote for their story that the show was apparently 'on the verge of collapse'.

'What about the other papers?'

'They haven't written anything – yet – but don't expect to go home any time before eight, I'm surprised they're not already on the phone. I told Michael and Liv to stick around at the conference and help as much as they could. It's not only about the papers, I want him on all the breakfast shows tomorrow and, in the afternoon, I want a film crew out with him as he joins the search party.'

'And what would you like me to do?'

'Keep the show on the road and keep Braithwaite at bay. Make sure he doesn't give any interviews, lock him in a cupboard if you have to but for God's sake don't let any journalist within fifteen metres of him.'

'Right, thanks.'

'Oh and, Violet, there's one more thing I need to ask you... it's just. Well, at the conference those police officers did say it was important to tell them anything we might know about Minnie's disappearance. Don't you think we should mention those girls I met at the factory? They seemed to imply that they knew where she was...'

Violet hesitated. 'Can't you hang on? One more day? If the press conference leads them to Minnie anyway and she decides to come home, of her own free will, then nobody has to be any of the wiser about the role the show played...'

He wondered what to do. One more day, he thought, but then again, one day could be the difference between life and death, between her coming home or...

In the end, Edward agreed, at least to Violet's face.

He left work once again exhausted, fed up and frustrated by the constant moral conundrum he was presented with.

14

Even if Edward had somehow missed *The Lion* front page, rammed into his face by the commuters who were hemmed in beside him on the Tube carriage that morning, there was no avoiding Violet or indeed Mags who were both clutching copies, as Edward pushed open the door to the production gallery.

MISSING O'SHEA GIRL PHONES HOME:
'I'm Alive And Want To Be Left Alone'

- *O'Shea in clear as girl leaves voicemail for Mum*
- *Says she ran off when Mum refused to leave 'abusive' stepdad*
- *Exclusive interview. A mother's agony: 'She's alive but I've still lost my only daughter.'*

'Thank fuck for that,' Mags said. As *The Lion* had indeed so eloquently put it, Minnie was alive and very much wanted to be left alone. Jo had gone too far, it seemed, in initially allowing her husband Stan to stay in the house and Minnie had walked off in anger, promising never to return whilst he remained in the house.

'We should have phoned social services,' Braithwaite said to Edward and Violet, despairingly, over coffee. 'Had her put in foster care until her mother provided evidence that she could properly look after her daughter. We behaved irresponsibly by allowing her to come on the show.'

Violet did not look impressed.

The crazy week, however, wasn't over yet. Now that they had more time, Mags – supported by Violet – had decided to scrap some of the follow-ups for the next week and replace them with actual shows. This meant spending the next two days scrambling around for good stories.

Violet had bartered with Mags and they had agreed on replacing just two of the week's episodes with new material and, by the Friday recordings, they finally had a week's worth of shows. The first girl had had breast enhancements funded by state health-care. Michael had shredded her to bits of course while Liv had tried to understand her motives. The woman had – in due fashion – ran off the stage.

Next up were two brothers who'd apparently turned their lives around because of the *O'Shea Show*.

Violet took them through to the green room while Edward headed up to the gallery, taking his seat beside Braithwaite. The studio lights came up and the audience filed in.

Since she'd not been on the original shows it was felt Liv's presence on the first story would be redundant so Edward grabbed her a quick coffee while the techies set up.

When he returned from the coffee shop, the recording was about to start.

'My next guests appeared on the show three years ago with

their mother,' Michael began. 'Luke and Kyle came to hear the truth about who had stolen their mother's jewellery and over a thousand pounds in cash. We put our detective on the case and live on stage we revealed how we'd tracked down the jewellery to a pawn shop and trawled through hours of their CCTV: despite their innocent pleas both Luke and Kyle, ladies and gentlemen, were seen quite clearly handing over the jewellery. Take a look, guys, at one extraordinary show.'

The techie next to Edward pressed a few buttons and the lights in the studio dimmed as the projector screens came alive with a montage of clips: interviews shot before their first appearance three years earlier, clips from the show itself and dramatic footage sent in by their mother of her chucking out their belongings from the family home after the first recording.

'A family in turmoil. Let's see where they are at three years later.' And out onto the stage came the two brothers. They looked considerably different from how they had in the footage. They were thinner and their hair was more overgrown.

The audience didn't know whether to applaud or boo.

The two sat down in chairs with a cheeky grin.

'So, before we get on to what happened with your mother and what your relationship is like now, give us a bit of background on the journey from the day you were kicked out with your bags packed. I mean what was that like, it must have been awful?'

'Yeah, to be honest,' the smaller one said. 'I remember being close to tears and thinking what the hell are we going to do. We literally had nowhere to go. It was…'

'Rock bottom,' the other one interjected, both of them surprisingly humbled.

'Never seen anyone like that on stage before,' the techie said to Edward. He agreed. Even Braithwaite looked slightly overwhelmed.

Edward turned back to Michael who'd asked the brothers where they'd gone on the day they were kicked out.

'We wandered around for hours on our own. We honestly didn't know where to go. The only thing we had was our phones so eventually we thought we've got to find a place to kip even if it's just for one night. So we found the address of our nearest homeless shelter. It was about four miles away but it felt a lot further.'

'We stayed there for about a week,' Kyle, the younger brother said, 'and it was rough. We were with drug addicts and awful people. So we decided we had to get jobs and we applied everywhere. Eventually, we started working as bin men and then applied for a council flat.'

The story continued and Edward watched as they described their climb out of poverty and into reasonably well-paid jobs as furniture salesman. Luke, the elder brother, was even tipped for promotion. Then came the key question and the one which, Edward suspected, might even cause grown men to cry in front of several million people: what was his relationship with his mother like?

'I haven't been back to that house since we were kicked out.' Luke was welling up and Kyle went to console him.

'Cry me a fucking river,' said Mags.

'I thought you liked it when they started blubbing, boss,' one of the techies said.

'Yeah, when they're a fucking cancer patient and we're palming them off with the latest Xbox to while away their last days, what kind of men are they?'

Edward could see that Braithwaite was riled. He too clearly found Mags' comments distasteful, to say the least. But there was little either of them could do.

Back down on the stage Michael appeared a lot more sympathetic.

'So, guys, I guess this is really important, we do all we can when the show is over but at the end of the day if someone doesn't want to talk then we can't really make them. Let's start with this, though, if there is anything you could say to your mum what would it be?'

'That we're so so sorry. We're not trying to make excuses and all that but we were so young… we've learned so much in these past three years.'

'You know we do all we can on this show to help people. We did try with your mother for several months after the first show ended and she didn't want to speak to us. You know that was her decision but I've got news for you, look over at that screen over there.' Michael pointed to the giant screen which slowly faded into a panel of glass and a tough-looking woman standing behind it. 'Because we tried again. No one on this show knew what I was up to but I went round to your mum's house personally and I begged her to speak to you and to try to find it in her heart to forgive you and, ladies and gentlemen, here she is: Anne-Marie is on the show.'

There was a stunned silence in the gallery.

Braithwaite was grinning. 'The reunion was my idea.'

Edward nodded. It didn't surprise him that Michael had taken credit for Braithwaite's big idea but it did surprise him that Braithwaite had managed to keep it all under wraps.

Back in the studio, the mother said she was prepared to forgive her children and the three of them burst into tears. It was, all in all, an excellent result.

When the recording came to an end Edward and Violet stewed over the show. There was never a dull moment working on *O'Shea*, they concluded.

Edward felt like the week had been one long, never-ending day. He wanted some company. As Violet packed up her things, Edward hesitated slightly but then thought, screw it.

'Drinks?' he asked.

She shook her head. 'Sorry, I'm knackered.' She headed off down the gallery stairs.

'Tomorrow then?'

But she didn't seem to hear him and Edward was forced to make his own way out of the studios and to the street. But as he was beginning to despair at having once again to head back home and spend the night alone, his phone vibrated.

True to her word, his friend Cate had texted back and was inviting him to meet her at a restaurant near Millennium Bridge in an hour.

~

He sat down and she immediately asked how he was.

'Fine,' he lied, trying to forget about the show and the empty shell of a life he was leading or the emotional rollercoaster he continuously seemed to find himself on. But she wasn't easily fooled. They ordered drinks and then she pounced.

'Edward,' she said, firmly, 'I can see it in your eyes. *The Michael O'Shea Show*. What's going on? I mean it can't be worse than working on the newspapers, can it? At least you have more money.'

Working for newspapers was a tough and stressful gig but it was nothing compared to working on television. He wasn't only reporting the news, he felt as if he was actively exploiting people, so much so that he had – at the very least contributed to – one vulnerable girl running away from home.

'I can't take it,' he said, almost breaking down.

The server brought out the drinks and Edward unburdened himself. He told her everything. When he had finished Cate grabbed hold of his hand.

'It is insane. Forget the money. You need to get out, as soon as possible.'

'I know,' he conceded, 'I know.'

'I think you should hand in your notice. Start looking for another job tomorrow. From what you've told me if you don't get out soon then you might end up getting in some kind of trouble with the police. They're asking you to do things you don't feel comfortable with, it's not worth it.'

Cate's advice was logical. But it wasn't as simple as that. Dropping out so soon after joining the team would hardly get him a good reference and he doubted he could find a new job very easily which may well mean having to move out of his flat.

'I can't leave yet.'

The server came over again and Edward ordered the steak.

'I'll keep an eye out for something, Edward,' Cate said, 'but I honestly think you need to get out now. Look at you… I can see the bags under your eyes, the greying hairs.'

'Thanks for the compliment!' he said, though the truth was that at that moment, Edward felt he was as close to a breakdown as it was possible to be. Nothing – not even the intoxicating smell of steak as it made its way through the crowds and to his table – could replenish the energy that the week had taken from him.

So a phone call was all it took. One voicemail message and this had all gone away, for now. No questions asked. The girl would be presumed safe. Getting her to record the message, to make out she was okay, had not been hard. It was obvious, of course, that they'd still want to find her, she was underage after all, they'd try to trace the call. But that was all part of the fun; the miles of travelling to find a suitable payphone, and the satisfaction that they would spend the next few weeks wasting their time searching an area that had nothing to do with her disappearance.

Alas, such trouble for a girl that was becoming a bore anyway. Soon new prey would be needed and, as it happened, a new batch of fresh, delicious meat was about to be delivered...

The big news on Monday morning was that the Jessica Butler story was back on the cards. Strangely, it had been Violet's idea. Mags and Michael had briefed her that, that week, more than ever, they had to prove that the show had a purpose, that it did and could change the lives of their guests for the better. It was premature, Violet had said, but it would be the heartbreaking week. There would be celebrity specials with C-listers telling of their recovery from drugs and – another cheeky dig at *The Lion* – how certain downmarket newspapers had destroyed their lives. There was also going to be a special show about a nine-year-old with a brain tumour. They were going to shower him with presents and fund life-changing experimental surgery in America. Tears, Edward thought, remembering Mags' comment, would be appropriate on this one. But the weeks' worth of shows would start with tough love in the form of Jessica Butler.

'I like it. I like it a lot,' Michael said when Mags mooted the idea in front of him on Monday morning as he sipped coffee in the gallery, combing back his hair. 'When I lead her to that taxi and I've told her straight: it's either my way or the highway, it's at that moment that people will finally get it, the naysayers will realise that they can criticise and moralise and cast judgement, but tough love, straight talking, honesty, these are the only tools that will help people to help themselves. That's what I'm about, that's why, despite all of the crap, I keep going...'

'Fucking hell. Since when did we become the gospel channel?' Mags said. Even Michael cracked a smile.

The meeting dispersed and Violet went back to working at the desk. Edward joined her.

'I've got another meeting this afternoon,' she said.

'Oh?'

'Nothing big. Just upstairs – the exec – wanting a debrief about last week. Anyway, the point is we need to go and see the Butlers and get them booked in otherwise we're not going to keep on top of the schedule.'

'So you want me to go on my own?' Edward asked, slightly alarmed.

'You've done enough visits to know how they go but – if you must – take Braithwaite with you. It could help sweeten them up if they have their doubts, but only if you think you can control him.'

'I rather think my ears are burning!' said a distinctive voice as he entered the gallery.

Violet gave a rare smirk.

'I'll leave you to it.'

Unlike so many of his colleagues, Edward understood why Braithwaite behaved like a thorn in the show's side.

'This really is one of those rare journeys where the train takes longer than driving,' Braithwaite explained. He had offered to drive Edward to Barrington-Stoke and so they were pulling out of the garage. 'It's such a remote place, I should expect you would have to make a lot of changes and take a taxi at the other end if you'd gone by rail.'

'Yes,' Edward said. 'The Butlers seem like a nice family though, don't they?'

'Yes, they are. They are friends of a friend, which is how they got hold of me. They rang me up to see if I could help get them on the show. Jessica does seem in rather a bad...' he stumbled slightly, 'well she needs our help. They've tried everything.'

'I suppose that is what's good about this show,' though Edward knew he didn't truly believe his own words, 'it does do some good, it helps people solve their problems.'

'Yes, I suppose so...' Braithwaite said.

They pulled into Barrington-Stoke after a good hour and a half. Mr and Mrs Butler were on the driveway, watering their hanging baskets as Edward and Braithwaite approached.

'Good morning,' Mr Butler said, waving to them as Edward and Braithwaite got out of the car and headed inside.

'Jessica is at school,' Mrs Butler explained, leaving them alone in the lounge whilst she made tea in the kitchen, 'but she'll be back for her lunch break.'

'We've agreed on that,' Mr Butler added, taking a seat in the lounge. 'We ask her to come home so we know she's being fed.'

'Have you ever caught her trying to make herself sick?' Edward asked.

Braithwaite looked annoyed but Edward knew he couldn't stop him doing his job.

'No,' Mr Butler said, firmly, 'no, I haven't.'

Mrs Butler returned with the tea.

Edward took a cup, then outlined how the story would run. 'We want to put surveillance on Jessica, so we can see what she is really up to.'

'To make sure she's not on drugs?' Mr Butler asked.

'Yes, but we're pretty sure that she isn't, it will be mainly to see how many times a day she's eating, whether we think she is throwing up all of her food.'

Mr Butler seemed uneasy. 'And you think that this will be the best way to help her see she has a problem, to confront her?'

'Yes,' said Edward, trying not to linger on an – understandably – distressing part of the show for too long. 'We've also got a doctor who specialises in eating disorders, he's going to give his analysis on stage. We're hoping that with Michael, Dr Braithwaite and you telling her the same thing, she might see sense and realise she needs to change.'

'What will the support be like when the show is finished?'

Only Braithwaite could answer this question. 'It will be the best help we can provide,' he explained, 'but it will involve you not seeing Jessica for quite a while.'

'Oh…'

'I have organised a residential clinic for her in Cornwall. She'll have her own room and she'll be looked after by the best doctors and nurses until she's made a full recovery.'

'Will we be able to visit her?'

'Yes but only after the first two weeks. I've spoken to the clinic and they think it's really important that Jessica is left alone so that she can get over the worst of it.'

'And when will the treatment begin?'

It was one question that Edward did know the answer to. During the initial discussions about this story, Michael and Mags had suggested a follow-up episode a week later in which cameras followed Jessica's 'journey' to recovery and her first few days at the clinic. However, everyone was now adamant that Jessica should be taken off in a car to the clinic during the show. It would send home the message that eating disorders were serious and that if people wanted to change their lives it wasn't enough to do it tomorrow or the day after, they had to do it *today*. He told Mr Butler what would happen and he did not look happy.

'You mean you want us to ambush our own daughter?' he said, incredulously. 'She would never forgive us.'

'When it's all over, when she's recovered, I'm sure she'll thank you,' said Edward, tactically.

'You don't know my daughter.'

Edward smiled. 'But she looks up to Michael O'Shea, doesn't she? She will listen to him, he will make her see sense, I promise.'

'What about clothes for Jessica, if she's going away?'

Edward told her they could be sent down to Cornwall the following day and not to pack anything; it would look suspicious. Nobody wanted Jessica getting wind of what was really happening.

When Jessica appeared at lunchtime and she tucked into the smallest cheese sandwich Edward had ever seen, not even finishing it, Edward tried to put her at ease as he told her she'd definitely be on the show. He deliberately avoided explicit mention of the line of questioning she'd face or her illness, much to Braithwaite's outrage, and instead focused on her meeting with O'Shea, and how he could help her with her media career. Of course, that wasn't a complete lie, when she was better and if she put on a dramatic enough performance, he had no doubt Michael would see to it that she appeared on some reality show or other.

Finally, after half an hour of discussions and another cup of tea, Edward and Braithwaite were ready to leave. 'Thanks so much for your time,' Edward said, shaking Mr and Mrs Butler's hands, though he felt rather uneasy at doing so. He felt as if he was stabbing them in the back, though he tried to forget about it.

On the journey home Braithwaite was incensed about the deception – something he had known nothing about until then – and Edward simply did not have the heart to mount a defence about something he knew deep down was entrapment. So he let Braithwaite rant on and tried to be as cordial as possible. The only thing that satisfied his conscience and stopped him from conspiring with Braithwaite to sabotage the show was the sight of Jessica Butler's ludicrously small cheese sandwich. She was a girl that needed help, whatever the cost.

~

The week leading up to Jessica Butler's appearance was far less manic than the previous week. The celebrity stories were easy to arrange. There was no need to do any prior research. Michael, who had that week been far more involved in setting up the shows – perhaps trying to keep a low profile by spending his days in the studio rather than attending his usual press junket where he could easily be ambushed – had insisted that the celebrities be allowed to tell their own stories without interference.

Perhaps feeling a semblance of guilt that he did not want to admit, Michael also personally arranged everything for the boy with the brain tumour. He took a film crew down to the hospital where he was staying and instructed Edward to order as many balloons, decorations and party poppers as the show's budget would allow. The boy's story was going to take the form of a party. He would be blindfolded and led into a studio where an audience composed entirely of his family, friends, and supporters would erupt into applause. The stage would be decked out with a cake, the decorations Edward had bought and, of course, presents. Lots of presents.

For once, Edward actually wanted to prepare for the show and he made sure he did all he could to make it perfect. There may have been a cynicism attached to the initial decision to have him on, but poor Freddie Bell – the nine-year-old with the brain tumour – didn't have to know that. All that mattered was that he had a special day and got the funding to have his operation in America.

By Thursday afternoon, however, a strange atmosphere had overcome *The Michael O'Shea Show*. Everybody was pitching in to help with the last-minute preparations so they could go home early. Braithwaite volunteered to book the taxi that would take Jessica Butler all the way to the clinic in Cornwall – it would reach the secluded retreat for eight or nine in the evening he assured them – and in the same spirit, Mags offered to walk to the station and arrange for the Butlers' train tickets to be sent by courier.

Of course, the Butlers were perfectly capable of driving to the studios, but Violet had insisted that they come in via train.

'No turning back once you're on a train, if Jessica does have any last-minute doubts.'

By half past four, they had all but finished the arrangements for the recording and, other than a few more balloons that needed blowing up and placing on the stage, they were ready to go.

'Er...' Unusually it wasn't Braithwaite that was stumbling; Michael seemed to be at a loss as to what to say. 'I guess that was good work today, guys. See you tomorrow.'

A compliment from Michael O'Shea, whatever next...

17

Edward could spot the Butlers making their way towards them from quite a distance. Jessica had straightened her hair and fixed it in place with a cute polka-dot headband. And she had complemented it perfectly with a smart cream blazer and a plain dark-blue dress that made her look almost nun-like. In fact, it was as if she was dressed for an interview. Of course, to her, it was an interview, an audition for what she saw as a life-time career in the media.

'Good morning.' Edward beamed, and Jessica went to shake his hand.

'Did you have a nice journey down?' Violet began, asking her parents and they said there were no complications.

'I'm afraid you're not on until the end of the day,' Edward said.

They did not seem best pleased but there was little that could be done about that. There was a tight schedule – aside from an hour-long break for lunch – the shows would be recorded, as ever, back-to-back and they weren't about to risk pausing the show whilst they waited for delayed trains to arrive. Everybody on the show today would be here first thing, even those on last.

It was a rather unfortunate scenario given that it gave Jessica's parents an entire day to mull over the situation and potentially decide they were going to pull out at the last moment. But a solution had been found. The Butler parents were shown to the channel guest suite – a dining area with guests from other shows on the third floor – whilst Jessica herself was given an 'exclusive' tour of the building and allowed to meet a few celebrities. It added to the illusion that Jessica was being brought onto the show to talk about her media career but also kept her separate from her parents.

Finally, four o'clock came and Jessica and her parents were brought up to separate green rooms where they had microphones fitted.

The decision had been taken to go for a full four-on-one assault with Mr and Mrs Butler, Michael and Liv all trying to ram home the message to Jessica about her eating disorder.

'Now, my final guests are two parents who are at breaking point. They suspect that their seventeen-year-old daughter, Jessica, has an eating disorder. But she won't admit it and she is becoming increasingly thinner and, they suspect, increasingly cunning at disguising her unwillingness to eat.

'Jessica has only agreed to come on the show because she is a massive fan and because we've told her we can help her become famous. She has no idea what this is really about. So without further ado, let's get Jessica's parents on the show.'

And Mr and Mrs Butler walked feebly onto the stage, the audience clapping and cheering as their faces turned pale.

'Don't worry about them,' Michael said, pointing to the audience, 'they don't get out much.'

Mrs Butler forced a smile.

Liv sat down on the chair beside her and held Mrs Butler's

hand. 'I'll cut straight to the chase. You believe your daughter has an eating disorder?'

'We think so,' Mrs Butler said.

'So I guess the obvious question is when do you think her problems began? Did it all come out of nowhere?'

Mrs Butler looked to Liv for reassurance who nodded. 'She's always been a happy girl and she used to eat healthily. We used to take her out for a roast dinner on Sundays and go to restaurants. She was okay really until a few months ago.'

'And that's when things started going wrong?'

'We noticed she wasn't eating as much, small things but it never really bothered us.' Mrs Butler's voice was so gentle that the techie next to Edward said he had to turn her mic to full volume. 'We never thought that something funny was going on but there were times – looking back – when we perhaps should have questioned what she was doing. We'd ask if she wanted a dessert and she'd say no when she'd usually want one. We'd say we were thinking of going out and she'd turn it down... but we thought she'd just made alternative plans, you know, to go and be with her friends.'

'When did you realise things had got more serious?'

'We noticed she was spending her pocket money on these magazines.' It was Mr Butler who was speaking up about his daughter.

'Gossip magazines?'

'Yes, ones about celebrities. So we quizzed her about it and she said she wanted a career in the media, to be famous and that these magazines were going to help her do it. We told her she should focus on her exams so she had all her options open, but I think we rather misinterpreted what she meant when she said these magazines would help her.'

'What did she mean?'

'She meant that these magazines had led her to the conclusion that the only way she was going to lead the lifestyle she wanted and to work in the media was to look and behave in a certain way.'

'To lose weight?'

'I think it started off that way but then it escalated and now she just focuses on her weight and how to get out of eating anything at all. It's like an obsession. It doesn't matter how much weight she loses I don't think it is ever enough.'

'So how bad have her eating habits become? How much does she eat a day?'

Edward had put all of this information in the production briefing Michael was supposed to read before every show. For some reason or other, he actually seemed to have paid attention to it today.

'We do make her come home for dinner on school days so we can make sure she definitely eats something.'

'Really. Does she always come home without a fuss?'

'Yes, always, but we think that she's secretly making herself sick, bringing it back up again or hiding her food down her top or in her pockets. But we can't watch her all the time. We can't police her. She thinks we're bugging her and that we're working against her but we're not.'

'We're just trying to help her,' Mrs Butler said.

'We know, babe,' Liv said, clasping her hands firmly. 'Michael's only trying to get the full picture for the viewers at home.'

Michael didn't react. He clasped his hands together. 'Right, folks, shall we get Jessica on the show. Liv is going to bring her out.' And, sure enough, cameras followed Liv as she made her way to the giant screen which faded into a glass panel and a door as she approached.

Jessica was sat on a comfy chair, sipping water from a plastic cup. Well, she was until Liv grabbed hold of her hand and walked her out onto the stage.

'Good to have you on the show, Jessica,' Michael said. 'We've got your parents here...'

Her expression dropped.

'They've been telling me about your eating habits.'

Edward could see the seething anger, the bubbling fury.

Braithwaite was jittery. He got up and paced around the gallery.

'Sit down, Braithwaite,' Mags screamed. 'Sit the fuck down.'

Back on the stage, Liv was playing the good cop.

'Jessica is an average teenager who wants to be famous, aren't you? Nothing wrong with that.'

'Let's hear from the horse's mouth. What's the deal, Jessica?' Michael said.

'I err...' She stumbled slightly, and a look of fear crept across her face. She jolted and forced herself to sit upright; to her, today was an interview, every word she said would be judged.

'They hate me,' Jessica exclaimed, 'Mum and Dad, want to control me, stop me going out and having fun. They're always in my face.'

Edward had not heard Jessica speak like this at home; he can't have been the only one to have realised that her antipathy towards her parents was all a carefully constructed front. She wanted desperately to be the bad girl but it wasn't washing.

'No, darling, that's not true, we just want to help you. You're not well.'

Jessica fidgeted, it was if she was deliberately trying to psych herself up.

'Why won't you leave me alone?' she said. 'I'm seventeen I want to lead my own life.'

Her parents looked shocked and saddened.

Michael was having none of it. 'Hang on a minute, you're trying to turn the show around and get out of what we're here to talk about. First of all, your parents have done everything for you from what they've told me and what my researchers said when they visited your house.'

'Yeah, I know what you're all about,' Liv said, 'you're trying to paint yourself as the victim here.'

'This isn't about the poor little posh girl being victimised by her controlling parents,' Michael continued, 'it's about you taking responsibility for your illness. Because you are ill, aren't you?'

'No I'm not!' Jessica exclaimed.

'And you're sure about that, are you?'

Jessica shrunk back into her chair.

'There's nothing you want to own up to? Your eating habits are completely normal? You eat three good meals a day, you swallow and digest it all? Tell her, Liv, tell her what we know.'

'We've been watching what you've been up to. Let's watch a clip from our private detective to see what he found out.'

One of the techies dimmed the studio lights and the screens lit up with snippets of surveillance cameras intercut with the silhouette of a private detective narrating what he'd found: he explained that he had followed Jessica when she was not at school and at weekends to find out what she was up to. The detective explained that he never once saw Jessica eating or buying food, even when she was with friends, and that he had got footage of Jessica placing food her friends gave her into a bin when they were not looking. He had also called upon a female accomplice to follow her into the bathroom and record what she had heard: what sounded unmistakably like her flushing food she'd been offered down the toilet. But the strongest evidence was reserved for the end of the film: the private detective had spotted Jessica meeting up with another girl one to one. The girl looked thin and exhausted and, when Jessica's parents heard their conversation they broke down in tears, the two girls talked explicitly about their plan to break into the media industry by losing weight and how no one else understood them. They even talked about the tactics they were using to disguise the fact they weren't eating.

The lights went up to gasps from the audience.

'Well, Jessica, what have you got to say for yourself?' Liv asked.

Jessica ran off the stage, her tears spewing eyeliner and foundation all over her face. Liv jogged on after her, inviting the camera crew to follow her. The projector screen above the stage lit up so that the audience could see what was happening behind the scenes.

Jessica came to rest in the corridor outside Michael's dressing room. She covered her face with her hands and Edward couldn't help but feel for her. The tragedy of it all moved him; the complete public breakdown of her life. And wasn't he responsible for it all? Hadn't this been a car crash of his own making? But his self-doubt and guilt about what he had done would not stop the show.

'You've got to listen to me.' Liv tried to grab hold of Jessica's hands. 'I know it might seem awful but your eating habits are all out in the open now. You have a serious problem and you can't keep pretending anymore. We want to help you. Yeah?'

Jessica removed her hands away from her head.

'So come on.' Liv led Jessica back onto the stage to much applause.

After several moments of Michael and Liv moralising and trying to get Jessica to realise the effect of her eating disorder on her parents, Michael pounced.

'There is a way for you to get better. It won't be easy but it's your only chance.'

Jessica looked confused.

'But to take it you've got to really want to change your life. Is that what you want?'

Jessica said nothing.

Liv continued.

'Babe, we've sorted the best help for you, it can make you better, get you eating properly.'

'And *if* you succeed and get back on your feet I will arrange something for you: meetings with producers, some contacts of mine. These people could kick start your career in television. But only if you get better? Is that a deal?' Michael said.

'Er...'

Michael and Liv grabbed hold of Jessica's hands.

'Come with me, then?'

Mr and Mrs Butler, already in a flood of tears, collapsed in each other's arms: because they knew what was coming. They got up as well and they, tailed by the cameraman, made their way backstage, through the green room, out into the dark corridor full of wires, past the gallery steps and then out to the garages.

'Open the garage doors,' Michael said to Jessica, and when she pulled them back, she found a single silver people carrier, waiting to take her away.

'The only way you're going to get better. We've booked you into a specialist clinic by the coast in Cornwall. The treatment will last as long as it needs to. It will be tough. But one thing is certain, these people will make sure you get better.'

Jessica looked as emotionally exhausted as her parents. She went to them and collapsed into their arms. 'Will I be able to see them?' she asked, her voice slightly muffled.

'Not for the first two weeks,' Michael explained. 'The first two weeks will be the hardest of your life. They will be made even harder by the fact you will have no contact with anyone, other than a phone call once a night, but I promise you, if you do this, you won't look back.'

Jessica continued to stay huddled in her parents' arms.

'So what's it going to be?' Michael snipped.

It took Jessica several moments to drag herself away from her parents.

'Come on, make the right choice!' Michael said.

Finally, she agreed to get into the car and as the doors slid shut, everyone, including Edward, was in tears.

'A brave girl,' Michael said. 'A very brave girl, don't you think?' He was talking to Liv.

'She's a tough cookie, she'll be all right.'

The cameraman tracked the car as it plodded out of the garage, over the road and across Blackfriars Bridge before it disappeared into the labyrinth of skyscrapers that skirted the Thames. The credits rolled over the scene and the theme tune gently crept in.

That was, at long last, a wrap.

But there was no self-congratulatory applause or shakings of hands nor even any sigh of relief. The entire production gallery was silent, dumbstruck by what had taken place before them.

Even on their way to Blackfriars station to drop off Mr and Mrs Butler, Edward and Violet barely said a word to each other. It was only as they returned to the studio that Violet broke the ice, with one entirely unexpected word.

'Pub?'

And with barely another word between them, they collapsed onto the bar of The Blackfriar before taking refuge on a table near the back.

'You see it all on this show, don't you,' Edward said, sipping his beer.

'Indeed you do,' Violet said, 'indeed you do.'

Edward took more gulps and there was silence for several moments.

'I hope Jessica gets on all right.'

'They'll look after her in Cornwall.'

'You don't think Michael and Liv were pushing her too far? Do you think it was all worth it in the end? For getting her into the clinic and making her see sense, I mean?'

Violet shrugged. 'It's not in my job description to think about that, and it's not in yours either.'

Edward sighed. He knew he would get no further reaction from Violet and it worried him slightly. How could anyone be so cold, so heartless, so uncaring as to think only about their own position and not about anyone else, however vulnerable? But, he supposed, as she had hinted on so many occasions before, that thinking in *those* terms was the only way it was possible to do that job. It made Edward wonder...

'Why did you apply for this job in the first place?' Edward enquired.

'Money,' she said, 'stability. Don't want to be homeless or on benefits. What about you?'

All obvious and valid reasons, Edward thought. His motives had been similar. Though he wasn't entirely motivated by the stability and money that the job offered. He had been genuinely excited about the prospect of working on television. Admittedly he hadn't been a massive fan of the show before he'd decided to work on it, but he had thought that perhaps he could help people, empower them to better their lives. Whether that was true of what they had done today, he didn't know. Had they truly helped Jessica Butler get help for herself? And was humiliating her on national television a price worth paying... so many moral questions.

Edward wondered whether to confide in Violet what he had admitted to his friend Cate the previous week. In the end, the drink seemed to make his decision for him.

'I'm thinking about getting out,' he said.

Violet barely reacted. 'Why's that?'

'The job isn't what I was expecting.'

'What *were* you expecting?'

'I don't know but I... I feel as if... as if I've lost all of my morals, that I've sold out completely...'

'I felt like that too when I started,' Violet said in a rare moment of candour. 'It comes with the territory. Just try not to think about it.'

'If you think that, why do you stay?'

'Because I don't have rich parents to back me up. Because we don't live in an ideal world. Because if I didn't do this job somebody else would.'

'So, you think I should stick around for a while longer?'

'I don't presume to tell anyone anything,' said Violet, 'but if you want a good reference, keep your mouth shut, keep out of Mags' way for another few months and quietly hand in your notice. Do not do what the last few researchers have done and make a big scene before your departure. Now,' she finished off the last of her vodka and Coke, 'more drinks?'

Edward smiled and headed to the bar.

18

The journey to Cornwall was a long one. In fact, by the time the car carrying Jessica Butler had crossed into the remotest parts of Devon, the sun was already beginning to set.

It had taken some speed to catch up with the taxi as it meandered through the empty country lanes even though the driver of the grey saloon was not familiar with the route. The driver of the taxi – a Mr Thomas Mallaky – had been paid a lot of money to make this journey, so far from his usual London patch and down these narrow country roads almost certainly guaranteed to be empty as nightfall set in. But Mallaky would never see the pay cheque, that was for sure. He would have to be killed, obviously, but that shouldn't be particularly hard. It wasn't as if he was carrying the President of the United States. His only passenger was a nobody, a haughty adolescent with delusions of grandeur that were about to come crashing down. The tiniest drops of the drug and she would be out, faster than being shot at point-blank range.

As the night properly began to set in and the last remnants of the day faded away, the taxi came into view. There it was on the horizon, the only thing for miles, tugging along without a care in the world, the driver blissfully unaware that the last few moments of his life were slowly trickling away as surely and as rapidly as the setting sun.

Mallaky leaped into fourth gear and in mere seconds overtook the taxi. Then, almost instantly, with one quick swish from a gloved hand, a smoke grenade broke up the scene. The taxi veered off the road and the driver skidded round in panic until at last, no longer able to keep control of the vehicle, he crashed into a nearby oak tree.

The taxi had not been overturned and the windscreen had barely been cracked but the airbags had been deployed and the shock had stunned both passenger and driver into a panic. That was all that was needed.

'What happened?' Mallaky screamed. Jessica was in hysterics. The stupid brat, how on earth did she have it in her to scream so loudly?

'Who's there?' Mallaky asked, as he spotted a bright torch amongst the smoke, someone walking towards him. He raced to turn on his headlights but before he could get a good look at just who stood before him, he collapsed. Nobody but Jessica Butler heard the three bullets penetrate his skull, the Cornish wilderness took care of that.

There wasn't a moment to lose and the driver was bundled up into the boot of the other car.

'It's bedtime,' said the voice of someone she knew yet couldn't quite place.

Jessica tried to get away but ended up in a crumpled heap on the floor. How foolish, how stupid to even try when she was so weak. She screamed when she saw that he was holding a syringe.

'Now hush, little girl, we wouldn't want to disturb the neighbours, not that they can hear you.' She was lifted gently onto the back seat of the saloon car with her head pressed up against the window. It was as if she had simply fallen asleep of her own accord. For now, at least, nobody would suspect a thing...

19

When Edward awoke the next morning, it wasn't to the sound of bells from the church opposite his bedroom or even his own alarm clock, but to a ringtone. His mobile was vibrating furiously on his bedside table.

Violet had fallen asleep beside him. She stirred at the sound of his groggy voice answering the call.

'It's fucking happened again...' Mags said, practically screaming down the phone.

'What? What do you mean?'

'Jessica Butler. Gone, vanished.'

'You mean she's walked out of her therapy?'

It took several moments for Edward to establish from Mags' rant that Jessica had never even made it to the clinic. The car that had taken her to Cornwall had been found smashed up about thirty miles from its destination and both driver and passenger were missing.

Edward told Violet what had happened and it seemed to defuse any of the awkwardness of the fact they'd both woken up in bed together, somewhat worse for wear. Violet's perfectly brushed hair was out of place and her make-up had run down her face.

'This is mad. How can she have disappeared? We put her in the back of that taxi, we saw her drive off.'

'She must have gone AWOL,' Edward decided. 'Overpowered the driver to try to get out and he crashed the car.'

At that moment Violet's phone rang as well and, no doubt because she didn't want her boss to know where she'd spent the night, she pretended to Mags that she was completely surprised by the news of Jessica Butler's disappearance.

'We need to head to work.'

'You don't want breakfast?'

Violet gave Edward a bemused look. 'I need a flannel,' she said.

Edward nodded, confused.

She had time to wash the previous day's make-up from her face and reapply it but not enough for even half a bowl of cereal and a cup of tea. Violet returned looking fresher than she had done before and he wondered if anybody other than himself would be able to guess that she had not changed clothes in over twenty-four hours.

Once Edward had freshened up and changed his suit – something Violet assured him he had only five minutes to do or she would leave without him – they were out of the door and headed for the Tube station.

As they took refuge in the crowded carriages, thankful to get seats, Edward finally broached the elephant in the room.

'We didn't...'

Violet arched an eyebrow. 'We didn't what, Edward?' She laughed.

Edward stuttered slightly and Violet said nothing more as he followed her through the Tube station, savouring the last few minutes of humdrum before the chaos that was inevitably about to unfold.

~

Such was the severity of the situation that by the time Edward and Violet arrived at the studios, the entire crew including the technical team had been summoned to a specially booked-out conference room, complete with white leather chairs and a stunning view out onto The Strand. The channel director Mr Griffiths was due to join them at nine.

'There's no way around this,' Mags said, clearly agitated at the fact she couldn't have a cigarette. 'This is bad, this is fucking bad.'

'But I don't understand,' Edward said, deciding it was pointless sitting in silence, however much abuse he got for speaking his mind. 'Surely we haven't done anything wrong? It's not like Minnie, it's not as if we could have done any more to safeguard her. We did everything we could, we did all the research and then put Jessica into the car. It's horrendous, I know, but if she wanted to run off then what more could we have done? We could not have done anything to stop this happening.'

Everyone but Braithwaite, who seemed even more sheepish than usual no doubt because – legally – it was his responsibility to look after the guests when the recordings were finished, looked at him.

Mags went to reply but Liv stepped in. 'Let's just get a few things straight here – Edward isn't it?'

'Yes.'

'Well, Edward, our show has been the subject of at least two major police investigations. One of them was caused, in part, by your incompetence. Jessica Butler will be all over the papers by the end of the day. Do you think anyone cares about what really happened? All people are going to see is another girl we humiliated in front of millions of people. If you don't get this cleaned up, it won't just be you marching out that door, sonny, we'll all be out of a job. So if you still want to be here tomorrow I suggest you stop making excuses for your own shoddy work, shut your trap and get on with your job. Understand?'

Edward could do nothing but nod. Liv's expression, however, completely changed as the door to the boardroom opened and in walked a middle-aged man, carrying an iPad and a leather briefcase.

'Mr Griffiths,' Michael said, getting up to shake his hand.

'Thank you, Michael,' and he proceeded to sit down. 'As you know, we are in an incredibly serious situation. The clinic phoned the police in the early hours of the morning when it became clear the girl was not going to arrive. It might simply be that she ran off because she didn't want to attend the clinic you arranged for her, which will inevitably lead to serious questions about the integrity of the show and the network. But it could well be that somebody is targeting young girls who have appeared on the programme. There is no evidence that the two disappearances are related at all, at the moment, but it is a possibility. So once again we can expect there to be critical reports in the media when it is made public, later today, no doubt focusing on our failures to ensure guest safety. The episode involving the girl will not be broadcast of course until further notice and it is of paramount importance that the recording is not leaked. We must do everything we can, therefore, to prove that the disappearance of either girl was in no way caused by any mismanagement on our part. I, therefore, propose that we launch an immediate investigation which will review how effective our safeguarding procedures are and whether there was anything that could have been done to prevent this.'

Everyone around the table had been left open-mouthed.

It was Braithwaite who asked the first question. 'What will this investigation involve?'

'I am taking legal advice but it is very much agreed that there will be an independent panel and one of the members of that panel will no doubt want access to the studio on filming days in order to assess for themselves whether our provisions are adequate.'

~

'This is most distressing,' Braithwaite was saying back in the gallery. The meeting with Mr Griffiths had gone on for another hour. He had proceeded to explain in horrifying detail how the inquiry would proceed.

'The Butlers rang me up in tears. I feel that we should go round there and…'

'Don't you fucking dare!' Mags screamed. 'There'll be press swarming over that house. And I know what you're like. Won't be able to help yourself, giving quotes, shitting verbal fucking diarrhoea all over *The Lion*'s backside. You can stay here where I can keep an eye on you.'

'This is bad,' Edward said.

'You don't fucking say,' Mags snapped back.

Michael and Liv had both been given instructions not to leave the building in the afternoon.

'It's not over yet,' Michael said. 'We're not finished. The show can survive.'

It was a horrific situation. For all the humiliation and downright cruelty of Friday's recording, there had been a sense of relief that Jessica Butler had finally been packed off to get some help. Now Edward was facing the reality that instead of helping her change her life, he could have helped destroy it.

Michael walked back into the room. 'The police are officially launching an abduction inquiry and have named the taxi driver – Thomas Mallaky – as a suspect.'

Nobody, other than Mags, knew what to say.

'I hope for the love of God when they catch him he's armed, then they can shoot the bastard there and then, no questions asked.'

'We should have checked the driver,' Edward said to Violet. He was racked with guilt: how could he have let this happen? Why hadn't he done more to stop this?

'It's not our fault we didn't investigate another company's employee, if indeed he is responsible. Really no point beating yourself up about it.'

Edward sighed.

20

The car wound its way around Graysmead, to the tall collection of towers at the very edge of town as the last remnants of daylight faded into the horizon. The car reached its destination a good few streets away from the estate. They didn't want to draw attention to themselves. It was best to be discreet, to walk on foot, though it wasn't as if they were expecting a visitor from The Michael O'Shea Show.

Inside, the talk turned quickly to the purpose of their meeting.

Tiffany was alone in her flat, lest her baby, left sleeping in its cot.

'You didn't make enough of an impact last time. It's all about the impact you make. I can coach you. I can make you famous, rich beyond your wildest dreams but only if you play it my way. This time people will remember you...'

'Tell me what I have to do...'

21

It was, to quote Mags, the shitstorm to end all shitstorms. Front page splashes across the board.

'There's a press conference at half nine,' Violet said as she put down the phone, pointing to the screen from which the techie usually watched the show as it was broadcast.

'Will Michael be there?'

Violet nodded. 'And so will Liv but that looks like all the PR they'll be doing; the newspapers and the TV stations aren't interested in any more interviews. Most of them told me to get lost and that they'll run what the hell they want, using more colourful language.'

'That's not great but I sp–'

Edward and Violet stopped; they could hear footsteps on the production gallery steps and sure enough several seconds later there was a knock at the door.

'Do I have the right place? This is the *Michael O'Shea Show?*'

Edward went to open the door and in walked an elderly lady with a stern look on her face and a clipboard.

'I am the director of the independent panel into standards and procedures,' she explained. 'I was told I would be allowed access to the filming of the show for a few days.'

This had been discussed at the meeting with Mr Griffiths the previous day but Edward had no idea that her inspection would begin so quickly.

'Yes, of course,' he said. 'Can I get you anything? A cup of tea?'

'That won't be necessary.'

Violet and Edward paused. Suddenly it dawned upon them that their every move was to come under scrutiny. How on earth could they plan for anything if they were constantly being watched? And what to do now? Did they watch the press conference? Should they comment on Michael and Liv's performance? In the end, they simply tried to ignore the inspector, pulled their chairs closer to the screen and began to watch the scene unfold before them.

Michael's performance was, as usual, slick and heart-wrenching. Despite their refusal to interview him directly, the press had turned out in force and he posed for photos at the conference table with Mr and Mrs Butler, who were understandably beside themselves with anguish. What was nice was that the Butlers were not once critical of the show. In fact, they went to great lengths to talk about how much support they had received in the run-up to Jessica being sent off to Cornwall. At the end of the conference, the detectives dropped the bombshell that the disappearance of Minnie Jenkins was still being treated suspiciously, despite the voicemail she had left, and nobody was ruling out the theory that the two disappearances were related. Suddenly the room erupted with a scrum of questions and accusations from the reporters. In the end, Michael brought the conference to a close rather swiftly and walked out.

Edward gave Violet a knowing look but she did not return it, nor did they discuss the press conference at all. The truth was neither of them had any idea how to manage the unfolding crisis.

'Look at this.' Mags placed a stack of newspapers down on

Violet and Edward's desk. It was a sight, unlike Edward had ever seen. Pages and pages of coverage. *The Lion* lead with 'O'Shea in Meltdown' whilst *The Owl*, a highbrow broadsheet, questioned whether the television industry as a whole was regulated enough.

Edward flicked through the pages but one story caught his eye.

'O'SHEA IN NEW TEENAGE SEX SCANDAL' 'EXCLUSIVE: I FATHERED O'SHEA'S BABY'

Embattled TV Star Michael O'Shea is today being accused of failing to practice what he preaches as The Lion *exclusively reveals he has been accused of fathering a baby with a teenage girl and cheating on his long-term wife Karen.*

Twenty-year-old Tiffany Roe has claimed she had a secret romp with O'Shea when he came to visit her home town of Graysmead for a story that was never aired two years ago. The girl, who was initially dropped from the show for editorial reasons, but finally made it to air with her first appearance on the newly revamped O'Shea *with her twin sister, said she confronted the besieged presenter about the issue backstage but now feels she has to speak out.*

O'Shea regularly lays into cheaters on his show and has been known to describe parents who don't pay child maintenance as 'worthless scum'. He has also spoken out against older men who enter into relationships with teenage girls and has refused to fund his own brother's trial for sex crimes against young girls.

Tiffany was eighteen at the time of the alleged affair, a few months older than Jessica Butler, the girl who police believe was abducted on her way to an eating disorder clinic after an appearance on O'Shea's show.

'I was young and naïve, I saw that he was off the telly and I wanted him.'

Michael and Liv returned from their press conference as Edward had finished reading the story. Braithwaite joined them soon after; the entire team was assembled, ready to attempt to find some way through the fog of chaos.

Edward knew he had to mention the story he'd finished reading but he knew better than to bring it up with Michael, so he discreetly passed the paper to Mags who glanced over it. Edward noticed the inspector, trying to get a glimpse of what Mags was looking over.

'This is a mess, a FU...' Mags started.

Violet cleared her throat and put her hand in the air. 'This is the inspector from the standards committee.'

The inspector gave Michael a stern look. He at first seemed at a loss for words.

'How long will *she* be here,' he said.

'I have been advised that I can have as much time as I require,' the inspector replied. 'Nothing less than a complete, transparent picture of how the show is put together will help me write my report. And I must warn you that if you attempt to obstruct me or restrict my access in any way then you will render my investigation redundant.'

There was a stunned silence across the gallery. Edward had no idea of how to proceed. They were being attacked on all sides. In the end, it was Braithwaite who broke the ice.

'This story...' he started, having clearly read it over Mags' shoulder.

Edward could have banged his head on the table.

'What story?' came the inevitable response from Michael. So much for subtlety.

Mags sighed, heavily, and passed the newspaper across the table. 'I assume it has no basis in fact?'

Michael scanned it for several moments. 'I'm not even going to dignify that with an answer. That name though, wait a minute. Look at this.' Michael reached into his pocket and pulled out his phone. 'Do you know what? Cancel her trip to Florida.'

Both Violet and Liv gave Michael the same stern look, trying to remind him of the inspector.

But he wasn't having it. 'Look...' and he pulled out his mobile phone.

'Tiffany Roe is one of many people who thinks she has the right to bombard me with abusive messages every day, all because she's been on the show once and wants more attention, thinks she knows me, day after day, spouting lies and lies. And now the idiots at that paper...'

Violet cleared her throat and Michael trailed off.

'Here...' he said and passed the phone around so that Edward, Violet, Mags, and Liv could see what was on the screen. Amongst a torrent of abuse in the 'blocked' category, almost every other message was from Tiffany in various guises. Her usernames varied from Tiffany126 and Tifferz to BABYOSHEA but all of them described Michael as a hypocrite and made reference to the fact he owed her money for her baby.

Edward wondered why the girl had chosen this moment to go to the papers.

'Oh, she won't have been that clever. Either some scumbag journo or other will have trawled through all our guests or this would have been kept in a drawer for months until the right moment... for maximum impact.'

'But if these allegations are simply not true why can't you put out a statement to that effect?' Braithwaite asked.

Edward could tell Michael wanted to launch into a tirade but he was resisting.

'I'm not going to dignify her with a response. Why should I?'

'You could do a paternity test,' Braithwaite suggested.

'Wait a minute. We're still looking for shows to fill up for the rest of the week, aren't we?' Mags said.

'Yes,' Violet said.

'So what if we turn this around,' Mags said, 'invite her onto the show.'

'I just said that I don't want to dignify her with a response, I don't even want to put out a statement, let alone let a stalking maniac into the building.'

Liv stepped in. 'But we could turn this into a story about the nature of the press. If you prove, live on stage, that she's a liar then you get people at home to understand that the papers are trashing your name... think how it will play.'

'And the girl?' Braithwaite said. 'We'd need to make sure that she was looked after, given the help that she needs when the show is over.'

'I don't give a flying fu–'

Violet talked straight over him. 'So, this will be a show to illustrate the damaging impact of Tiffany Roe's behaviour. It will examine how easy it is to make allegations sitting at home on a computer and to forget about the real impact that they can have.'

'What she said!' Mags piped up.

'That's settled then,' Liv said.

It was long past six. The inspector had bid them all goodbye, thinking that the day was over, but it certainly wasn't. Edward, Violet, Mags, and Braithwaite had all signed out through the front reception but had then crossed the road and had snuck into the garage compound. At last, they were free to let rip and come up with a course of action without fear of signing the show's death warrant.

Michael's iconic Jaguar car took up so much room in the garage that the group actually had to get into his car.

'Look what we have been reduced to!' Mags screamed.

'Let's try to keep our heads,' Violet said. 'We have a plan. A good plan.'

'A plan? What plan could possibly fix this mess? They're insinuating, implying, ALLEGING,' and Mags placed her hands above her head and made emphatic quote marks, 'that Michael is a paedophile, that he likes young girls. And let's not forget about the reason we're all here. They've hired that inspector to shut us down. It's the same bitch that did the vote-rigging inquiry on *Who Deserves a Million?*'

Who Deserves a Million? was a short-lived reality show that a rival channel had produced a few years back. Contestants, unaware they were being filmed, would, over the course of several months, be presented with all kinds of moral dilemmas: an expensive watch might be left lying on the ground and only those who handed it in would make it through to the next round. In the final, the public had to vote for the person they thought most deserved to win a million pounds based on their performance in the previous tasks and a short three-minute video in which the contestants begged for the money.

After *The Lion* received a tip-off they ran an article suggesting the vote was rigged and the contestant who was to win the money was decided, prior to filming. The subsequent investigation found the network had indeed been rigging the vote: the producer of the show was sacked and only a heavily toned-down version of the programme – in which the prize money was substantially reduced and a panel of judges picked the winner – was allowed to be broadcast. In the end, the whole thing was shut down due to poor ratings.

Michael seemed remarkably calm. 'I've done nothing wrong. Mags has sold me on the Tiffany paternity story.'

'Okay,' Violet said, 'I appreciate we're in a tight spot but we will come out on the other side if we have a good game plan. Getting Tiffany on to do a DNA test on her child is a very good idea. We also have a good angle that can help us demolish the claims one by one. The press and the channel will never get their way if we have the public on our side. Jessica Butler has probably run off because she doesn't want to go through with the programme at the clinic. We could riff off that and talk about

133

Michael's disappointment but that it's ultimately up to her, only she can help herself. The immediate issue we have is if Tiffany refuses a DNA test. If she's lying why would she want to humiliate and expose herself live on television?'

'Oh I don't think getting her on board will be an issue,' Michael said – Edward could tell that he'd been biding his time, his anger building. 'Attention-seeking scum like her love the limelight, it's what makes them tick, they're so desperate, they'd even risk being humiliated. She'll no doubt assume that, even if she is exposed, people will be interested in her comeback, how she reformed, all the usual sycophantic shit that comes with the territory. The reality is that people couldn't give a toss about lowlifes like her, isn't that right, Braithwaite? You're the psychologist, the expert on these matters.'

'She obviously has a mental disorder that would need to be treated.'

'First-rate fucking nutjob, up for anything,' Mags said.

'Exactly,' Michael replied.

'H-hang on, hang on!' Braithwaite said. 'We have to be careful. Look what happened the last time we invited vulnerable people on the show.'

'For the last fucking time, Braithwaite. We will give her the help. We'll palm her off with whatever doctor she needs, give her whatever she wants. And make sure it's twice whatever *The Lion* have offered her, which by the way is far more than she deserves, but only IF she plays ball.'

'Right then, tomorrow we need to go and track her down. We will have to film an interview with her as well as her and Michael taking the swabs of DNA.'

'Don't go easy on her either,' Mags said.

'I'm afraid that might be rather difficult, what with the inspector. I would imagine that she would want to come with us. But,' Violet explained, 'perhaps we could avoid the usual way of doing things. If we go around trying to find dirt on her it won't do our reputations any good...'

'All right, fine,' Mags said, 'lay off the shit shovelling, just focus on her. It doesn't really matter anyway, whatever she says we're going to prove she's a liar.'

It was getting late and the absurdity of the situation was taking its toll. They were having a work meeting, hours into the evening, in a parked car so they could avoid being overheard by an inspector they were supposed to be co-operating with.

'I think we should go home and get some rest,' Violet suggested. Mags too seemed to think sleep might make it easier to think clearly and so finally they all departed the car, leaving Michael and Liv to make their own arrangements home without being spotted by the press pack, a permanent fixture of the main road.

'Today, we're going to do things differently. I'm going to prove just how low some people are prepared to sink. Let's take a look at what I'm talking about.'

The projectors lit up, the lights dimmed and a short film began to play. Frantic music played as the audience was reminded of *The Lion* exclusive: 'O'SHEA IN NEW TEENAGE SEX SCANDAL' intercut with fragments of an interview Edward had recorded with Tiffany and a short clip of Braithwaite taking a swab of Michael's DNA. As the music reached its climax, a final tagline: 'Two sides to every story, one test, one result.'

'So, now we're all up to scratch, let's get Tiffany on the show, guys,' and the audience erupted into booing as Liv brought out a confident-looking Tiffany onto the stage. She was wearing a sleek black dress and had barely applied any make-up to her face. She looked like the innocent victim she clearly wanted to portray.

Michael, Liv, and Tiffany parried back and forth for several minutes.

'Liv, you've known me for how long, in all that time, have you ever seen me so much as kiss another woman?'

She smirked and shook her head.

'No, but that's not what this is about. It's not about whether you've been unfaithful and are you the father of this girl's baby. We all know that's not true, this is about Tiffany and why someone would choose to make such vile allegations. Her life has been a rollercoaster…'

'You know, I've had just about enough of this. We had Tiffany on before, with her twin and the folks at home might have had some sympathy for her but why should they care about her now? She's made vicious allegations against me and I'm going to prove it!'

The audience burst into applause as Michael took an envelope from the techie and vindicated himself.

'Surprise surprise, I owe you nothing, love! Proven, right here, I am not the father of your baby.'

Tiffany had obviously braced herself for what was coming. 'He's lying! The test is rigged.'

'Oh please!'

She bowed her head in shame but it was hard not to wonder whether she was acting, whether this was all part of her plan.

Michael relished in the triumph. 'Isn't the truth of the matter you were sleeping here, there and everywhere? And a whole host of people could be the father?'

The audience burst into rapturous applause and hollering.

'See, ladies and gentlemen, she doesn't deny it. It's true, isn't it?'

'But, Michael, the emotion in this case is running high. I just think this entire situation is never going to be settled until we try to understand why Tiffany lied in the first place.'

The audience clapped, half-heartedly, but Michael wasn't going to allow this be resolved just yet.

'Might as well milk the cow for all it's got,' Mags whispered to Edward in the gallery, quietly as she could, hoping the inspector didn't overhear her.

'This is one-sided,' Michael explained, incredulous, 'this is not about her, it is about me and all the other men that Tiffany has damaged with her lies.'

'Yeah!' some of the audience members chanted and then the inevitable happened. Tiffany walked off. Liv ran after her and the cameras followed her backstage.

'Look, Michael's just trying to get at the truth. Isn't that the reason you came here today? Walking away now, it's only going to make things worse. Think about that little kid of yours, he deserves to know who his father is. And whoever that person is, we're going to need to arrange contact centres and all sorts to try to make this work.'

Tiffany didn't reply but they were close to convincing her.

'Come on,' Liv said, grabbing hold of Tiffany's hand, and they headed back out to the main studio again for round two.

Edward pulled off his headset.

It was definitely time for a coffee. Maybe Violet would come with him. And sure enough about a minute later he heard foot-steps on the gallery stairs. But it wasn't Violet.

'I would like to observe the aftercare programme,' clipped the inspector. 'Where can I find Doctor Braithwaite?' Edward was deliberately vague, directing her to Michael or Liv, who would no doubt be better at handling the inspector than Braithwaite.

Several moments later Violet made her entry.

'Where have you left Tiffany?' Edward asked as the inspector stalked off.

'Tiffany insisted on going to see Michael and Liv for auto-graphs and advice.'

'Oh?'

'I told her to go and find him in his dressing room and then to wait in the corridor so I could give her train tickets to get home.'

'Fair enough,' Edward said, turning into the staff dining room. They queued up to get their coffee. Edward had decided he quite fancied a lemon muffin as well. The staff dining room was mediocre compared to one of the coffee shops on The Strand but that was all he had time for. As Edward got closer to the front he realised something was up. More and more people seemed to be gathering around the widescreen television. As he reached the front of the queue Edward could see why.

'BODY FOUND IN O'SHEA SHOW DISAPPEARANCE CASE' ran the strapline below the reporter who was stood in the woodland of what looked like a vast country park, amongst the pouring rain. Edward's stomach turned over. He no longer wanted a muffin or a coffee. The knowledge that Jessica or indeed Minnie had met their end in what would inevitably be gruesome and painful circumstances and had been left to rot in some random country park, miles from where they lived, made him sick. But as the report continued, the photos that popped up onto the screen were not those of either girl but of a small man, smiling, wearing a baseball cap. Edward left the queue so he could see what was being said.

'...a taxi driver for seven of his twenty-nine years, Mr Mallaky was described by his boss as reliable, enthusiastic and loved by all his customers. But in recent weeks he was the main suspect in the disappearance of Jessica Butler, a seventeen-year-old sixth-form student suffering from an eating disorder whom he had taxied to Cornwall after her appearance on *The Michael O'Shea Show*. There was also speculation that he could have been behind the disappearance of another girl who appeared on the show. But all that was put to rest this morning when police confirmed they had discovered a body at a country park, later positively confirmed as that of Thomas Mallaky.'

Edward felt relief but not for long. For it was shortly followed by guilt. Guilt that he'd ever suspected Mallaky in the first place but also guilt at his own relief that it was Mallaky's mangled body that had been found rotting amongst the woodland, rather than that of the two girls.

'So tell us what this means for the investigation?' the reporter asked a top criminologist who had joined him.

'Firstly, this will obviously become a murder investigation: the wounds to Mallaky's body could not have been self-inflicted. It is clear that whoever took Jessica Butler wanted to remove the taxi driver as he got in the way of his abduction plans, there can be no doubt about that. Incidentally, the police force investigating Minnie Jenkins – the other missing girl – have made a statement. Minnie, if you remember, also appeared on *The Michael O'Shea Show* but the search was called off when she phoned home claiming to have run away of her own volition.

'Police are now treating this call as suspicious and have revealed that it was made from Cornwall as well. This means that it is highly likely that these murders are related and that the perpetrator is deliberately seeking out victims from *The Michael O'Shea Show*. And if we are to assume that is the case then I should think the police will be considering whether there was any inside involvement since the person who kidnapped Jessica Butler and, perhaps, Minnie Jenkins as well, almost certainly had access and control over their whereabouts on those evenings.'

Even the correspondent seemed stunned.

'So what are you saying? That someone who works on *The Michael O'Shea Show* is responsible for murder and – at the very least – abduction, possibly even three murders?'

'Let's not speculate too much but I think it is at least a strong possibility that that is the case. I would be surprised if we didn't see police attention turn to the channel.'

There were gasps and shocks from the whole room. Violet had her hand over her mouth. This was too much.

'Someone needs to speak to Michael and Mags,' Edward said, thinking pragmatically, though why he was volunteering to tell the great Michael O'Shea that his empire was collapsing all around him he did not know. Nevertheless, he made his way back past the gallery steps and the green room and to a small brown door: Michael's dressing room.

Edward knocked but there was little point, the door was already half ajar and he wasn't in any mood to wait for a response… but as his eyes came into focus he knew there was no escaping the scene that stood before him: there was Michael O'Shea, only he wasn't alone, his hands were placed firmly around Tiffany's neck. The game was up.

23

'Get out!' Michael screamed. He released his grip on Tiffany so suddenly that she almost fell to the floor. She gasped for breath and scrambled towards the door as fast as she could, slamming it behind her.

'It was you?' Edward said. 'All along it was you...'

Michael lunged for Edward and before he could react he had pinned him up against the wall.

'Listen to me very carefully, buddy, all right? Breathe a word of this to anyone, and that goes for your girlfriend too, believe me your life won't be worth living.'

Bravery was a virtue quite lost on Edward Lewis in this present moment. He had always imagined that if he happened across a robbery, a murder or indeed an assault on a vulnerable girl that he would intervene and rush to save the day. But all Edward could do was babble.

Michael leant in closer, grabbing hold of Edward's cheeks, pinching them together, his heavy panting breath warm and wet on Edward's neck.

'I'm a well-connected guy, I can have you fitted up...' Michael panted, he was salivating over every syllable, 'really... wouldn't... take... much.'

Michael let go of his cheeks and Edward gasped for breath, almost delirious. Michael straightened himself up; it was as if nothing had happened. Edward almost thought he was going to apologise. Instead, he walked out of the dressing room and left Edward alone and dazed.

In the staff dining room, Edward stood still once again. All around him people were talking, chatting about the criminologist's revelations. Outside, the press had gathered and even from the back of the room, away from the long windows, Edward could see helicopters flying around the building. Everyone was contemplating the same thing and yet Edward had the answer. The terrible burden of the truth weighed him down, divorced him from reality, left him mute.

He looked around for Violet and made a half-hearted attempt to find her. But in the end he was glad not to see her, lest he blurted everything out. The canteen fell silent as Michael waltzed in, accompanied by Mags. He was calm, relaxed. Meanwhile, Mags looked like her life had fallen apart.

'It's a mad world out there, folks. They say someone on this show was responsible for the murder of that taxi driver and probably those two girls. Personally, I don't believe it. I don't know what the future of the show is at this point. All I know is we can expect the police to be everywhere. It's going to be a busy day tomorrow, so I suggest we all go home, get some rest and think about what we're going to do next...' and as he finished, Michael O'Shea's eyes seemed to linger on Edward.

Rest? Edward thought, how would he ever sleep again?

24

The scene in front of the *People Network* studios the following morning was more frenetic than Edward had ever seen it. All eyes were on the dozen or so uniformed policemen who were walking in and out of the front entrance carrying out sealed boxes.

Inside, the atmosphere was tense. The police had raided the offices at dawn. According to the receptionist in the entrance lobby, when she had arrived that morning, it was to the sight of a police sergeant sitting in her chair. He had informed her that nobody would be allowed down to the basement.

Her authority all but gone, she had taken up a plastic chair in the middle of the atrium with the hundreds of other staff who worked in the building. Nobody here was under arrest, the police sergeant informed Edward, but it was advisable to stay here and wait to answer some questions.

The veiled threat was obvious. Anyone leaving the building before they had been questioned would be viewed with intense suspicion. Edward had little choice but to sit down and wait his turn.

Michael was nowhere to be seen. Of course, he would have

been interviewed first, no star guest was going to be forced to slum it out down here, that was a given. But the more he looked around, the more he realised how alone he was. There was no Mags, no Liv and – once more – no Violet. The only other members of staff that Edward recognised were the few techies and Braithwaite who seemed engrossed in an audiobook.

Where was Violet? Why wasn't she here? Had she already finished with her interview?

Edward was overcome with nerves. His legs felt like they were going to crumple. He was glad of the chair, however, impractical and rickety as it was.

'They say they're going through people in alphabetical order,' the receptionist explained.

'And where are we up to?'

'They'll get to L soon enough,' she said. 'Not worried, are you? Paul on fifth has friends in the newsroom, he says he thinks the person responsible for all of this specifically sought out this show to carry out this crime. That means they're looking for someone who has worked here less than six months...'

It was too much. Edward leapt off his chair and ran all the way through the atrium and to the bathroom at the back of the room, not even bothering to read the signs above him to determine which bathroom was which. In the cubicle he vomited with more vigour than he ever had done before; it was as if he was expelling all of the anxiety, all of the stress, the panic into this one toilet bowl. It was an exorcism.

It was not until he felt completely cleansed, exonerated, that he arose from his purgatory, and gasped for breath. But he was no longer alone. There beside him as he leant against the open cubicle door catching his breath was Violet; he had walked into the girls' bathroom.

'Worried about your interview?' she said. 'That you'll get found out?'

It was the first time Edward had seen Violet exhibit any real emotion.

'How could you ever live with yourself?'

'Live with myself... get found out... Violet...'

He came to his senses and noticed the white powder still sneered around her nose. 'You're high,' he said. 'You don't know what you're...'

'Don't patronise me.'

Edward couldn't believe what was happening, he felt the world spinning and he turned his head towards the bowl again. This time he had nothing left to give.

He knew he had to be brave.

'It's not me. It's him... I went to his dressing room but when I opened the door, Michael had his hands around Tiffany's neck. He said he was going to fit me up if I told anyone. What are we going to do?'

Violet said nothing for several moments.

Edward trembled. 'Violet... you have to believe me.'

'Are you sure? He definitely had his hands on her neck?'

'It is possible they were play fighting, I guess...'

Violet arched her eyebrows.

'His face was red,' Edward continued. 'I've never seen anyone that angry. Oh, Violet.' He buried his head into her shoulders, but she didn't react. 'What are we going to do? I can't go on pretending, knowing what I know... I need to tell the police.'

'Not sure that's the best idea.'

'Why not?' Edward let go of her. 'We need to tell them what we saw so they can arrest him, bring him in for questioning. They're looking for someone who worked on the show, and Tiffany... she might be in danger.'

'Fine,' said Violet, 'you tell them. I'll see you tonight in the usual spot.'

'If I'm not still giving an interview to the police, maybe they'll need more help with their enquiries.'

~

'What can you tell me about the murder of Thomas Mallaky and the disappearance of Jessica Butler and Minnie Jenkins?' the officer asked. Edward was in a room on the highest floor of the building – a boardroom – overlooking the city. You could see the skyline for miles into the distance and the Thames glistened in the sunlight. Behind a large table with enough space to fit at least thirty people there was a buffet counter with a big spread. Tea, coffee, cakes, sandwiches and all manner of other snacks, not that Edward was offered any of it.

'Shortly after I heard the news that the taxi driver had been murdered, I walked in on Michael O'Shea with his hands around one of the girls on the show today. I believe he could be behind the other disappearances and the murder of the taxi driver...' It came out quite matter-of-factly. There was no emotion in his tenor.

'That's a serious allegation you're making there. What did you say your name was?'

'Edward Lewis.'

'And your role at this network...'

The officers weren't asking a question. They had a file and a clipboard of every person they hoped to see that day.

'You're picking up on one small thing, Edward, and drawing a whole host of conclusions that could turn out to be false. Michael O'Shea a murderer, after all the work he's done for charity? I've noted your information down. Now...'

'What?' Edward was incredulous. 'Is that it? What will happen next?'

'I'll pass on your complaint,' the man said, 'and *if* it's deemed serious enough, someone will investigate. Now... where were you on the night Mr Mallaky was found dead?'

Edward was reduced to a stunned silence.

'Can you answer my question, please, Mr Lewis, where were

you on the night of the murder? I need you to give me as much information as possible.'

And so Edward was forced to account for all of his movements and to submit to a forensic investigation about his personal life, his opinions on other colleagues who worked at *People*… the questioning was relentless. He didn't get the impression the officers were asking any more of him than they had done of his colleagues, but he still felt violated. And whilst one officer asked the questions, the more junior of the two made extensive notes. At the end of the final question, the officer got up and thanked him for his time. It felt more like a job interview than anything else.

As Edward closed the door behind him, he crumpled to the floor, tears streaming down his exhausted face.

25

When Michael O'Shea was finally able to sneak away from the studios to buy some lunch, donning heavily rimmed sunglasses and a thick winter coat so as not to be recognised, he knew he was in trouble. Not because anybody had spotted him – he had borrowed Mags' rundown blue Vauxhall and his disguise seemed to have worked – or even because one day earlier the police had raided the studios of his beloved show, poured scorn over his reputation and accused someone associated with his show of murder.

He was in trouble because of the fridge, metres in front of him. He was by the checkouts in a petrol garage on the edge of the city where he had come to grab a sandwich and there, in all its glory, stood a specially discounted display. Freshly stocked with all manner of alcoholic beverages, it seemed to eye him up, basking in the late autumnal sunlight, pleading with him to seek refuge in one of its many refreshing cans. He could barely contain himself. The stress of the past day or so had taken its toll on him, he longed, ached for a drink and it took all of his willpower to resist.

'That will be £4.87, please.'

'What?'

Michael hadn't even noticed that the cashier had processed his shopping. He was within breathing distance of the fridge.

'£4.87. Card or cash?'

Michael handed over a fiver, collected the change, then went back to Mags' car. Even though the show had been effectively cancelled for the foreseeable future, Michael had been in meetings all day with top executives from the channel. This was no longer an ordinary crisis that could be quelled in time, it was a firestorm that threatened to destroy the entire channel, not that anyone of those grey suited pricks could see that. They were too busy following protocol, briefing everyone; if anything would kill the channel it would be bureaucracy.

There was one positive anyway: no more media appearances. The executives at the channel had told him he was to keep a low profile, no more getting up at 5am and dancing like a monkey. For a few days at least he no longer had to pretend that he liked those insufferable forty-year-old hags who insisted on interviewing him at ridiculous hours in the morning for their breakfast shows or that he had even the slightest flicker of sympathy for those pathetic, talentless morons who turned up to audition in front of him, expecting him to make them millionaires overnight because their parents had filled their heads with delusions of grandeur from the moment they had been born.

He should have counted his blessings. But of course, he couldn't: there was a much bigger problem. What to do about Edward Lewis and what he'd seen. It was, however, a problem that looked as if it was about to get a whole lot worse.

When he got back to the studio and to the dressing room that had been a sanctuary in the past few weeks, one of the few places where a tabloid journalist couldn't point a long-lensed camera, his phone rang. It was a London number.

'Is that Michael O'Shea?'

'Who's asking?' he said, grumpily.

'Hi, Michael. It's DS Mackintosh from the City of London police.'

'Bill?'

Michael did a double take.

Bill Mackintosh had been one of the detectives he'd followed on the documentary series he'd made about crime. They'd been on a crusade through London, closing down drug dens and then camping out in the houses, waiting to catch unsuspecting punters in the act. Michael and Bill had become fairly good friends and he was supposed to be taking him for coffee to discuss a follow-up show... until all this shit had come about.

'I'd like to talk to you. It's just a formality; I'll do my best to be discreet of course. When's best for you?'

'What's this about?' Michael asked. It didn't sound like a social call. 'Look, I'm free this afternoon,' Michael added before the detective had time to reply. 'How discreet are you talking?'

'I'll come in plain clothes, on foot, through the back entrance.'

'Fine,' Michael said, 'I'll let you in through my garage, what time can I expect you?'

'Five o'clock sharp. I presume today's show is cancelled?'

'Yes, until further notice.'

Michael put down the phone and closed his eyes. He had to act cool: ride it out... because if he didn't, who knew what could happen.

As far as Michael could grasp, the press hadn't picked up on the officer. He might have been dressed in plain clothes but if he had come through the front entrance then there was always the chance one of the crime hacks would recognise him.

Michael invited the detective into his dressing room, offering him a seat on the sofa.

'I'm afraid we've got to go through the formalities first, Michael,' the detective said. 'I hope you understand. Can you tell me your full name and date of birth?'

'Michael Matthew O'Shea, MBE, 18th July 1975'

'And I do need to tell you that you do not have to say anything but anything you may say can be used in evidence.'

Michael stood up, his blood boiling. 'You're arresting me?' he snapped. 'You said this was informal.'

'I am not arresting you,' the detective said. 'I have to give that caution to everyone we interview. It just means that if you said anything relevant, anything that might help us catch whoever kidnapped those girls, we can use it in court.'

Michael gave him daggers.

'Look, Michael, we don't think you've done anything. But…'

'What?'

Of course, Michael had hoped it wouldn't come to this but now his worst suspicions had been confirmed.

'Your researcher Edward, basically what he's saying is that he walked in on you and you had your hands around one of the girls you had on the show. I take it that's…'

'Well yeah, that's utter bullshit,' he lied. 'I have people on my show because I think I can help with their lives. What would be the point in having them on if I screwed them up even further?'

'But Tiffany Roe did come to your dressing room?'

'Yes, she wanted to get my autograph, a lot of guests do. My other researcher, she dropped her off there. Why would I go assaulting someone if I knew my researcher could come back any minute to pick her up?'

'Sure,' the detective said, sympathetically. He seemed to be buying the story, so far. But just as Michael was thinking about a way to plant an idea into the detective's head that would not only exonerate him completely but destroy those two scumbag researchers, the detective did his work for him and asked a question so obviously pointed, so clearly loaded, Michael had to try very hard not to smile.

'So, why do you think your researchers are making these allegations?'

'I think they're panicking.'

'Panicking?'

'Yeah, making up anything they can think of to turn the spotlight off them.'

'You think?'

'You tell me, officer. But why don't we stop and look at the facts for a minute? Two girls on my show go missing in a short space of time and everyone assumes it's that taxi driver. You find the taxi driver and realise the only people who could have done it are people directly involved with the show. And at the exact moment you announce this our number one researcher attempts to dish the dirt on me. I know who I'd be wanting to talk to if I was you, detective.'

A smirk had grown over Mackintosh's face. Michael knew he'd won.

'And one more thing,' Michael said. 'If you want to find these scumbags, I'd suggest paying a visit to my brother.'

'Why's that?'

'My brother is a liar and a fantasist. The spastic twat has always been jealous of me. Edward and his cokehead slag of a girlfriend will know about this – they read all the papers – and they'll be trying to put words in his mouth to stitch me up.'

'Well,' DC Mackintosh said, 'looks like the net's closing in on our prime suspects.'

'And if I'm right, don't you forget who gave you the tip, yeah?' Michael could not resist a smirk.

'Thank you for your time.'

'Not at all…'

'We will keep you informed. And, as a way of thanks, maybe

we can see about getting you even better access for your next documentary with, say, the commissioner?'

'Apology, most certainly accepted,' Michael said.

And the detective saw himself out.

The stage was set.

26

Had it not been for a text message from Violet, reminding him of his appointment at The Blackfriar, he would have been in danger of forgetting the horrific scene from the day before that the police had been so disinterested in.

'I had a feeling this might happen,' Violet said, rubbing her nose, which hadn't gone unnoticed by Edward.

'You do, you do believe me?'

'Yes, if you think it matters...'

'It matters because those girls deserve justice.'

Violet shook her head, exasperated. 'Spare me the crusade...' She necked back a drink.

'How can you say that? It's like you don't care.'

'Get real, Edward. You did your bit. You told the police. Up to them if they don't want to listen. But we're small fish. Do you really think *People* are just going to hand over their highest-paid star on the hearsay of two researchers? Think of the scandal, the lost money. If someone has to take the fall for this, it will be us. If you stick your head out too much they'll...'

'Cut it off?'

'If you want to pursue this, be my guest... I want another job at the end of this.'

Edward changed tack. 'And what about your cocaine addiction?'

Violet closed her eyes, momentarily. 'Addiction? Stop being so dramatic. We all do what we have to do to get by. You should try it...'

Edward fumed. The very idea that *he* should try drugs.

Violet's phone buzzed. She flicked through it and started to watch something. Edward was intrigued, Violet invited him to look over her shoulder.

'...in his first interview since the scandal broke, Michael O'Shea pulled no punches,' said the reporter as establishing shots of his plush London home played over her words. Then the cameras cut to the interior of Michael's home. He was sat by the fireplace, with a concerned look on his face, his model wife, Karen, beside him, clutching his hand.

'...the channel didn't want me talking to the press.'

'So why have you decided to break your silence?'

'Because everybody knows me and respects me for telling it how it is, for offering the viewers the truth. I can't hold my tongue on such a serious issue.'

'Isn't it best to let the police do their job?'

'The police are doing a very good job but there's a cloud of suspicion that is hanging over this show, hanging over me.'

'And how have you been coping with it?'

'I've barely slept. The idea that kids that were on my show were abducted in that way. I feel for the parents and I've offered as much support as I possibly can. I'm in contact with them. We also have the highest standards of care and support after filming is finished, but we can't be held responsible for what happened. The disappearances, the murder of that taxi driver, folks at home have to understand that we all make choices, the only person or people responsible for these horrific crimes are those who carried them out.'

'And you mentioned that the police are doing a good job. Do they have any idea if they have any suspects lined up?'

'Yes,' Michael said. 'They have a suspect and they are gathering evidence. I think they'll be making an arrest any day now. Personally, I think two people are responsible for this crime. A double act.'

'And who do you think they might be?'

'This might shock you and viewers at home – and I know the police have a job to do – but I'm going to tell you who I think abducted those girls and killed that taxi driver.'

The reporter was out of shot but Edward could tell she was hanging on to his every word as everybody watching this exclusive was.

'I think it was the two researchers on the show. Edward Lewis and his girlfriend Violet Dearnley.'

Edward began to shake and was suddenly aware of everyone else in the pub who'd no doubt soon see this interview. Even Violet looked shocked by what Michael had just said.

'You're right – that is a shocking allegation to make. They could sue you for slander and the police could arrest you for interfering with their investigation.'

'I'm well aware of the risks but I think it's important for me to speak out, to let viewers know several facts about this case. That two days ago Edward Lewis came to visit me, drunk, in my dressing room, and admitted to being behind a plot to frame me, that he was jealous of my success. His whereabouts have yet to be accounted for, it's clear that he knew the route of that taxi and so did the girl he is currently dating, Violet Dearnley.

'We have suspected for a while now – though we gave her the benefit of the doubt – that she has a major drug problem and that she has been regularly taking cocaine at the workplace. The police are investigating them, but I'm not convinced that they are doing enough. My only concern here is for the girls' families. They deserve justice, to know what happened to their beautiful young daughters. And they will never get those answers unless Edward and Violet do the right thing…'

'Do you have a message for them?'

'Do the right thing, buddy. I don't know what motivated you, whether you were jealous of me and you murdered those girls to frame me or you murdered them and thought you could scapegoat me, but you've worked on my show long enough to know how I operate. You know you did the wrong thing. Come clean, give yourselves up, it's the only way.'

There was a stunned silence between Edward and Violet as she turned off the phone. Edward looked around him furtively, wondering who else in the pub may have seen the interview. Everybody seemed to be enjoying their drinks, as if nothing had happened.

Violet looked pale.

'I don't know who to believe anymore…' she said. 'What's to say you didn't admit to all of this in his dressing room? That you're the liar.'

Edward closed his eyes.

'I…'

'I need to think very carefully about my next move,' Violet said.

'We need to run. In a few hours, by the time everyone has seen this, we're going to be the most wanted people in the whole country.'

'You will be but I won't be… not if I turn you in.'

'You know I didn't do it. You know it wasn't me.'

Violet closed her eyes in resignation. 'Give me your phone.'

'What?'

'Give me your phone, Edward.'

He reluctantly handed it over, wondering whether to trust her and then Violet took out hers.

'Follow me,' she said and left her pint on the table, slipping out onto the main road. It was cold outside. 'Keep your head low, downtrodden...' They walked for a few moments before they reached the banks of the river Thames. She threw both phones into the sea without warning. Then she dragged him by the hand until they reached a cashpoint. There was no time to question her.

'Take out as much as it will let you,' she instructed.

'Why? Violet, what's happening?'

'The police are going to make a choice,' she explained, 'us or the great Michael O'Shea. And since Michael just turned most of the country against us, what do you think will happen if we walk around like normal? We need to get as far away from here as we possibly can.'

Edward did as he was told and took out three hundred pounds in cash. She did the same.

As they headed off down streets, through alleyways, past landmarks he recognised and some he didn't and eventually into Stepney Green Tube station, Edward tried to piece everything together.

'This is mad,' he said; an understatement if ever there was one. It was all so wrong. They weren't the ones who should be on the run. 'What about Tiffany? She could be in danger.'

'Michael won't do anything to her while there's so much attention... another body would not look good,' Violet said. 'It would look too suspicious.'

'Tiffany could be the key. If we could just get hold of her and convince her to go to the police.'

'You have such a naïve view of the world,' Violet screamed.

The few people in the Tube were staring at them. Edward lowered his head, frightened at the thought of how many of them had seen that interview.

'But we have to trust the police. What if we had blown the whistle on the show before? Complained about the way Michael exploits all the guests? Then maybe he would never have abducted the girls, killed Mallaky.'

'Oh, please! Do you really think if we'd gone to the police earlier it would have solved all of this? They would have laughed at us, charged us with wasting police time…'

'Not the police then, maybe the independent regulator…'

'Independent regulator.' Violet laughed. 'You just don't get it, do you?'

'I…'

'Nobody wants to know. It doesn't matter how many regulators or how many officers we go to, unless we have evidence nobody is going to investigate. Michael is too powerful, too famous, too rich.'

The Tube doors opened, the train whizzed off down the tunnel and then there was silence; there was no one on the platform and Edward had nothing left to say.

27

'Where are we going?' Edward whispered. They had arrived at Victoria Coach Station.

'As far away as possible from London.' Violet was studying the departures board, looking for a particular coach.

She led Edward to the end of the station where there was a coach about to leave for Edinburgh.

'What are we going to do about Michael? Minnie, Jessica? Other girls?'

'Nothing. We're going to lie low and forget about all of it.'

'What? We can't! Michael, he's a...'

Violet shrugged. 'We told the police, didn't we? Did our bit.'

'We have to investigate!'

'Investigate what? The only way to prove Michael has done this is to persuade Tiffany to testify and that doesn't prove anything about the other girls...'

The coach was about to leave.

'Are you coming?' the driver asked.

Edward thought about letting Violet go but then sighed and joined her.

Some people were travelling alone and had already plugged

their phones into the power sockets, others were chatting between themselves, some were reading books, but all of them seemed to have not a care in the world as Edward sat down next to Violet. And as the coach passed through Marble Arch several minutes later and headed out of the city, Edward wished more than anything that he too could empty his mind of all that he had witnessed in the last few weeks. Instead, he did the only thing he could and nestled down into the window, trying desperately to fall asleep.

By the time he awoke, groggy-eyed, they had reached the motorway and were well on their way up north. They were not due to arrive until the early hours of the morning. If he had still had his phone then perhaps he could have booked a hotel in advance but Violet had put an end to that.

'We'll have to take whatever is available, I guess. Don't you have any friends that way?' Edward asked.

Violet shook her head. 'I'm not that well connected. Don't you have any friends up north?'

'No, I grew up in Kent.'

'Lucky you.'

The bus was pulling into the station. The time for small talk was over.

As they jumped off out into the unknown, Violet led the way and up the steep sloping streets.

The rain was coming down hard, the skies grey… Edward hoped they could find somewhere fast – and comfortable – though he knew this was unlikely. After trying three hotels off The Mile they finally found a cheaper bed and breakfast further from the centre. The room they were offered was pleasant and clean but nothing out of the ordinary.

'Here,' Violet said, handing Edward a hip flask as she walked to the bathroom to get ready for bed.

'What is it?' he asked, regaining his composure.

'Vodka. You need it to calm your nerves.'

He took a couple of sips and returned it to her as she climbed into bed.

He wondered why he was doing this but couldn't be bothered to argue and before long he was fast asleep…

∼

Any prospect of a quiet morning soon evaporated with an urgency and panic unlike either of them had ever felt before when, as Edward always did first thing, he turned on the news.

'My God,' he said, shaking so violently he felt as if his entire body was going to crumple to the ground. 'Oh my goodness.'

Violet came running over from the bathroom when she heard the reporter speak, the toothpaste dripping from Violet's open mouth. The strapline said it all.

'O'SHEA DISAPPEARANCE: RESEARCHERS PRIME SUSPECTS?'

The reporter was live outside the *People* studios where the sun was only just starting to rise.

'Police this morning have issued a statement saying they want to talk to this man and this woman in connection to the disappearances on the *Michael O'Shea Show*.' To Edward's horror the screen flicked to a zoomed-out photo of him in sunglasses on holiday in Florida – his Facebook profile picture – and then briefly to a photo of Violet looking several years younger and with slightly shorter hair and a fringe. 'The two people in these photographs are Violet Dearnley and Edward Lewis. Police have confirmed that they are researchers on the show and that they haven't been seen since Tuesday when they failed to turn up for work. They are believed to be travelling together. It comes after Michael O'Shea gave a bare-all interview last night, in which he explicitly named the researchers…'

'So what does this mean for the investigation?' the presenter in the studio asked the reporter.

'It seems highly likely that the police want to question Violet Dearnley and Edward Lewis because they may well be directly involved in the disappearance of the two girls. Police haven't said whether they want to interview them as witnesses to what happened or suspects, but police believe that these kidnappings can only have been carried out by someone who either appeared on the show or had knowledge of how the show operated. It is also worth noting that they both failed to turn up today. Now I think the question many people will be asking is did they run off because they knew the heat would now be on them?'

'And tell us, how do people get in touch if they see either of these people? Or what should they do?'

'At this stage it seems that…'

Violet grabbed the control from Edward's hand and turned it off.

Violet rummaged through some cheap clothing she'd picked up from a supermarket in London before they had headed for the coach station.

'Here,' she said, throwing him a thick blue hoodie, 'put this on and keep your hood up at all times.' Then Violet pulled out the pair of sunglasses that she always carried and a headband and placed the glasses firmly around her eyes and pushed her hair back with her band.

'You really think this is going to work?' Edward asked, though he couldn't deny such small changes did make Violet look quite different.

'Only if people don't get a good look at us.'

Edward was losing his cool. 'What are we going to do? Where are we going to go?'

Violet appeared calm. 'We need to clear our names.'

Edward gathered up the remainder of his clothes into the rucksack he'd bought and then the two of them were off, wanted for crimes that they had not committed.

28

'I said the only chance we'd have of persuading the police to investigate Michael was through Tiffany. Actually, I was forgetting about something.' Edward had spent several hours working on his theory.

'Oh?' said Violet.

They were passing through the tall back streets of Edinburgh Old Town, tall and discreet.

'There's another person who could implicate him,' said Edward. 'Michael's brother, Phillip.'

Violet chimed in. 'I suppose it's possible that Phillip's penchant for young children stems from watching his older brother. But,' she cautioned, 'we don't know that for sure and Michael will know we're likely to go and visit his brother in Manchester if he can implicate him.'

'So that's where we are heading? Manchester?'

'Looks that way.'

'How are we going to get there without being arrested?'

'By being discreet, by buying tickets in a different name. And by sitting at the back of the coach, in the corner. We keep our hoods up, curl up in a ball and fall asleep and no one will suspect a thing.'

'You've really thought this through…'

Violet nodded.

Edward was uneasy as they boarded the coach this time. He tried to steady his chattering teeth, his shimmering body, knowing what would happen if he attracted unwanted attention.

When they finally hopped off the coach in Manchester, fear of being recognised and accosted haunted Edward and Violet's every movement. They hadn't dared stay in a hotel in case the staff had recognised them. So they sat down in the corner of a relatively empty park.

'How are we going to find Phillip?' said Edward.

'If we can wait for him after his trial, we can follow him and find out where he lives.'

'And how will we know when he's next up in court?'

Violet handed Edward a local paper. They'd passed by a news stand on their way there, but Edward hadn't seen Violet pay for anything.

'I couldn't exactly have walked up and paid for it when all his other papers have my face plastered on the front page,' she explained. 'I swiped it.'

'But if you'd been caught,' Edward protested.

Violet shook her head and shrugged.

'But I wasn't, Edward. Here.' She opened the paper on page eight where there was a half-page lead:

TALK SHOW BROTHER IN COURT

The sex abuse trial of Phillip O'Shea, the brother of the famed TV host Michael O'Shea, began today as the prosecution outlined their case against the 38-year-old at Manchester Crown Court. O'Shea from Manchester is charged with five counts of sexual assault and downloading indecent images of children. Jonathan Edwards QC, for the Crown, said that police had uncovered over five-thousand different indecent images of children on O'Shea's laptop, downloaded from the internet. The trial will continue tomorrow.

'So all we have to do is watch him go in, wait for him to come out and follow him home?' Edward said.

'Yes.'

'Without getting caught.'

Violet feigned a smile.

That night they didn't sleep. Fearing that wandering around Manchester city late at night might not be the best idea when the police were on patrol, ready to break up the inevitable fights when closing time came at many of the bars, Edward and Violet took shelter in the only place they could: a toilet cubicle. No one came around to lock up and the stragglers from the pubs were no doubt far too drunk to think about using a urinal or a cubicle. So, Edward and Violet rubbed their hands together and tried to keep each other warm, far too on edge to fall asleep even if their surroundings had indeed been considerably more comfortable.

When the sun started to rise, they sprayed some deodorant over each other and made a move. Edward was developing a beard which Violet approved of, claiming he would be recognised less easily as he'd always been clean shaven.

At the courthouse, they at first took to loitering around the small side street at the back.

At last, ten o'clock struck and from afar they caught sight of Phillip O'Shea.

He was disabled and was using crutches. There were a few

reporters following him. Just one photographer had shown up to get a snap of Phillip, who was moving so slowly and flanked by a solicitor trying to give him some last-minute advice, that it was hardly difficult for the photographer to run ahead of them both and get the shots he wanted.

After a few minutes the photographer ran off, satisfied with his catch, and Phillip O'Shea had disappeared behind the double doors and into the courthouse. It seemed that in the eyes of the press he had been guilty from the moment he was accused, the story had ended weeks ago and there was little appetite to report confirmation of what was already true, especially since the press currently had a bigger, more scandalous story to follow...

As four o'clock approached they made their way back to the courthouse and set about waiting for Phillip to emerge. This time there were no reporters to greet him or anyone for that matter, and he was left to stumble down the stairs on his crutches, alone.

Edward and Violet followed him, discreetly and quietly, down the back streets of Manchester and towards the suburbs. When he thought no one was watching he stopped hobbling and picked up pace, placing both crutches into one hand.

Phillip remained oblivious for the entire time until at last, he arrived at his home: a small terraced house, surrounded by moss and overgrown shrubbery. There was no one about apart from a couple, arguing in the front seat of a car. The windows were still single glazed and covered in grime and the door itself was rusty and needed replacing. A light went on in the living room: Edward and Violet made their approach.

There was no doorbell so all Edward could do was knock heavily, hoping Phillip would hear.

It took a good five minutes for him to get to the door and they were greeted, as expected, with suitable disdain.

'What do you want?' he hissed, having swiftly taken to his crutches once more.

Edward opened his mouth to speak but, stupidly, had thought

little about what he might say. It was only as he stood there in the doorway that he realised he may be face to face with a paedophile; the lowest of the low, the 'scum of the Earth', to quote the words of Phillip's brother. But of course, it wasn't as simple as that. It never was.

Edward remembered being played an archived clip of a once-loved musician, as he took a reporter on a guided tour of his home, filmed a few months before his exposure as a serial child abuser; Edward didn't know why he had expected to see seedy photos of children hanging from the walls, shut curtains, and secret rooms, but of course there was nothing remotely abnormal about where the now disgraced DJ had lived. Despite his dark secret, day-to-day he lived like any other man.

Phillip's house, although cluttered and messy, was much the same. It shed no light on the accusations levelled against him.

'We want to ask you a few questions,' Violet said.

'I'm not talking to journalists!' Phillip snapped.

'We're not,' Violet said. 'We want to talk to you about your brother, we worked with him.'

'My brother? What's he got to do with this?'

'If you let us in we can explain,' Violet said. Phillip did not look convinced. 'Please,' she added, 'we won't stay long.' He contemplated his decision: curiosity clearly got the better of him.

'Fine,' he said, hobbling backward so that she and Edward could make their way in.

The inside of Phillip O'Shea's house was just as neglected as the outside. The white walls had faded to yellow and the carpeted hallway did not look as if it had been hoovered in quite some time. The living room was no different either. In fact, it looked as if it was stuck in the 1970s. The television was chunky and small, there were extravagant paintings on the wall, and the sofa was curved and pink. And all around were cabinets of rubbish: Elvis Presley records, unlabelled videotapes, piles of discarded bills and unopened junk mail, half broken mugs and dog-eared books.

'Can we sit down?' Violet asked.

'Tell me about my brother,' he said, without answering her.

Violet and Edward took seats, regardless.

'It's really important you tell us the truth,' Violet explained. 'We believe your brother might be involved in some serious crimes.'

'What sort of crimes?' he asked.

'Similar to the sort that you've been accused of,' Violet said.

His eyes widened.

'You've seen the stories. Two girls from Michael's show have gone missing,' said Violet, 'and a taxi driver has been murdered. We caught him with his hands around the neck of a third girl. We're sorry.' Violet was humble. 'We need to know, have you ever seen your brother do… *anything*?'

'Yes,' Phillip said, after a slight hesitation. 'Yes. I saw him.' He took another break. 'I saw him…'

She was taken aback.

'When?' Violet probed but, before he could answer, everything stopped. Suddenly, the house was ablaze with blue lights and police officers of every rank were swarming into the house. Edward was pushed to the floor beside Violet and, before he could even catch his breath, he was being pulled up again, the caution he had heard so many times before on television washing over him like a particularly potent cocktail he knew would hit him soon enough.

'Edward William Lewis, I'm arresting you on suspicion of the murder of Thomas Mallaky, the abduction of Jessica Butler and the abduction of Millicent Jenkins. You do not have to say anything but anything you do say may be given in evidence.'

He was in a dream, he was watching himself from a telescope afar and yet he could still feel his arms, the cold metal pressing against his wrists as he was led away into the police van.

29

Her lifeless body was easy to cut. Protection had to be taken, of course. Thick black gloves that could be easily burned, a knife sharp enough to hack it clean off without creating too much of a mess, a vial to collect the blood and a plastic sheet to stop the excess from seeping onto the floor. This could not turn into a hatchet job. Not now, not after so much preparation, not in the final stages...

30

The morning brought with it another police van. Taken from his cell and bundled into it before the sun had even fully risen, Edward was told little about where he was going or what had happened to Violet, only that he was heading in the direction of London.

The press seemed to know more than he did. For, right on cue, as Edward was taken outside into the yard he caught a few snatched glances of the paparazzi, already camped outside the police station in droves. He tried not to look at them as he was handcuffed and bundled into an empty van. His isolation from Violet was deliberate, he'd been told, so that he couldn't confer with her – though he and Violet would surely have had plenty of time to concoct a story during their escapade around Manchester, had that indeed been their plan.

It took what seemed like an eternity to get to London. Through the bars on the windows and the cage in which he was imprisoned, Edward could barely see a thing, only glimpses of the motorway or the grey blocks of flats as they got closer to the city. Above the engines, Edward swore he heard a helicopter circling around. The paparazzi clearly hadn't missed a trick, though why any unsuspecting viewer would be inclined to watch Edward's complete journey from Manchester to London he didn't know.

He was thankful when he was finally led out of the van and into another police yard. Inside the station he searched once again for Violet, hoping to catch a brief sight of her so that he could be sure she was okay. But there was no such luck. *Maybe she hadn't been arrested at all?* Maybe the police were only interested in him.

'Follow me,' the officer said. The custody suite at this station was a lot bigger and it was modern too. There was no hint of the Victorian architecture at all, just lots of plain white walls, plastic flooring, and thick metal doors.

'Do you wish to see a solicitor?'

'No.' *Perhaps not the most sensible option*, Edward thought, but he was confident, despite having spent several hours in a cell already, that, if he told the truth, justice would prevail.

'You may be required to give another interview. For now, I'd like you to tell me where you were on the evening of Millicent Jenkins' disappearance.'

'I was...' It took Edward a while to remember. 'I was at home in my flat. We had done a show with Minnie and we had put her and her family onto a train. But that's not the point...' Edward protested, 'I didn't do this and neither did Violet. I saw Michael O'Shea put his...'

The officer held up his hands.

'Silence, son,' he said, 'you're here to answer my questions.'

'But I've just told you–'

'Did you sexually assault Minnie Jenkins?'

'Of course not!'

'Did you murder her? After you assaulted her did you kill her? Where have you hidden her body?'

Edward could see this was going nowhere. He refused to answer.

'Did you falsify a voicemail message in order that her parents would think that Minnie was safe?'

He shrugged. 'No. Of course not.'

'Where were you on the evening Jessica Butler disappeared?'

This time Edward did have an alibi. He explained that it was the night he and Violet had gone back to his flat and that there would be CCTV showing him getting the Tube, that there must be a record of him leaving the studios. He couldn't possibly have driven all the way down to Cornwall and caught up with Jessica Butler's taxi. But his alibi didn't appear to satisfy the officer.

'Anyone who worked on the show could have found out where Jessica was going,' Edward protested. 'It wasn't a secret. It was Michael who did this. You're going after the wrong person. You need to interview Michael O'Shea.'

Another officer walked into the room and whispered something to the detective questioning Edward. They both stood up.

'Interview terminated…' he said, turning the recorder off, and he led him out of the room.

'Can I go?' he asked.

'Not a chance, mate,' the officer said, laughing.

'What?'

'It's the cells for you.'

And, his worst nightmares confirmed, Edward, alone, without even a glimpse of Violet, was led into a room no bigger than a bathroom and the door slammed abruptly in his face.

'I'm innocent,' he protested, and he felt like banging on the cell door, creating a racket, but he knew it would be of no use. All it would serve to do was play against him in court… Yes, it was becoming more and more obvious where the interview was heading. Oh, why hadn't he listened to Violet? Why had he ever pursued Michael O'Shea? It didn't seem to matter how much he protested, how much the evidence pointed in the other direction, he was being fitted up for a crime he didn't commit.

Later that evening, as he lay in his cell, his face full of tears, Edward reflected on the world he saw around him, the cynicism, the lies, the exploitation that he had been a part of. He had cared little for the people who came on the show. And he had done little to improve their tragic lives. He was disgusted with himself for thinking only of what would make good television, of what would allow him to keep his job. He had been burnt by the fire that he had helped to fuel; maybe he deserved everything he got...

31

E dward was led into the interview room again but this time there were two detectives. They started the tape and asked once again if he would like a solicitor. He declined.

'What can you tell us about your time working on the *Michael O'Shea Show*, Mr Lewis?' the female officer asked. 'Did you see anything suspicious?' *What was this? A change of tack? Good cop, bad cop?*

'Am I not a suspect?' Edward asked.

'You've been arrested on suspicion of murder, abduction, and rape. If you're innocent you should answer our questions and assist us with our investigations as best you can.'

Edward had no idea what his rights were: surely he had to be informed whether he was a suspect or a witness? But he didn't know for sure. For the first time, he felt exposed without a solicitor. He had no way of knowing what traps he was about to walk into. What if this was a cunning way of getting him to implicate himself?

The officer repeated the question. 'What can you tell us about your time working on the *Michael O'Shea Show*?'

Edward wasn't sure he could answer such a vague question so

he simply repeated what he knew to be the truth. 'I walked into Michael O'Shea's dressing room and I saw him with his hands around a young girl. Her name is Tiffany. If you arrest Michael and give her protection, a safe house, then she'll tell you...'

'We have tried to trace Miss Roe and, would you believe it, we can't find her.'

'Check the recordings. She was on the show. Check the notes we made, the CCTV from the studio.'

'There is no doubt Tiffany Roe appeared as a guest on the *Michael O'Shea Show* but, conveniently perhaps, television production companies do not make a habit of installing CCTV in their star guests' dressing rooms...'

'What!'

How could this be happening to him? How could he have been set up so easily, so glaringly obviously?

'You have to do something!' Edward screamed as the realisation that he might not be getting out at all started to dawn on him. One thing was for sure, now he definitely needed some legal advice.

He changed tack again: 'Tiffany is in danger, so is her twin. If you don't find her, she could be Michael O'Shea's next victim.'

'You are here to answer my questions,' the officer said, shutting Edward down. 'That is what you have to do if you want any chance of getting out.'

So Edward caved and asked for a solicitor. The interview was suspended and he was sent back to his cell to wait. Only guilty people ever needed solicitors; nobody innocent ever had the kinds of conversations Edward was about to have, nor did they sit in a room for half an hour weighing up the balance of evidence against them, contemplating whether to give a no-comment interview.

In the end, Edward decided he was going to answer the questions, despite the advice of the duty solicitor who had been allocated to him. Edward had decided that he was a truthful man, an honest person and that the best he could do was to co-operate and hope that his interrogators would eventually come around.

'Tell me everything you remember about the night of the first disappearance, that of Minnie Jenkins.'

Edward narrated everything he could. How he and Violet had mounted a lengthy PR campaign to stop the papers getting hold of the story and how he and Braithwaite had gone looking for her. He told the entire truth, he knew there was no use withholding anything or trying to embellish what had happened but he knew it sounded patchy as he said it. Why, if he was so innocent, had they tried to stop Minnie's mother Jo phoning the police for over a week? And since he knew the girl's address it was surely quite possible that he could have parked up outside and whisked her away one evening?

After an intense two-hour session, exhausted, Edward was sent to his cell once again where he reflected on his predicament. Years of being an avid fan of *The Blue Beat* – a rival crime show to the one Michael O'Shea presented – had taught him one thing: police officers could not hold him forever, at some point they either had to charge him or let him go.

And he sensed that moment was approaching. Soon he would know if he was to be charged with killing the taxi driver, abducting Minnie and Jessica. Of course, no one ever got bail for murder. This was it: he'd had his final chance to plead his case, either he got out today or he would spend at least the next six months in prison, waiting for the fight of his life. There would be no reprieve, no period in which he could pack up his life as he knew it before accepting his fate.

Hour after hour went by and he found himself becoming like a meerkat; every time he heard an officer on the suite, the rattling of keys, the sound of boots marching towards him, he thought it was his time.

Then, at last, the doors to his cell opened.

'Follow me,' said the officer.

Edward could do nothing but close his eyes and hope for the best.

3 2

The telephone rang five times before an officer at the station picked up. The pre-recorded staccato tones of Microsoft Sam rang through the receiver, devoid of any emotion. Strange how one call was yet again to change everything...

'Hello, officer. You might want to check Michael O'Shea's secret garage. It is located on the outskirts of Manchester and registered in the name of Matthew Jones. You may find something that will help you with your investigation into the missing girls.'

The officer went to reply but before he got a chance the person occupying the phone box had dashed off into the pouring rain outside. The glass door clinked shut. The sound of feet slushing through the water reverberated through the area and when, in the minutes or hours to come, the police arrived to investigate, they would find the receiver, still dangling in mid-air...

33

The two men stood before Edward and it took him an age to take in what they said.

'You're free to go, son...'

'Free to go?'

Edward was stunned. He had prepared himself for the worst.

'We've had to make some special arrangements.'

'Special arrangements?'

What the officer meant was that the outside of the building was swarming with reporters. The longer they had kept Edward, it seemed, the more journalists had arrived, perhaps anticipating a statement from the police announcing that he had been charged. A taxi had been booked to take him back to his flat as there was clearly no way he could walk or take the Tube. And he had been advised to leave London as soon as he could if he wanted to avoid the attention of the press.

As Edward was led out of the custody suite and made his way towards the public reception, the flicker of camera flashes caught him off guard.

'Your public awaits!' The officer at the reception said. Edward was not in the mood for jokes. He said nothing, held his head up high and headed out. But it wasn't the lights that took him off guard. Reporters were screaming and shouting for quotes whilst presenters did pieces to camera. It was impossible to concentrate in the racket. He felt as if he could not even hear his own thoughts.

Finally, he scrambled for the taxi that had been arranged for him and an officer slammed the door behind him. The police station, the cameras and then the City of London all faded into darkness and Edward sat still as he tried to come to terms with the realisation that his life as he knew it was all but over…

HOW THE TABLES TURNED ON MR O'SHEA'S SANCTIMONIOUS PANTOMIME FOR STATE DEPENDENT DELINQUENTS

-We look back at the life and legacy of Michael O'Shea as 'the trial of the century' begins

It has been an unfortunate stain on our country for a great many years that Mr O'Shea's daily parade of emotionally deprived, drug-addicted, state-dependent delinquents has continued to be a cause célèbre of certain sections of our media. The ratings hit was nothing more than a shameful pantomime of the underclass who dream of a better life, who thrived off Mr O'Shea's rags to riches tale, who felt that they too would be showered with wealth and privilege, if they just used their fifteen minutes of fame to their advantage. Today, however, the illusion of Mr O'Shea as a moral crusader – the man who shamed people into turning their lives around by simply 'telling it like it is' – will come crashing down as allegations of his staggering hypocrisy will once again be thrust centre stage as his own trial for murder, kidnap and rape begins in earnest.

No doubt regular readers of this newspaper will remember the dramatic turn of events late last year when researcher Edward Lewis was released without charge while his former boss spent the evening in a prison cell, charged with the murder of Thomas Mallaky and the kidnap of Minnie Jenkins and Jessica Butler. Hours before, police officers were seen searching Mr O'Shea's five-bedroom mansion where he resides with his model wife Karen and two children – a thousand miles from the council estates and drug dens of his guests. Then later in the evening came the news that police had searched a garage on the outskirts of Manchester following an anonymous tip-off. What they found there, one can only speculate, but it was indeed enough for him to be charged only a few hours after his arrival and soon we will know whether it is enough to convict him.

THE LION, P.1

THE MAN WHO GROOMED A NATION

- 'Broken' O'Shea in the dock

-Prosecutors slam fallen star as a 'cold-blooded murderer'

Opening one of the most talked about trials in modern history, Hugh Kenner QC, prosecuting, today destroyed Michael O'Shea's reputation as he set about trying to convince the jury the fallen star was guilty of rape and murder. Referring to his weekly daytime show and his role as a judge for Make Me a Star, *Kenner said, 'Mr O'Shea used his fame to groom an entire nation into believing he was a moral crusader, a man simply trying to help people resolve their differences and better their lives.' But this was a lie, he said. Mr O'Shea was not just a serious sexual offender with a penchant for adolescent girls but an 'opportunist and a cold-blooded murderer who used his status and his show for the gravest of acts.'*

The researchers on the show, Edward Lewis and Violet Dearnley, appeared to be in the clear as Kenner described how they were 'unwittingly' used to gather information about young vulnerable teenagers on the pretext that they would appear on the show where O'Shea would offer to help them whilst all the time his true motive was to abduct them, rape them and kill them.

But the most shocking part of the opening statement came right at the end when he revealed that 'damning DNA evidence' would prove O'Shea's guilt beyond doubt. Kenner told the jury they would hear how O'Shea raped and murdered fifteen-year-old Millicent Jenkins and seventeen-year-old Jessica Butler and that he also murdered the innocent taxi driver, Thomas Mallaky, who he said 'just happened to be in the wrong taxi, on the wrong journey, on the wrong day,' and 'was brazenly slaughtered, his body dumped, left for the deer'.

The trial continues tomorrow.

THE LION, P.1

HE'S LIV-ID!

-O'Shea furious as co-host refuses to defend him

Olivia Dessington-Brown will not come to the defence of her former friend and co-host Michael O'Shea at his trial for murder and rape.

The move comes as O'Shea's legal team set out his case in their own opening statement in which they made the astonishing defence that O'Shea had been engaged in a decade-long affair with his co-host despite being married with two children. His secret rendezvous with Dessington-Brown on the nights in question, he alleges, explains why he does not have an alibi for the murder of either girl.

The trial continues.

Inside the Strange World of TV Quacks

Occasionally in British public life, we get an insight into some little facet of truth, a rare admittance of how society really operates, and today – at the trial of Michael O'Shea – we got exactly that, an extraordinary exposé of how so-called 'experts' are bullied and cajoled in the mad world of television.

Bernard Braithwaite, a not wholly innocent and strange character with a penchant for stuttering and verbosity, told the trial today how he was handpicked by Michael O'Shea for his show.

O'Shea 'had come to my rehabilitation clinic when I was a psychiatrist,' he explained. It was here that O'Shea tempted him with such a large sum of money to come and work on his show that Braithwaite felt he could not turn it down. We can see the tacit agreement that took place, no doubt without a word ever being spoken. Mr O'Shea's show, the court heard, was recovering from yet another scandal, this time involving a guest who ransacked the set and attacked his best friend on stage. Mr O'Shea needed to prove that the show was looking after its guests or the courts and the network would no doubt have discreetly shown him the door. Desperate that such a new regime should not affect his ratings or his proclivity for scandal and salaciousness, O'Shea hired the useful Dr Braithwaite, to act as his 'yes man'.

Despite his protestations that he was 'worried' that his boss might have 'ulterior motives' and his hope that he could 'make a difference', the unadulterated greed with which Dr Braithwaite entered into this agreement with Mr O'Shea directly influenced the tragic circumstances that are currently being considered by the jury.

So this paper has little sympathy with Dr Braithwaite's admission that he was the subject of bullying by Mr O'Shea.

'I suppose he saw me as a direct challenge to his authority and to his career,' he began, with such delusions of grandeur it is hard to wonder why he never considered a career in television himself. 'So I would have to say that he undermined me regularly. He made some very cruel remarks towards me and to other members of staff. Wherever he could, he made sure to ignore my decisions and make me feel worthless.'

'Do you think Mr O'Shea made guests on the show feel like this too?' the prosecutor asked.

'I think so,' was his reply, carefully calculated, no doubt. 'I cannot speak for them of course but there were many people who were booked onto the show who I felt would be inappropriate and they seemed to leave feeling emotionally shrunken and deflated.'

'So, Dr Braithwaite, if what you are telling me is correct, why did you continue to work for Mr O'Shea? Why did you not resign?'

Indeed a question which gets to the heart of the matter. How many more so-called 'doctors' have sold out on their principles for the sake of making a quick buck in this never-ending gold mine of debauchery? And how much longer can we turn a blind eye to the under-regulation of broadcast media in this country?

THE LION, P.1

O'SHEA'S EMPLOYERS GANG UP

-Shocking revelation at court as Braithwaite says O'Shea IS capable of murder.

Michael O'Shea's fortunes took a dramatic turn for the worst yesterday as the doctor in charge of looking after guests on his show admitted he did believe O'Shea was capable of rape and murder.

Under examination, Bernard Braithwaite said he thought there could be no doubt that O'Shea was guilty because he was 'different' with the victims. 'He liked to wow them, I think. I suppose he didn't have to groom them, really: they were so starstruck by him, they came to him. The younger girls would often want his autograph. He would never have to ask them outright to come and find him but it was always made clear that he would be available after the show in his dressing room.'

Asked if O'Shea manipulated the situation, Braithwaite added: 'I certainly saw situations arise where he could be alone with young teenage girls.'

Later, O'Shea's other employees were forced to admit their doubts about the besieged presenter.

Senior Researcher Violet Dearnley described how O'Shea behaved aggressively towards other staff on the show, including Braithwaite. The jury was then shown footage of fifteen-year-old Millicent Jenkins' appearance on the show. Asked whether the tape showed that O'Shea was deliberately trying to 'provoke' the girl into running away so that he could abduct her, Dearnley said no.

'Michael rarely read the case files on each guest in detail until the morning of the show.'

'But he was aware of whom was on his own show in advance? He made the final decision?'

Dearnley continued: 'Yes, he would have the final say and the cases would be discussed with him in advance. He did not show any particular interest in any of the cases where the girls were abducted.'

Jurors also heard from an ex-employee of the show who survived just one week under the heavy pressure of the show before he dramatically attempted to kill himself.

Johnathan Langton, twenty-six, took to the stand to retell the events of two years ago. Readers might remember our exclusive coverage. Two guests ransacked the O'Shea Show and destroyed half the set. A subsequent court case resulted in the show's producers being told to clean up their act. Langton, however, had warned O'Shea and his producer about winding guests up before they appeared. 'I was concerned that this wasn't right but they simply told me to "f*** off",' and he was even spat at. O'Shea and his producer got so annoyed at him that they locked him out of the gallery where the show is controlled. Whilst recording took place, he attempted suicide and was forced to resign. O'Shea was a 'monster' he said, 'who was obsessed with power and status'. The trial continues.

THE LION, P.5

O'SHEA EXCLUSIVE – POLICE 'GIVE UP' ON SEARCH FOR BODIES

It's been well over six months since the disappearance of Minnie Jenkins and Jessica Butler and with their bodies still no closer to being found, The Lion *understands the police and the CPS have now accepted they will not find their remains before the conclusion of Michael O'Shea's trial. Police have already poured vast amounts of resources into searching the area surrounding O'Shea's garage on the outskirts of Manchester, where a car belonging to him and a single thumb belonging to Millicent Jenkins were discovered.*

Hundreds, if not thousands of hours of CCTV have been scoured for clues and a daily patrol of sniffer dogs have continued to comb through the woodland. Divers have even searched local reservoirs, lakes, and rivers in a twenty-mile radius. But still nothing. Police say they are confident they can still secure a conviction.

'We would obviously like closure for the victims' families,' one officer told us.

THE LION, P.1

O'SHEA'S BROTHER ACCUSED

-How Michael taught younger brother sick paedo fantasies

The courtroom in the O'Shea trial today became the venue for a dramatic family drama as Phillip O'Shea, younger brother to the embattled presenter, accused him of teaching him how to abuse children.

Phillip O'Shea, who himself has a conviction for offences against children, said his brother used to hang around the school gates looking for innocent victims to bring back to the apartment the sick siblings used to share together.

Asked if anybody witnessed this, he said there could be potentially hundreds of parents and children who spotted them at local schools.

Despite being quizzed for several hours, Phillip O'Shea could not recall the names or appearances of any of the alleged victims and none have come forward despite numerous appeals but asked if he believed his brother was capable of rape and murder, he said yes.

THE LION, P.1

O'SHEA'S DNA COURT SHOCK

The prosecution ended their case against Michael O'Shea by turning the tables on the former presenter and laying out damning DNA evidence against him that he would usually hand out to guests on his own show.

In a truly shocking twenty-four hours in court, prosecutors first successfully got Mr O'Shea to admit he would have known in advance exactly where Jessica Butler was going on the night she was abducted and that he also had access to the home address of Millicent 'Minnie' Jenkins.

Next came the extracts of Michael's first police interview. The officers can be seen asking him how many properties he owned. He tells them about his family home and his villa abroad but not about his garages and denies he has a lockup, even when asked directly. The interview, the prosecution alleges, proves O'Shea is a liar.

But the final twist of the knife came when prosecutors presented evidence that O'Shea's DNA had been found on the severed thumb believed to belong to Minnie Jenkins, which had been discovered in his garage. A cardigan, also found in the lockup, had traces of both O'Shea and Minnie's DNA.

THE LION, P.4.

O'SHEA ON THE DEFENSIVE

From our reporter in the courtroom

It took just a day for O'Shea's team to lay out their own evidence because there was so little of it. The ex-presenter did not deny being at the garage, no doubt because the evidence that he owned both the garage and the KA was overwhelming. There was an answer for even the most incriminating evidence. His brother's testimony was not credible: Phillip allegedly had a vendetta against Michael because he had not funded his own trial for abuse crimes. The garage was not a murder scene but a secret rendezvous point: for Michael told the court that he had been having an affair with Liv. So desperate was he for these details of his private life to remain a secret that he lied to the police, worried that if he had to appear as a witness, his affair would be made public and his marriage would be over. This is why he had no alibi for the nights in question.

Michael had one public social media account and the few private text messages he and Liv had sent each other had been on secret pay-as-you-go phones which they had both taken great care to dispose of every week. And why had Liv not testified that all this was true? Why had she not corroborated his claims? It was simple, Michael argued: who on earth would implicate themselves in a murder inquiry by voluntarily placing themselves at a crime scene?

An unlikely scenario but readers of The Lion *will make up their own mind as the trial continues.*

Tomorrow: *the defence cross-examines the witnesses.*

THE LION, P.1

O'SHEA COURT SHOCKER: RESEARCHER'S COKE AND SEX SHAME

-Top researcher denies she was high during filming

Michael O'Shea's defence team today poured scorn over a researcher who had testified against him, claiming she was addicted to cocaine and moonlighted as a high-class escort. Under oath, Violet Dearnley denied she used the Class-A drug and regularly saw men who had paid to have sex with her via a mobile phone app.

O'Shea's defence team argued the absence of mobile phone records was suspicious, as too was Dearnley's refusal to submit to a drugs test. They presented damning photographs of her taken by a private detective showing her meeting with men in a bar.

But prosecutors claimed the researcher disposed of her phone in haste after her colleague Edward Lewis admitted his suspicions to her that O'Shea was behind the disappearance of the two girls. Dearnley feared that O'Shea might try to track her down and kill her so threw her phone into the River Thames. Furthermore, prosecutors argued, there was no evidence that money changed hands or that Dearnley slept with the men she met up with. Prosecutors also told the jury that the private detective was not an impartial witness since he had previously been retained by the O'Shea Show.

The defence for O'Shea argued Dearnley's judgement could not be trusted since she may have been high on drugs during the times she was working on the show. Prosecutors also argued her work as an escort impinged her reputation and diminished her credibility as a witness in the case.

34

He was not an idiot. He knew it had been over for a long time. No amount of mudslinging was going to change that. As he was led into the gallery which had, in recent weeks, subsided in numbers and was now packed to the brim, Michael knew there was no point getting his hopes up.

There was complete silence; not even the faintest flicker of a juror's hand could go unnoticed by the pack of reporters in this room. In walked the judge and finally, the infamous words rang around the courthouse as he addressed the jury:

'Have you reached a verdict upon which you are all agreed? Please answer "yes" or "no".'

'Yes.'

'On the first count against Mr O'Shea, the murder of Millicent Jenkins, does the jury find the defendant guilty or not guilty?'

'Guilty.'

'On count two, the murder of Thomas Mallaky.'

'Guilty.'

'On count three, the murder of Jessica Butler?'

'Guilty.'

'On count four, the rape of Millicent Jenkins.'

'Guilty.'

'On count five the rape of Jessica Butler.'

'Guilty.'

The court gasped but Michael did not. Even if, in those few short seconds, before the jury foreman had delivered his verdict, he thought he was about to get off, every facet of Michael's life had already collapsed in upon itself; his marriage, his reputation, his career, his chances of ever seeing daylight again.

He looked around, vaguely amused at the absurdity of the situation: he could almost smell the print as journalists around him raced for the most shocking adjectives, the word allegedly now so markedly absent from their reports.

'Take him down...' said the judge.

Michael O'Shea had wasted away in prison, his face, gaunt and pale, the beard he had grown wild and out of control. But at least the baying media outside would be denied this final portrait of him, his face hidden behind the blacked-out glass of the prison van.

35

More than thirty minutes had passed since Michael had been led away. Edward was stood in the cloisters at the back of the building, staring out at the cobbled courtyard, incredibly aware of the helicopter circling around above, no doubt streaming the scene live into people's living rooms. He had lost Violet in the crowd but she had figured out where he had gone.

He had bought a packet of cigarettes earlier in the day.

Violet eyed him from a distance, tentatively opening up the box, trying to work out how to use the lighter.

'I never really understood people's proclivity for these things,' he said, 'until this morning.'

She snatched the packet from his hand and took one herself. He could no longer be bothered; he knew he would hate his first puff and that he would be left painfully short of breath as the smoke filled up his lungs...

'The verdict... I don't feel any better,' he muttered.

'It is what it is.'

'I still feel guilty,' Edward said, softly.

'Then you've thought about this too long.'

They stood in silence for several moments as Violet finished her cigarette. Violet started to move back into the building but Edward didn't follow her. She raised her hand in farewell and he wondered if he'd ever see her again…

36

'...He rose to fame during the trial of disgraced talk show host Michael O'Shea where he worked as the director of guest rehabilitation. Some have speculated that he is tipped for a show of his own but for now, he's on tonight to promote his new book: *Under The Spotlight: A life Behind the Cameras.* Please welcome Dr Bernard Braithwaite, everyone.'

There was a warm round of applause as a much more comfortable Braithwaite, dressed in blue jeans and an unbuttoned cardigan, stepped out onto the studio floor. He bowed gracefully and raised his hands to quell the noise as Jim Cartwright began his interview.

'How've you been, my friend?'

'I'm well, thank you.'

'Good, that's what we like to hear! Now tell us all about this book you've written. You actually started it whilst the trial of Michael O'Shea was going on, didn't you?'

'Yes, I think really the book was...' Braithwaite paused, ostensibly to collect his thoughts, though Edward could tell he was simply trying to stop himself stuttering. 'It was a way of reflecting on everything I'd seen happen over the last few months. I do feel that when tragic and unexpected events happen in our lives we've got to find some way, first of coping and coming to terms with them and then of understanding, of shaping a narrative out of what has happened to us and this, I suppose, is my attempt at doing that.'

'Absolutely, and these events were just so shocking, weren't they? I mean for us, as viewers, to hear about what Michael O'Shea had done... it left you with such a sense of despair, he's even been on this show, on this very sofa, but for you, it must have been so much worse.'

'Yes, I suppose that is what everyone is interested in and what I have tried to devote a fairly substantial chunk of the book to, a memoir of my time working on the show and how that juxta-poses with, well... the truth.'

'If you ever saw anything which might have been suspicious...'

'Exactly, yes, and I honestly could not think of anything. He seemed like the perfect husband and he did a good job at convincing us all that he was only interested in improving the lives of his guests.'

'So, what was your view on the trial as it unfolded?'

'Like everyone else, I had no idea what to think. You can't really speculate about the outcome, you have to let justice take its course. I offered to help both sides with all that I could remember so we could get to the truth. But the verdict has been out for over two months, you have to accept it and I do I accept it entirely of course. He was found guilty by a jury.'

'But he has appealed against his conviction and his legal team have released statements in which he is adamant that he is inno-cent. Even now, is there not a flicker of doubt in your mind?'

'No, the DNA evidence, I think, does prove it and, as I said, he was found guilty by a jury so that is as close to any kind of closure we're going to get. I can't imagine anyone considering quashing his conviction based on the evidence we heard.'

'And what about the show itself, do you miss it?'

'Oh of course. Though the trial features in the book, most of it is about the good experiences I had on the show. It was so rewarding and, I will be quite honest with you, Jimmy, I did really enjoy my time...'

'And rumour has it that we might be seeing you back on our screens pretty soon actually. What can you...'

Edward turned off the television. He was lying in bed, alone. A complimentary copy of Braithwaite's book was still lying face down on his coffee table. The rumours were true. Braithwaite was to get his own show. Same studio, same time, and, if he had his way, the same backstage crew as well. Edward had gotten a phone call the same day that the book had arrived, asking him to consider returning as a researcher. He'd asked for time to think about it, feeling at that moment, frankly, overwhelmed and still quite sick of hearing about Michael O'Shea.

Financially, returning was definitely the best choice. But Edward had already turned down an opportunity to write about his experiences on the *O'Shea Show* for *The Lion*, though Violet had accepted. Edward hadn't spoken to her since that day at court but he had happened upon her article, plastered over the front page. It wasn't as if Edward blamed her – or Braithwaite – for cashing in. It was a tough world and they'd all suffered at the hands of Michael O'Shea. They deserved a shot at fame and riches but Edward didn't know if he was ready to do the same. He imagined Violet already had another job, somewhere in the City. But he was wrong...

It took only three days to coax Edward back into the studio; the price was right. So there he was sitting beside Violet, signing the paperwork. Violet acknowledged Edward but said little. She seemed awkward and he could not help wondering how she had spent her days during their long absence without work, how many people had she slept with or how she was funding her cocaine addiction?

Braithwaite had promised to 'do things properly', to 'right the wrongs of the past'. Edward didn't know how far he believed that. But the experience on the *Michael O'Shea Show* had made him re-evaluate everything. Edward was determined to take more responsibility for the decisions he took in his working life and he had reasoned that there was nothing wrong with taking an opportunity so long as he was true to himself, so long as he was happy to throw in the towel if he saw something he felt uncomfortable with.

So here he was, about to make the preparations for the new series. One of the things that had most persuaded him to return was safety in the knowledge that Braithwaite's show would be a world away from O'Shea's. In fact, the channel seemed to have done a complete U-turn in order that the new format should fit Braithwaite's personality.

There would be no shouting or confrontation, guests would be brought out separately to each other, offered tea and coffee and, most unusually of all, there would be no studio audience. No more pantomimic chanting, no patronising clapping: just Braithwaite sat quietly on a stage trying to counsel people as best he could. It was everything the *Michael O'Shea Show* was not.

What was more – and Edward suspected, the main reason the channel had agreed to the show – Michael's notoriety was almost guaranteed to double the viewing figures. Anyone interested in the trial would be watching, eagle-eyed for more scandal. There were even rumours that Braithwaite would present a special from Michael's prison cell, where he would convince him into finally confessing all and giving up his appeal, revealing the location of the bodies...

As well as a pay rise, Edward and Violet had been given their own office and a garage, perks of the job, he supposed. While

Edward had not been able to afford it, Violet, Edward noticed, had bought herself a cheap car. The interviews she had given to *The Lion* had been more lucrative than even Edward could have imagined and it was more than double the money they'd offered to him to sell his story.

So as Edward walked down the corridor, which had been decked out with a plush new carpet and 'no smoking' signs, Edward paused for a moment before he entered his new office. The moral conundrum which he faced on a seemingly daily basis had been resolved: they would fix people rather than break them.

Violet was inside, busy at a new computer, presumably compiling information for the first set of shows.

'Hi,' Edward said, tentatively. If it had been anyone else he would have gone over for a hug, without hesitation. She smiled, briefly.

'Braithwaite has already suggested some guests for the first show,' she said. 'There's a young mum who's just split up from her boyfriend and she's pregnant with his child. She was friends with Minnie's mum.'

'Oh that's strange, you wouldn't think she'd want to come on given what happened...' Edward trailed off. Braithwaite appeared at the door. He had grown a beard, appeared to have lost weight and was sporting a new blazer.

'We were just talking about the first guest.'

'Good. It really is quite tragic. I'm going to try to get her to tell me the entire story and then quiz her a bit about her childhood. But we have gone to great lengths this time to ensure that the guests feel comfortable and are looked after. We've scrapped Florida so that we can spend more money on professional help. We've also got a new producer. Dave used to produce *Who Deserves a Million?* before it got cancelled.'

'Oh... I see.' It wasn't really a surprise that Mags had decided against returning to the show. Not given how fiercely she had defended Michael in the trial and, Edward thought, fondly, how strongly she loathed Braithwaite. For all her unpleasantries, her cynicism, her chain-smoking, her insatiable appetite for swear words, somehow Edward knew the show wouldn't be the same.

'I shall leave you to it,' said Braithwaite, 'but if you do have any problems you know where to find me.'

'Thanks,' Edward said.

As it happened, the new producer was hardly the pinnacle of professionalism either. In fact, he quickly became known as the caveman, for his dirty black stubble, beer belly and proclivity to sit slumped in the gallery for most of the day, making sexist jokes and complaining bitterly, about the amount of work he had to do.

It was mainly left to Violet and Edward to put the show together: from the research right through to the recording. Strangely, though, this made the experience a lot easier. Half the battle before had been trying to second guess and then persuade Mags about their choices. Dave was so lazy that he rarely challenged them. The research was also a lot less full-on than it had been. They were no longer searching for the guests with the most compelling story: it was a case of deciding who needed the most help.

By the end of the week they were more than ready to record the first set of shows. Braithwaite came to see them that morning.

'Relax,' he said, 'take it easy. We're not in the business of exploiting people.'

'Thanks,' Edward said, though it soon became apparent Braithwaite's motives for speaking to the both of them was not just mere pleasantries.

Inevitably, a lot of the stories they had compiled for the first week were ones that would have ordinarily fallen by the wayside on the *O'Shea Show*. Their first attempt was the complete antithesis of Jessica Butler's story. A huge man, so overweight that he could barely fit through his front door and in need of a specially converted bungalow with wider doorways. Thirty-eight-year-old Alan's addiction to junk food had naturally caused a complete mental collapse and he had lost his job. What made it a good story, though, was the question of why he had suddenly descended into obesity.

The man was a fantasist. His entire life had been a lie. He'd married two different women and mortgaged two different houses, fathering children and using false names. He'd pretended to one wife that he was a teacher and to the other a private detective, using the latter lie to explain his long periods of absences. He had kept this up for a decade before he was found out when he mistakenly left a debit card with his real name in on a trouser pocket he had put out to wash. The whole affair had ended with a suspended prison sentence and his children and both wives refusing to have anything to do with him.

But what was staggering about the whole incident was that in the seven years since it had happened, he had refused to talk or even acknowledge that anything untoward had taken place. On his return from prison, he had sunk into depression, obesity, and unemployment.

Edward had hoped that Braithwaite would spend the first ten minutes of the show describing and highlighting the severity of the man's condition and the majority of the show trying to get the man to open up about what had happened and confronting him with the facts.

But it appeared Edward was to have no such luck.

'I thank you, from the bottom of my heart, for joining me today,' Braithwaite began, in an overly sincere piece to camera. Edward did not correct him, thinking it set the tone for the new show. The set had been completely re-designed. It no longer felt like a bear pit; there were pot plants and bookcases and instead of plastic chairs, there were sofas with a coffee table between them. As Braithwaite addressed the camera, Violet, off-screen, led Alan from his motorised wheelchair and onto the sofa.

Braithwaite explained his predicament but only briefly – he skirted around the most sensitive details – and focused not on the causes of the man's obesity but merely on practical ways to address it.

'Can we get back to the root causes of his obesity?' Edward said over the mic. 'Get him to open up about the identity fraud.'

But his advice appeared to have fallen on deaf ears. Fifteen minutes went by and still, Braithwaite was nodding passionately and offering up suggestions about how the man might set about changing his diet. Edward was quite happy for Braithwaite to approach the subject gently but to completely ignore the obvious not only felt like a disservice to the viewers at home – who Edward feared may well turn off in their droves – but to Alan himself. He couldn't go on ignoring the blindly obvious. If Alan went on pretending that nothing had happened, that the crimes he had committed had never taken place, Edward failed to see how he could even begin to get better. To use Braithwaite's own language, Alan wasn't addressing the core psychological issues behind his addiction.

The recording was coming to an end. There were just five minutes left. Edward reminded Braithwaite again. But he still refused to go into any of the details about the man's identity fraud. *How could they broadcast this?* The omission was so huge, it was almost comical. They had dropped a bombshell and not mentioned it.

When the recording came to an end and they broke up briefly, ready to bring on the next guest, Edward wondered what to do. Did he go downstairs and have a word with Braithwaite right at this moment? Did he leave it and accept that this was the way he wanted to run his show? In the end, he just couldn't leave it alone. So he sprinted down the gallery stairs and to his office where Braithwaite was going over some notes with Violet.

'Did you not hear me over the microphone?' Edward asked,

casually, though his unorthodox appearance backstage obviously gave away his concerns.

'Yes, Edward,' Braithwaite said, 'but I really didn't feel it was appropriate to go into that on national television. In fact, I do think we should ask the editors to take out even that small reference to the fraud. You have to remember this is such a profoundly different show to anything that went before, the interests of the guests must always come first and if I'd gone into any detail it could have backfired, Alan could have tried to kill himself when he saw it broadcast back, it could have made for a grave situation indeed.'

Edward didn't quite know what to say. He didn't want to challenge his new boss, especially on the first day at work but he was genuinely worried. Who would watch a show in which the very notion of conflict was met with disdain and censure? But then, perhaps this was a one-off, the man had a serious condition and was clearly fragile...

Edward shouldn't have banked so heavily on such a thought. This was the way Braithwaite would run the show, regardless of the rapidly declining ratings and regardless of what anybody else wanted. And once again, nobody but Edward and Violet seemed to care. Least of all Dave, the new producer.

'Make us a cuppa tea, love!' he shouted to Violet one day as she sat at the desk at the back of the gallery, putting the final touches to the following days recording with Edward. The techies were also in, rehearsing.

Violet ignored Dave. She was devising potential follow-up questions for the guests which she and Edward were going to try, no doubt unsuccessfully, to get Braithwaite to ask. When the two of them were finished they began to head downstairs, but they were accosted.

'Oi, where do you think you're going? What kinda woman are you? Come back and make me a cuppa!' Dave roared as Violet headed off downstairs.

'Enough!' Violet said, raising her hand, as she approached the gallery door.

'Oh! Hit a nerve, have I? Looks like we 'av a feminist, lads.' He was talking to the techies. They nodded in vague agreement, trying to ignore him. Violet was not impressed.

'Don't speak to me like that,' she said, clipping the end of her syllables short like a woodpecker snapping shut its beak.

Dave gave her the finger but by then she was halfway down the gallery stairs…

'We can't go on like this,' Violet said. They were in The Blackfriars. Edward was sipping cider, as was Violet, though hers was a non-alocholic brand. It was the end of the second week of recordings.

'We're doing more work now than we were before. At least Mags was good at her job.'

'Oh, the caveman?' Edward said, pretending he wasn't distracted. The name had stuck.

'Odious man. We should do something about him.'

'We should speak to Braithwaite.'

By some strange coincidence he walked through the pub door.

'I did wonder whether I'd find you here,' he said.

'Do you want a drink?' Edward asked, politely, hoping he would turn him down.

'No, really, it's quite all right. I can't stop and I'm driving. I did want to have a word with you before you went off; you did leave in rather a hurry. I just wanted to check that everything is running smoothly with you, if you had any problems?'

'Dave,' Violet said.

'He's only temporary,' Braithwaite said.

'The workload... it's too much. We can't produce the show and look after the guests at the same time. We need someone to make sure everything is running smoothly,' Edward explained.

'I see... I did rather wonder whether he was the reason behind your de-camp to the pub!'

'What about Mags?' Violet said.

Edward couldn't believe he was hearing these words, *had they not suffered enough?* But he knew she was right.

'I can try,' Braithwaite said, 'but even if she was to agree I mean I... she... I...' He took a gulp and composed himself.

'We understand,' Violet said, tactfully. Regardless of what had been said at the trial, it had been Mags, not Michael, who had hurled the most abuse at Braithwaite; they weren't about to kiss and make up.

'No, it's not that. I don't mind... I can work with her... I mean that *if* she did come back we could not abandon Dave. He does have a contract after all, albeit a temporary six-month one. They would have to work together. That may prove tricky and the show's budget would have to be... stretched.'

'Okay,' Violet said. Edward could tell she was exhausted and did not want to discuss work any longer.

'I'll try to talk to Mags,' Braithwaite said, and with that, all three of them left the pub.

37

'**G**uess Mags is not coming back, then,' Edward said.
       'No,' Violet said. And there, amongst the pile of news-papers and magazines full of abuse for the new format, was a single-page spread on page five of *The Lion*, open for them both to see.

EXCLUSIVE INTERVIEW. EX-O'SHEA PRODUCER: 'MY BATTLE TO CLEAR FRIEND'S NAME.'

-I'll Prove He Is Innocent

A long-time friend of child murderer Michael O'Shea who came to his defence at his trial, says the former talk show host is innocent of all charges. Thirty-eight-year-old O'Shea was found guilty of three counts of murder and two counts of rape but Marguerite Archer, also a former producer on the now-defunct show, known as Mags, insists he was stitched up.

'Me and Michael go way back. I know he wouldn't do a thing like this. It's a f***ing stitch up.' But the evidence, including a severed thumb found in a secret lockup he owned and a blood-soaked cardigan, suggests

otherwise and was enough to convince a jury that the talk show host should be sent down for life. 'They asked me to go back but I wouldn't do it. It's beyond betrayal, it's not just stabbing him in the f***ing back, it's like creeping up behind him, hacking his head clean off with a knife and pissing all over his dead body.'

This week saw the launch of a new talk show fronted by Bernard Braithwaite, the doctor on the O'Shea Show. 'He was a weasel, always sneaking up behind people. I wouldn't work for him, cashing in on it all. He's just out for what he can get.'

'It's all we need,' said Violet, turning the computer monitor so that Edward could see the email attachment she was browsing. It was the ratings from the previous week. They peaked on Monday but then went dramatically downhill.

'Wow,' he said.

'Yes,' said Violet, 'we need more interesting cases not Mags mouthing off, it's going to kill the show and then we'll both be out of jobs, back to square one.'

'But how do we make it more interesting? Braithwaite doesn't seem to want to listen to us,' Edward said.

'The irony is Mags wouldn't let Braithwaite get away with this, she'd stand up to him. We need her.'

'But she won't play ball if she believes all this stuff about Michael being innocent.'

'So what do you suggest we do?'

'I don't think Braithwaite going to speak to Mags is a good idea.' The very suggestion now seemed ludicrous. 'The quotes will have been exaggerated but it's still not a good idea.'

'What about if we go to see her instead, talk to her, bring her round?'

'We can try, I doubt anything will come of it. Maybe Braithwaite can just hire another producer.'

There was a knock at the door. It was Braithwaite.

'Here.' Violet handed Braithwaite the viewing figures. He

pulled out a pair of glasses and studied the sheet for several moments.

'Hmm,' he said, 'I suppose they aren't really encouraging, are they? But we started off well and you know the figures aren't everything. So long as you do keep an eye on them.'

Violet was aghast.

'The guests for this morning's recordings will be arriving soon. These pair are damaged. They are brothers, abused as children, but now they are at each other's throats. I really would like some time to work through their problems so please don't interrupt with too many questions. I do have quite a clear idea of what I want to say.'

Edward took up the slack.

'And there's this,' he said, handing him the copy of *The Lion*.

Braithwaite studied the paper once again but remained unmoved. 'I see.'

'So...' said Violet.

'That's unfortunate, it can't really be helped, can it? She is entitled to her own opinion, as I am entitled to mine and you are entitled to yours. No point worrying about it.' Though just what Braithwaite's views on Mags were remained a mystery.

As Braithwaite closed the door behind him, Violet turned to Edward.

'It's suicide, he's going to kill the show. He's going to do it. We have to get her back on board. She's the only one who can talk sense into him. She'll make him put through her changes whether he likes it or not.'

Unfortunately, however, tracking Mags down was not that easy. For starters, they had to wait until the following weekend. They were working so hard and Dave was so utterly useless that, what with managing the studio floor as well as doing the research and having to fight with Braithwaite about the entertainment value of some of his guests, they rarely left the studios before 9pm. On Saturday morning, though, Edward and Violet, who had explained that she had spent the time during the trial passing her driving test, set out on the road to find Mags. Her last known address, according to the network database – which was still not password protected, despite the reassurances of the studio executives that it would be harder for employees to access personal information about one another – was a flat in Clapthorpe, a suburb about forty minutes away.

When they arrived, Edward and Violet found her modern apartment building, clad in white and spiralling four stories into the air. Edward pressed the buzzer. There was no answer. He tried again. Still nothing. So he tried one of the other flats.

'I don't give out details about residents to people I don't know,' snapped one of Mags' neighbours.

'That told us.' Edward tried another flat. This time a far more civilised response:

'I'm sorry, love. I don't know. Have you tried the pub?'

'The pub?'

'Yes, The White Horse. It's about a ten-minute walk.'

'This early in the morning?'

'It's only a suggestion. Sorry I can't be of more help.'

They took her advice and sure enough in the smoking shelter (*where else*) was Mags puffing away on her own.

'Fuck off,' she said, throwing her cigarette down onto the floor and stubbing it out with her feet.

'We saw what you said in the paper…'

'I know why you've come.'

'We just wanted your advice about something.'

'You shopped my mate, had him done for fucking child abuse, and then you want my advice? Fuck off!'

Edward tried a different technique.

'Why do you think he's innocent?'

217

She shuddered slightly and pulled another cigarette from her pocket. 'He wouldn't do it.'

'But all the evidence and I saw him, I walked in on him. We didn't stitch him up.'

'It must have been wrong. I've seen him.'

'What?'

'In prison, I went to visit him. That man did not kill those children.'

'Okay, well we'll say no more about it, but look we're not here about that, we need you to come back, to work on Braithwaite's show. We can't cope. It's all going downhill, we're overworked and he won't listen to us. The producer is useless.'

'You want me to work with Braithwaite, that slimeball? Are you having a fucking laugh? Bernard Braithwaite understands nothing, NOTHING about people in this world. No one wants to talk about the truth anymore but *he* did: Michael would always tell it how it is. He knew that no amount of counselling would stop these people. They shag everything that moves out of sheer boredom, they piss their benefits up the wall, pawn their grand-mother's jewellery for a few lines of crack...'

'We're trying to–'

'Trying to what? Save the show? Save your pathetic little jobs? Bet you got a pay rise, didn't you? You're all at it, cashing in on his misery, suits you down to the ground that he's rotting in some cell. Now fuck off out of my sight...' She lit another cigarette and Edward, fearing she might try to throw it at him, thought it best to leave.

'That was productive,' Violet said when they were back in the car.

'Do you really think she's right? That Michael's innocent.'

'No. She's confused, upset about her friend. That doesn't mean she's right. We're just going to have to go at this alone, find a way to get Braithwaite to see sense.'

'And I want to talk to you, Danielle,' the lights had been dimmed and a spotlight shone down on Braithwaite and his guest, 'about your relationship with your father.' The silence was eerie but there was little tension high above in the gallery where Edward was sat with the techies, co-ordinating the show.

'We need to get off this ASAP,' Edward said over the mic.

'The ad break is roughly around now,' the techie said to Edward. 'If you want him to leave a cliffhanger you better get on to him.'

'Wind up the stuff about his childhood, let's get on to what she did to her stepmother to get back at him. You need to mention her sexuality and the fact she slept with the stepmother.'

Braithwaite seemed to take no notice of Edward and continued to question the girl about how her father abused her. Twenty minutes passed. Still nothing, just Braithwaite talking her through ways she could come to terms with her father's abuse. It was as if he could not stomach any kind of confrontation at all.

By the end of the show, Edward was trying hard not to shout down the microphone: only now did he understand Mags' frustration. In the final five minutes there was a brief mention of

Danielle's 'slightly irregular' preferences and no mention of the fact that she'd slept with her stepmother. Obviously embarrassed, Danielle began to stutter and Braithwaite suddenly changed tack, ending the show abruptly.

Violet was backstage waiting to greet her. She'd forgotten to turn her mic off so Edward could hear Violet escorting Danielle out of the studios, pointing her in the direction of the Tube station. He made himself a coffee as he waited for Violet to come back.

'I'm off.' Dave swiped his denim jacket from the table with one motion and reached inside the pocket for the remnants of a sausage roll he'd eaten for lunch.

'Bye,' Edward murmured, wondering, if only momentarily, about the caveman's home life.

Edward took his coffee to the office and Violet arrived back a few minutes later. Her hair looked out of place, she'd parked pens behind her ears and she had bags under her eyes. Everything was up to the editors now. They had their own office upstairs in one of the fancier rooms of the building where a team of them worked on the entire channel's output. How on earth they were going to make the episode even remotely interesting was beyond Edward. It was a catastrophe, a nail in the coffin.

'There's no way we can broadcast this,' Edward said.

Violet said nothing. She didn't appear to be listening: she was too busy reading a letter.

'Did you not hear me?' Edward snapped.

Violet looked up and handed him the letter. 'It's inviting us to a meeting with the director of the channel to discuss a "way forward" for the show. First thing tomorrow morning.'

At that moment Braithwaite walked in with characteristically bad timing.

'Ah, I know you weren't all that happy with that episode, but I do think that's really helped Danielle and we got some really good emotional shots, I think.'

'There's a letter,' Violet said.

'Oh yes, I got that too. I'm sure it's nothing to worry about,' Braithwaite said, but he seemed agitated.

Edward knew Braithwaite was lying: he could tell he was deeply concerned about what senior management was going to say the following morning, as was Edward. For it almost certainly had everything to do with the declining ratings. 'I'll have a read a bit later, but I think I'm going to head off home and have a rest now. Have a good weekend, Violet, Edward.'

He closed the door and Edward shook his head in disbelief.

'He's killed the show. He's FUCKING KILLED IT.'

Violet held up her hands. 'Don't swear,' she said, calmly. Edward blushed. 'Let's go out.' She added.

'Now?'

'Yes, now. If it will stop you stressing.'

'But the show's about to... we need to... we need to prepare something for the meeting.'

'Forget it.'

'What?'

'Like you say he's killed the show. Might as well accept it and go out and...'

'And aren't you supposed to be driving home?'

Violet sighed.

'Are you coming up or not?'

They were in the busiest bar they could find. The music was loud and Violet was necking back the drinks.

Edward tried to keep up with her though he had no idea why.

Before Edward knew it, the night was running away with them and they'd forgotten all about everything.

'I gave up the coke,' she said on their third drink in.

'Well done,' Edward said.

221

'God, you're always patronising me,' she said, playfully.

'I'm just glad you were able to get over your addiction.'

She knew he was joking.

'I didn't have an addiction. But it's much better for my bank balance.'

'If you'd not come back to work on the show I would've had you back on as a guest, booked you into rehab.'

Violet laughed.

The music got louder and louder, the conversation more and more outrageous until suddenly and without warning, Violet started making out with him. Finally, it had happened.

'Come on,' Violet said, at about midnight.

'I, I...'

'We're just going to have to find something to pass the time until we sober up and I can drive you back home!' Violet said and Edward could do little to disguise his grin as they approached the garages which were behind a tall security gate. With one click of her fob, they slid back and Edward and Violet slipped through. In normal circumstances, it would have been eerie. Darkness had set in, there were no lights and every step he took on the pavement reverberated around the compound like a violin string. Violet's boots made even more noise. But the alcohol was making everything seem funny. In fact, it was hilarious. They looked at each other and burst into giggles as they made their way in. Edward had heard something and Violet had heard it too. Voices, breathing, rattling. Surely there wasn't anyone else working this late? It could have been people on the South Bank but it seemed unlikely.

'Did you hear that?' Edward whispered and his words were like a dagger, cutting through the silence.

'Could be a ghost. Maybe it's a sign.'

'A sign of what?'

'That we shouldn't have come back so early, that we should be out there...' Edward pointed to the city behind him, 'living life!'

Violet smirked and shook her head in shame at how drunk he was.

They crept towards Violet's garage door.

There it was again. It was a muffled sound, but it was definitely there, and then an unmistakable bang. It was as if somebody was kicking at the doors. But it wasn't coming from Violet's garage, but the one next door.

Edward approached, Violet by his side. Then, without warning, the doors to the garage next door slid up. They were about to find out what or who was inside. They moved further back, squinting into the dark, trying to see between the gap as it widened and widened. An engine started, Edward and Violet ventured further in. It was only as the garage doors reached the top of the frame that Edward could finally make out what he was looking at, but he had no time to react. Before he had a chance, the headlights on Braithwaite's car burst into life, full beam. Without warning, the driver hit the pedal. The lights went out and the world went black.

SOME WEEKS EARLIER

39

'Now fuck off out of my sight...' Mags had said to Edward and Violet, billowing smoke from her mouth like a chimney. She meant what she said. How fucking dare they come and find her like that? She didn't care how badly she needed the money, she was not going back *there* with *him* as her boss. And why did he even want to work with her anyway? She hated him. She'd made that much clear, hadn't she?

Mags couldn't stand snakes. People who whispered, who tiptoed and stalked about but behind closed doors they plotted and planned their every syllable, biding their time like life was one giant chessboard.

And that was just what Braithwaite had done and look at him now. The truth had already started to seep out. Instead of creeping back into his hole, the obvious place for a man who had no charisma and apparently not an ounce of common sense, he had miraculously ended up with his own prime time television show and a book deal. *Funny that*, Mags thought.

But it wouldn't last for long. Bernard Braithwaite was nothing like the man he'd trampled all over; prison was killing Michael O'Shea. It was unbearable. Michael was tough but not that tough.

Under normal circumstances, he probably could have hacked a few years in prison but for GBH, not as a kiddy fiddler. Nobody could survive that. It was outrageous. He had well and truly been done over.

She needed to see him, the rumour was that he was back on the bottle. It wasn't surprising, of course. But she knew first-hand how long it had taken him to quit. She needed to hear it from him, confront him and then try to knock some sense into him. He'd thank her later because she knew that he would have done the same for her if she'd ever shown an ounce of weakness...

When they brought him out, he looked even worse than the last time she had come to visit. There were bags under his eyes, his hair was out of place and the beard that he had been growing during the trial had now reached fruition, spiralling and contorting around his face like a forest.

'Have you brought any?'

So it was true.

If it hadn't been for the strict rules about bodily contact, she would have slapped him there and then.

'Is this what they've reduced you to? The great Michael O'Shea, a fucking alky, an alcoholic.'

One of the prison guards started to make her way over. The other visitors turned their heads. Mags wondered which one of them would contact the papers first. Michael said nothing. He barely lifted his head.

'Get a fucking grip!' she shouted. 'Do you think you're going to get out while you're on the bottle? I need you on fine form. I need you to go over everything that happened the nights those girls disappeared again.'

'What good would it do?' Michael muttered.

'I'll tell you what good it'll do. I'm going to prove you didn't do it. And when you're out, we'll campaign, we'll use it, we'll whip up a storm, get the death penalty brought back and *The Lion*, the fucking *Lion*, we'll close 'em down, we'll sue 'em for so much they won't have enough coffers left to cover the printing costs of one issue of their fucking pathetic excuse for an arse wiping rag of a paper.'

Michael's face flickered vaguely into shape. 'All right,' he said. He was trying.

'First, tell me everything about where you were on both nights.'

'With Liv,' he said, 'in that garage, having–'

'I get the picture,' Mags said, 'that whore,' she said, this time more quietly, so as not to get thrown out, 'scheming little bitch, we'll get her to admit it. Change her testimony.'

'All that does is place her at the crime scene as well, makes her culpable.'

'Good!' Mags said. 'I hope she rots, she deserves it.'

'Maybe…' He didn't sound convinced. Mags sighed, even after everything Liv had done to him he clearly still held a flame for her. 'But that does little to change the situation.'

'Who might have seen you?'

'I made sure nobody did.'

'You're too good at your job.'

Mags was silent for several seconds. She wanted to pace up and down the room.

'Think, think. Somebody must have found out about the garage. Somebody must have known, you must have let it slip,' Mags said, eventually.

'Not even you knew about *us*, let alone the fact we had a secret lockup. It was all supposed to be just that, a fucking secret.'

'If it was someone who worked on the show, then…'

'Then we can rule out Liv which leaves several options. You…' he said, flippantly.

'Thanks for the vote of confidence.'

'...one of the techies, Violet, Edward and Braithwaite.'

'The techies only come in on recording days, what grudge could they possibly hold?'

'You don't need a grudge, just a liking for teenage girls and a convenient opportunity to cover it all up.'

'Besides, they barely came into contact with me, how could they have seen so much and put all the pieces together, found out about my affair, the garage, and the schedule? We never told them *who* would be on the show, we expected them to turn up and film it and if they didn't know when Minnie and Jessica would be on, how could they have possibly engineered this situation?'

'So that leaves...'

'Edward Lewis, Violet Dearnley, Bernard Braithwaite...'

Mags smirked, she'd been thinking it all along.

'There's only one cowardly snake in the grass capable of pulling this off.'

'Oh, I think Edward and Violet would like to see the back of me.'

'They're jobsworths, they're hungry. They want to climb the ladder but they wouldn't do this. What have they gained from this? They put themselves out of a job and of ever having one again. Whoever did this is a sick fuck, Michael. Do they seem like sick fucks to you?'

'Correction. Whoever did this is a clever sick fuck, a sick fuck who can cover their arse and play the happy smiley game. Edward and Violet were more than happy to shop me at the first opportunity...'

'You should never have let that happen...'

'Don't you think I know that!'

Michael had lost his cool with that slapper, Tiffany, just as Edward had walked in. Mags had been forced to admit that, when she'd first heard about what had happened, even she had

had doubts. This was the one and only time she questioned her boss' innocence. But as it happened, Mags' suspicions of her former boss were partly her own fault. She'd been lax with the rules, allowed guests to wander in and out of the dressing rooms, collecting autographs as they pleased and, as a result, Tiffany had seen and then filmed Michael kissing Liv.

'You know she was trying to blackmail me, sell the story to the press. She could have destroyed my marriage, my entire show. Is it any wonder I had my hands around her neck? I could have done time for her, and trust that idiot to walk in at the wrong moment and put two and two together and get five.'

'The footage!' Mags screamed.

'Don't you think I've thought about it? Even if she hadn't have kept that quiet during the trial and it had come out in court, again all it proves is that me and Liv were having it off. It implicates her and makes it seem like we're having some sick murderous fantasy but it doesn't change the fact that somehow my DNA was at the crime scene.'

'How could that have happened? How could they get your DNA?'

'I can't explain it…'

'The point is if Edward and Violet went to the police about the garage when they were the ones behind the murders and knew about the garage, why didn't they shop you there and then? Why wait? Why run off and cast suspicion on themselves?'

'Because they're smart, because they wanted to muddy the waters.'

'I'll tell you who the traitor is. He's been staring at you all along.'

'Bernard Braithwaite is not clever enough to set this up, he's too much of a weasel, believe me!'

'You never even told me how you came to give that clown a job.'

'Can you blame me? The mess we were in…'

The time leading up to and following the first court case had been hectic, to say the least. They had been fighting for their survival.

'Fact: if we didn't do something to protect the interests of the guests, the show would have been shut down. The network was threatening to appoint someone of their own to interfere and, believe me, you would have liked that even less. I remembered Braithwaite distinctly when we'd gone to that drug rehabilitation clinic. He was so overbearing, it creeped me out. He practically bowed before me every time he entered the room.

'So, when we returned to do a follow-up piece, when we were running around, going to every fucking charity and drug clinic we could find, trying to highlight how responsible we were, we went back to that clinic where I'd first seen him and there he was packing up all his belongings. He'd resigned.' Michael mimicked quotation marks with his hands.

'There were rumours he'd been caught doing drugs himself, stealing from the clinic. I didn't know if it was true, frankly, I didn't care. So we had a little chat and I told him, there was a job going. He'd be paid well but he'd have to do exactly as I wanted. He agreed and hey presto...'

'Snakes like him are capable of anything!'

A bell sounded and Mags knew her session with Michael was at an end. She stood up and whispered, discreetly, 'I'll sort this for you! You'll be out and then it will be like old times.'

Michael forced a smile, placed his hand into the air in farewell, and then she was gone.

40

Mags' life had spiralled out of control since her contract with *The Michael O'Shea Show* had come to an end. She could no doubt have found another producer's job somewhere in London but she'd struggled to cope with the imprisonment of one of her best friends and the complete breakdown of her daily routine; the show had been her life. Slowly but surely, she'd run out of money. She probably could have survived another month or two if she'd gone easier on the booze and the fags. But the end of the road was near. She'd barely made a start at packing up her flat, even though the situation was now so desperate that the bailiffs would be round as surely as the sun would rise the following morning.

Her living room was a mess; a symptom of the chaos of her life. Her dining table was covered in dirty plates, empty cigarette cartons, unopened bills. And if she had been even slightly less observant, then Mags might have missed the unopened package hidden under it all. At the time she'd probably been too hungover to care to open it but now...

She pushed the rubbish to one side and rushed to see what it was.

'With my deepest compliments,' read the small slip of paper in the inside cover. It was Braithwaite's book. It was quite hard to believe that he'd sent her a complimentary copy. The arrogance of the man knew no bounds. Yet Mags was intrigued. She flicked through the solid 400 pages quickly, wondering what secrets they might contain, what clues were to be found. She knew she would read it eventually but right now she had a more immediate mission.

In her bedroom she had at least made a start of clearing out. She'd placed her clothes into a suitcase until all that remained was a row of coat hangers and a small wooden box. She grabbed it, opened it and there it was. A silver handgun, handcrafted and engraved with her grandfather's name. It had been a gift, left to her fifteen years previously.

Mags knew she was a hothead, but she'd never envisaged needing a gun before. She grabbed the weapon and Braithwaite's book and placed them into a handbag. *Oh, how times had changed.*

First. Olivia Dessington-Brown. The worst of the worst. She had knowingly allowed a child murderer to walk free and then watched indifferently as a man she was supposed to care about was locked up for life, just so that she could save her own skin.

It wasn't hard to track her down. A glance through the gossip pages of *Spice* revealed photos of her latest drunken night out. Even at half past four in the morning, as she stumbled into the back of a taxi, clutching a half-bottle of champagne, she still managed to look vaguely glamorous.

So that night, Mags headed out into the cold spring air and made her way to what was supposed to be one of London's poshest clubs. At least that was the way it marketed itself. Everybody knew that, in reality, it was a tacky place for Z-listers, the sort that wanted to court *The Lion*. With no show and no O'Shea to boost her profile, Liv would need the limelight. It was her lucky night: Mags would give the hacks more than enough to write about. When she reached the door, the way was blocked.

'Sorry, love,' said the bouncer, 'can't let you in if you're not on the guest list.'

Mags shook her head.

'Do I look like I've come to get rat-arsed?'

Indeed, she had deliberately not dressed up. The bouncer looked confused.

'I've come to collect a friend, get her out of trouble. She asked me to pick her up.'

'Who?'

Mags recited a celebrity she knew would probably be on the guest list but so obscure it would have seemed unlikely that Mags would have been making it up. The bouncer duly let her through.

Inside, the club was exactly as you would expect for a weekday evening. Loud music, a DJ, a smoke machine but an empty dance floor. There were no more than thirty or so people, some crowded into the booths at the edge of the room, others by the bar, but all of them sullen and disappointed there were no photographers to capture them in their finery: red dresses, thick mascara, high heels.

The woman Mags wanted stood out. By the bar, ordering herself a drink, she looked slaughtered already.

'Oi!' Mags shouted, heading straight for Liv. 'I want a word with you!'

Liv looked up slowly, both shocked at the sight of Mags and apparently bewildered by the booze. A few of the other girls, evidently bored, craned their necks to get in on the action.

'Why did you lie?' Mags asked.

Liv looked confused. 'I dunno what you're talking about,' she said, slurring her words.

Mags grabbed hold of her hair, ready to smash her straight into the bar if she didn't answer.

'I'll tell you what I'm fucking talking about, shall I? Michael O'Shea? You were with him that night, weren't you? You knew he was innocent but you let him go down so you could save yourself...'

'I- I-'

'The truth!'

'You don't understand. Will you just listen?' Liv's eyes were rolling all over the place. 'I could have been done, for murder! For murdering those kids, if I'd admitted I was there, we'd have both gone down.'

'Your evidence could have gotten him off! Could have gotten you both off, if you'd have told the truth. And what about the real killer? The real killer is still on the loose, you let a child murderer walk free!'

Liv seemed to regain her sobriety. 'Oh please!' she spat. 'Don't take the moral high ground with me, don't pretend you cared about those kids any more than I did. You're pathetic. I could see it and so could he. You're only here because you're in love with him. You think getting Michael off will win him over? If it was someone else you worked with, wrongly banged up in that prison, you wouldn't give a flying fuck. Well, I've got news for you, woman... he's taken, fucking taken! At least I knew that when I was with him, at least I didn't follow him around like a sad, pathetic puppy.'

Mags pulled back Liv's head and slammed it into the bar as hard as she could.

Liv stumbled from the bar. Her nose was bleeding and her hair was a mess.

By now everybody in the bar was crowded around them, open-jawed. The bouncer had rushed in to restrain them from each other but there was no need. Mags was already on her way out.

'Change your statement!' she shouted. 'Change your statement or your life won't be worth living, fucking believe me!'

41

Hunting down Tiffany Roe was easy. The police had returned her notes from the show in cardboard boxes when it was all over, and there it was in black and white, the address scrawled in her own handwriting, along with a dozen others. She'd written it down on a scrap of paper and put it in her pocket. She knew there was a real chance Tiffany had deleted the footage she was looking for and she knew perfectly well that even if she had it in her possession it would not change the verdict but it would give her satisfaction to know that she'd punished her for what she had done.

Without a car, the journey was long and arduous. There was a way of getting to *Graysmead* in the early hours, the last train out of London and then two buses. It took her almost two hours but finally, there it was; even in darkness the two towers still dominated the skyline from miles around. There were no lights on, every single apartment was dark and none of the street lamps appeared to be working.

But as Mags walked onwards, squinting as she struggled to make out the car park, ahead, she heard a movement which startled her and headed for cover in a nearby hedgerow, lest she should be seen. It was a car, leaving the car park. It had no head-lights and seemed to be moving deliberately slowly so as not to overwork the engine and cause alarm.

Daring to peep from behind the bush as it chugged slowly out of the car park, Mags could make out the model and registration number. She'd seen it somewhere before, she was sure of it...

Waiting a further five minutes for it to drive off into the distance, Mags quickstepped into the tower. The front door to Deacon Court was sticky so she was able to head straight in. She made for the lift and tried not to gag at the smell of cheap weed and mould.

Ascending floor by floor, she wondered how Tiffany might react. *Would she tell her everything straight away? Or would she hold out until the final moment, would she force her to pull the trigger?* Because Mags would. She knew she would do it if she had to...

When Mags reached Tiffany's front door it too was slightly ajar but it wasn't that which worried her. It was the smell – and the sight – seeping through the gaps in the frame – of thick, grey smoke.

Mags pushed open the door and instantly regretted it. Holding her breath as she went, she pulled off her jumper and wrapped it around her mouth and nose to at least give her some protection from the smoke. Then she turned on the torch app on her phone so that she could begin to see where she was going. The fire seemed to have started in the kitchen, by the oven. It was still only small but Mags could see it growing with every passing minute. She walked onwards, wondering if Tiffany was even in the apartment, perhaps she had deliberately set fire to her own flat...

'Tiffany!' Mags shouted. No response.

She made for the bedroom, pushed open the door and there she was. Tucked up in bed, fast asleep, not a care in the world...

Mags went over to the bed to shake her and finally, she stirred.

'W…w…' She came to. 'What's happening?'

'Your flat's on fire.'

'What? Oh my God.'

Tiffany walked straight over to her crib, to wake up Jayden, her baby and then she screamed; the cot was empty.

'What have you done with him?'

Mags had not anticipated the fire or the empty cot but she had to carry on, regardless.

'With who?'

'My baby!'

'I don't know about your baby. But no one is going anywhere until you hand over that footage…'

'What footage? My baby boy.'

Mags turned on the bedroom lights.

Tiffany went to scream again but Mags continued. 'Don't pretend you don't know what I'm talking about. I know you have a film of Michael and Liv. You could have gotten him off the hook. Hand it over!'

'I don't have it.'

'Hand it over!' Mags said. 'Hand it over or we're both going to die in this inferno.'

Mags could see Tiffany gaming the situation, she knew exactly what she was trying to do. So when she tried to make a run for it, sprinting for the door, ready to push past Mags, Mags pulled out her grandfather's gun. Tiffany froze.

'Don't think I won't!' Mags said. 'Where is it? Tell me where it is and I'll get us out. The clock's ticking, girl, the clock is fucking ticking!'

'I have a baby. My baby boy! I need to get out and find him. Please…'

Mags stood her ground. 'Then tell me, tell me where the tape is. Hand it over or help me find it.'

'I told you I don't have it. He took it.'

'Who? Who took it?'

'Bernard Braithwaite.'

Mags smirked. 'You've been colluding with him, haven't you?'

'What?'

'You set him up, Michael, you helped set him up! What did you do with the bodies? Did he have you do it for him?'

'I don't know what you're talking about. Look, please, let me go. My baby! I need to save my baby. You said you'd get me out if I told you about the tapes.'

'Let a child murderer go scot-free? Who the hell do you think I am?'

'A child murderer? I didn't have anything to do with the murder of those girls. What are you talking about? He just came round and told me if I wanted to get my revenge on him for setting me up, for humiliating me on telly instead of helping me mend things with my sis. He said if I wanted a real shot at fame I should go back on the show, pretend he was the father of the baby and that's when I saw him, with her, kissing, so I filmed it. I thought that's what Braithwaite meant, I thought that's how I could get my revenge. But then he told me not to mention it and he took my phone off me…'

Mags knew it was all over.

She should have left the girl to burn in hell or, better still, shot the bitch. But Mags knew it wasn't worth it, she knew she had to save her anger for one person and one person alone. Yes, Braithwaite would feel the full force of her wrath like no one ever had before.

'Get me out of this place, you mad psycho!'

Against her better judgement, Mags grabbed hold of Tiffany's hand and dragged her out of the bedroom and into the hallway.

In the living room the flames had engulfed everything. It was too late to stop it.

'What about my boy?' Tiffany screamed. 'Is he safe? Where's my boy? My little lad! I can't leave him in here.'

At first, Mags couldn't work it out but then it all made sense and suddenly she knew where she'd seen that car before, why she recognised the registration plate.

Tiffany started to cry, to scream. Wailing, Mags grabbed hold of her and dragged her out of her flat.

On the communal landing, Mags screamed at the top of her lungs, banging on as many doors as she could.

'FIRE, FIRE! OUT! OUT!'

By the time the groggy-headed residents had come to their senses and saw the flames licking at Tiffany's apartment door, Mags was already halfway down the stairs, on the phone to the fire brigade.

As she left the building, storming out of the front doors, racing as far away from the building as she could, Tiffany called out in vain to all who would listen:

'She tried to kill me! She's got my boy.'

But Mags knew better. She knew who had taken Tiffany's baby and who was responsible for setting the fire and she was going to make him pay.

In a lonely rundown corner of London, miles from Deacon Court, far away from the bars and the prying eyes of z-list celebrities and suspecting policemen, Mags sat silently, smoking, tears running down her cheeks.

The truth, at last; the world had conspired against Michael O'Shea. And she was going to prove it, even if it meant being locked up for a very long time…

4 2

It was just gone half past four in the morning, light was starting to crack through the small frosted window. She knew exactly where she would find Bernard Braithwaite, it was simply a matter of waiting.

She didn't know if Braithwaite's book would hold the key but she had an inkling, a knack that something in those pages would ring alarm bells. So in those hours, as she waited for the sun to rise, the book was her way forward. Because it had to be him, it couldn't be anyone else.

Of course, she could not read the entire biography in one evening but she knew the sections that needed her attention. Braithwaite had not just written an account of the last few months' events but had devoted most of his book to his early life, his hopes, his dreams. The arrogant bastard. As if anybody gave a shit about his childhood.

Nevertheless, Mags started going through the three chapters specifically devoted to the events leading up to Michael's trial. She scanned for any reference to Minnie, Jessica, and Tiffany. There was nothing out of the ordinary in the way Braithwaite had described Minnie's appearance on the show. Everything was as Mags remembered and as was recounted at the trial but as the book continued, and Mags slowed down to lap up every detail, she noticed two discrepancies. They were small and to anyone else, they would have seemed completely insignificant but to her they were gold dust.

On the day before Jessica Butler's story was recorded, Braithwaite wrote in passing how it had been Edward who had booked Jessica Butler's taxi but Mags had thought so much about that day, she knew that was not the case. It had been Braithwaite who had booked the taxi. She remembered him saying it. She had gone to the station to arrange the Butlers' train tickets whilst Edward had remained in the studio, setting up the stage for Freddie Bell, the boy with the brain tumour. Braithwaite had deliberately moved himself out of the crime scene. If he admitted that he had booked the taxi then surely it made him look guilty, he would have known exactly where Jessica Butler was heading on that fateful evening.

And what about the car that Mags had spotted leaving Deacon Court? That fire was not an accident, that much she knew.

Finally, the man had come unstuck. Perhaps Braithwaite had meant for Mags to read his book. After all, he had sent her a copy. Perhaps he thought he'd set up Michael so well that nobody would ever believe her even if she did attempt to expose Braithwaite.

What Braithwaite didn't realise, what he didn't count on, was that Mags couldn't give a flying fuck about the law anymore. She had satisfied herself that he had done it and that was enough. He was going to pay for everything he'd done, no matter how many years she got in return. He was more than worth doing time for. She'd wafted him away for years like the fly that he was, but he'd always come back, buzzing around in the distance. It was staggering that she'd left him alone all this time. She pressed her hand against her jeans: the gun weighed down in her pocket.

Dribs and drabs of light drifted through the toilet window as the sun rose over a new day. She knew it was nearly time to head out into the world.

She had to be careful. The police might be on the lookout for her, though, if Liv and Tiffany knew what was good for them they would have batted any officers away and refused to bring charges.

Mags climbed on top of the toilet shelf and out of the broken window through which she had clambered in and walked. No one disturbed Mags as the early hours of the morning turned slowly into the rush hour. She hopped on the nearest bus and sat stewing as it pulled into the capital.

By now Braithwaite would be in the studio. Of course, it may prove tricky to get into the building. But she was prepared for that. No more people were going to stand in the way of the truth.

When the clock struck half nine exactly she made her move and cleared out, hurrying through the crowds with her head bowed low so that no one could catch a second glance at her. When she finally arrived at the *People* building, she managed to get through the main gate with a crowd of workers making their way in from the Tubes. The guard barely glanced twice at her revoked security pass.

In the vast atrium, Mags bypassed the reception desk and headed straight to the basement stairs. The basement was unusually quiet. The studios were often more subdued on days when they weren't recording, it was perfectly normal, but there would always be someone from upstairs wandering the corridors, bringing dictates from above or packages for Michael, not that anyone took any notice. But today was different. There was silence even as Mags climbed the stairs to the gallery.

The room where she'd spent so much of her life, tearing her hair out, lambasting the ignorance and incompetence of guests and researchers in equal measure, now so tidy and ordered, but empty nonetheless. She scrambled back down the gallery stairs and headed for the offices. Michael's old dressing room, newly kitted out with a desk and a large bookcase, was now Braith-waite's office. It was locked. Mags could see inside. Nothing out of the ordinary.

Then she heard footsteps. Somebody was heading her way. She wondered what she should do. What if it was Braithwaite? Should she hide? Strike unexpectedly? No, she wanted an admission, confirmation, realisation that he'd lost everything before the light left his sorry, pathetic, droopy little eyes.

The footsteps grew louder as the silhouette in the distance came into focus. It was Mr Griffiths. Though she'd been considered a senior member of staff by Michael, she had only met the director on a handful of occasions. Indeed, he clearly hadn't got the memo about Mags' point-blank refusal to work with that weasel Braithwaite and he did not seem at all surprised at her presence at her former place of work.

'Ah Marguerite, isn't it?'

Prick, using her full name.

'I'm glad I've caught you. You do know there's an important meeting upstairs for *all* staff.'

'A meeting?'

'Yes, to discuss a way forward for the show. You did get the email? You'd better head upstairs straight away. You haven't seen Bernard Braithwaite, have you? Or any members of the production team for that matter?'

Mags popped her head into Violet and Edward's office. The lights had been turned off but the door was not locked, it was actually slightly ajar and Violet's distinctive pink clutch bag was still parked under the desk.

'They've not come in this morning,' Mags said, pretending she knew what the director was talking about.

'Not come into work? That's a very serious matter, a very serious matter indeed. The meeting was quite clearly scheduled. I am an incredibly busy man, as I am sure you can understand. I don't have time to deal with this. There are a million and one different programmes I am responsible for, just because you used to top the ratings figures, that does not give you licence to go around–'

'SHUT UP!' Mags screamed, suddenly realising she didn't have to listen to him anymore. 'Violet didn't go home last night!'

'How dare you talk to me like that... didn't go home last night? You just told me they haven't shown up for work today.'

Mags flung open Edward and Violet's office door and pulled out Violet's handbag.

'Nonsense. In fact, that's proof she is in the building right at this moment.'

'Ugh. Can't you see? Braithwaite, he's got them, he'll have them somewhere, he's probably killed them already.'

The director backed slowly away. 'Killed them? What are you talking about?'

'Braithwaite killed those girls, framed Michael and now he's going to kill Edward and Violet too.'

The director put out his hands. 'Come on. We were all shocked about what came out at Michael's trial but to go around accusing another member of staff... that's at best extremely unprofessional, at worst a serious slander on – until today anyway – one of this channel's key stars.'

Mags was just as confused as she was exacerbated. 'Until today?'

'My meeting, which you and your colleagues have done such a good job of boycotting – which hasn't helped your cause in the slightest, by the way – was to tell you all that we have decided not to renew production of the show for the forthcoming series. It would seem that we made the appropriate decision anyway given the spectacle I've just witnessed–'

'I've had enough of this.'

'What?'

It was time.

Mags caught her breath. 'We're going to search the entire

building!' she screamed. 'We're going to find Bernard Braithwaite and then I'm going to kill that bastard.'

'Have you lost your mind?'

Mags fell silent as she debated where to start looking, studying the corridor she was standing in. *Of course*, how could no one have noticed? The perfect hiding place. Detectives had spent months trawling the countryside, raking over miles of ground, knocking on doors but all this time they had somehow missed the one place that no one had thought to check...

Mags sprinted down the corridor and to the underpass to the garages. Griffiths ran after her.

If she remembered rightly, the detectives had only searched areas of the building belonging to Michael. And Braithwaite was no fool, he would have cleaned up, properly.

The garages, only used by people on the O'Shea Show, separated from the rest of the building by the underpass, were the perfect place to commit a murder. Braithwaite could slip in and out of the studio with no one raising an eyebrow with whatever or whoever in tow and, what was more, nobody would think to suspect the studios as the actual scene of the crime. Minnie had been snatched outside her home and Jessica Butler, miles away in Cornwall, why would anyone even consider that the killer might have returned to the middle of a busy city with CCTV everywhere? And how easy would it have been to have abducted Edward and Violet if they were working late one night? Drug them up, slip something in their tea and then drag them along this empty corridor when – predictably – no one would be around to see. It was all starting to make sense.

Mags rushed to the end of the underpass. There were four doors in front of her, each requiring a key code to get in, each one leading to a different garage.

'Which one is Braithwaite's?' Mags asked.

'If you break into the garage of another member of staff then I'll have no choice but to ring security and have you arrested...'

Mags ignored Griffiths and pulled out the gun from her pocket. She brandished it with so little regard, so little fanfare, that at first Griffiths didn't notice it, until the first bullet flew straight into the keypad, sending sparks flying.

'I'm calling security. A gun, an employee of mine carrying a gun.'

'Oh, believe me, if that bastard's behind this door, you'll be needing more than security, you'll need the police!'

'The police. Oh, you'd love that, wouldn't you? I don't care what vendetta you have, you are not going to ruin this company with any more scandal. I rather think you and your colleagues have done enough damage…'

She ignored him and kicked at the doors; they came right open.

Nothing. An empty garage.

Griffiths was on the phone but it didn't matter. Whoever he was calling, they didn't stand any chance of getting to the studios before she'd booted down every door.

Another door: this time, though, not quite an empty garage. She recognised the car inside: it was Violet Dearnley's. She hadn't left the building since the previous evening. That much was becoming clear, which meant she may well be behind one of the next two doors.

She pulled the trigger this time with a slight hesitation, knowing the power of it. Once again the door gave way and she took in the surroundings.

'My God…' Mags whispered. For once in her life, she was lost for words…

43

He was in a garage, that much was clear. As his eyes accustomed to the light he recognised the man in front of him: it was Braithwaite. But not the Braithwaite Edward had once known. He was no longer behaving in that timid manner. He was brazen, confident and his voice seemed to have modulated by an entire octave, he had lost even any hint of the stutter that had been the source of such ridicule for so long.

'Oh dear. I- I- r- really am so-sorry,' he started, apparently mocking himself. 'You'd never believe I was rejected from drama school, would you?' Braithwaite could see the confused look in Edward's eyes.

He couldn't move. There was nothing he could do. With his arms and legs tied up with duct tape and cable wire, he could only watch helplessly, his eyes slowly coming to terms with what was in front of him. First Violet. Her eyes were tightly closed. But even strung up against the wall, not a hair had fallen out of place. She was not the only one though. Edward was almost sick when he saw them. It couldn't be, it simply couldn't be. There, chained up on the opposite wall, were two young girls who should have been dead: Minnie Jenkins and Jessica Butler looked skeletal, broken.

Edward could say nothing, do nothing. He was not only aghast at what he saw but confused about how to feel. Should he have been relieved? Happy that the two girls, who he'd virtually forgotten about, were still alive after all? They were barely conscious, heavily drugged up on something. There was a cabinet in the corner of the room, full of needles and test tubes.

Edward shuddered at the sight of them. No, he wasn't glad these girls were alive at all. He wished they were dead so they'd never have to wake up and face the pain and the reality of what had happened to them in this garage. What Bernard Braithwaite had done to them looked far worse than death. Ending it all now would surely be the greatest act of mercy he could afford the girls.

Sat between the two walls was a car, Braithwaite's blue Honda Civic. There was space enough to see roughly what was going on, though not in great detail.

Braithwaite licked his lips and dimmed the lights even further as if he was about to tell a particularly spooky ghost story, only this was not a work of fiction.

'I think it's time I offered you an explanation,' he said.

Edward struggled to contain himself, wrestling against the duct tape which covered his mouth, even though he knew it would do no good.

'No one has missed these kids,' he said, pointing at Minnie and Jessica. 'People pretend to miss them, journalists pretend they matter, filing the odd story about them, but no one really cares if they live or die, least of all you and your pretty little girl over there.' He pointed to Violet. 'These girls, like most their age, wanted their fifteen minutes of fame and our fickle friend Mr O'Shea was more than happy to oblige, wrecking their lives, pretending he was better than them. I haven't done anything wrong. I am no child murderer, Edward. What do you take me for? You know me better than that...'

Edward struggled and Braithwaite laughed.

'Everyone thinks they're dead!' Braithwaite was jubilant, he didn't seem to be able to help himself, he clasped his hands together with glee. 'Everyone thinks *he* killed them. The great untouchable and I framed him. Finally, he's rotting away where he belongs: the filthy hypocrite. You see, he stood there on that stage, every day, pretending he was a paragon of virtue, moralising and shredding his guests to bits, mocking them, humiliating them in front of tens of millions of people, pretending he was better than all of them, whilst all the time he was playing away; couldn't keep his hands off Liv, could he? He had to have her, his wife and goodness knows how many other people.

'And such was his arrogance, Edward, that he thought no one had noticed. He thought he'd gotten away with it, persuading the channel to employ his very own bitch as a co-host just so that it was easier to sleep with her. I knew something fishy was going on even before she started working on the show. He spends so much time watching other people lie you'd think he'd know how to get away with it. But nothing escapes me...'

He glanced in Violet's direction for a brief second. 'I followed them one night, I know all about the tricks he plays to try to throw journalists off the trail and it really wasn't long before I saw his little hideaway, the garage, the different car... it was too good an opportunity to miss. Yes, I planned the whole thing. I kidnapped the girls! I set up the great Michael O'Shea. I shot the fucking sheriff!

'Minnie was the easiest. Her mother was so drunk she probably wouldn't have noticed even if I'd walked straight into the house and taken her there and then. I knew what was going on. You didn't need a PhD in psychology to have predicted what would happen that night when Michael allowed Minnie to go back home with her weak mother and her cheating, drug-addicted boyfriend. You see Michael pretended to care but as soon as the cameras were turned off, he couldn't care less. She ran for it, and I was there in my car, waiting to pick her up. It was dark, the streetlights were off, she didn't suspect a thing until it was too late.

'And then there was Jessica Butler. First, I made sure that our good friend Mr O'Shea didn't have an alibi... or at least one that his mistress would be willing to share with the world, making certain they were both heading for his garage that night, and then I put my foot down for Cornwall in a second-hand car I'd bought specially for the occasion. I knew the clinic was in the middle of nowhere. Nothing for miles around, deliberately so, no running away from that place, that's for sure. And definitely no way you'd be able to get your hands on any booze or drugs. Then the show really got interesting. The vultures circled; baying for blood, and it wasn't long before the media tried to paint the taxi driver as the murderer.

'And yes, before you ask, I did kill him. But so what? He deserved what he got. I did a bit of background on him. He was no saint. A child from an affair he'd conveniently forgotten about, a weed addiction and debt up to his eyeballs. He was scum like the rest of them. It was probably for the best. And then there was the icing on the cake: Tiffany Roe. A stroke of genius brought about once again by the great man himself. If he'd shown some tact instead of humiliating those twins like he always does, those deluded girls might never have spilled their secrets. But he was so determined to screw up their lives, he was so ready for round two even if it pushed them over the edge.

'So I paid the poor girls a visit. I told her that if she just went on the show one last time, if she played along with my little scheme, she could get what she wanted, a television career of her own. In fact, you know I think of everyone who will miss me, it will be those *Lion* journalists who will shed the most tears. Yes,' he laughed at himself, 'I've been feeding them stories ever since you started working at the show, Edward. All those anonymous sources at the show and it was I who advised Tiffany to go to the press claiming Michael was the father of her baby. I wanted her to do a DNA test. Yes...'

Edward was starting to make sense of it now and Braithwaite could see it.

'The great Michael O'Shea set up, condemned by one of his own DNA tests, who would have thought it? Yes, I switched the swab he thought I was sending off to the laboratory to confirm that he was not Tiffany Roe's biological father and kept it back for my own, perhaps slightly more nefarious purposes! But not even I could have anticipated what happened next, not in my wildest dreams.

'Tiffany stumbled across Michael and Liv kissing and filmed it on her phone. They didn't see her but she wasn't stupid. Later she headed for Michael's dressing room and threatened him with exposing their affair unless she was paid, handsomely. I was amazed. Who knew the underclass could be so entrepreneurial? Michael was not quite as amused by the situation. He snapped, told her she would get nothing and placed his hands around her neck. Who knows what might have happened next if you hadn't barged in, Edward? Who knows...

'A few sacrifices had to be made, of course; I had no choice but to cut off Minnie's thumb and cover it in Michael's DNA, and Jessica Butler's cardigan, such a shame we had to ruin it with Minnie's blood... Tiffany, though, well I'm afraid she had to go. The video she had of Michael and Liv could have wrecked Michael's conviction. I retrieved it, of course, but it's better to be safe than sorry. Don't worry though. No children were harmed in the making of this show!' Braithwaite laughed and his eyes drifted in the direction of the car that was taking up most of the space in the garage. Edward followed his gaze and through the window, he could see a baby, strapped in, fast asleep. It didn't take long for Edward to work it out: he'd rescued Jayden, Tiffany's baby, from whatever fate was in store for his mother.

'My only regret about the whole scenario at the time,' Braithwaite continued, 'was that you weren't put away as well, that I had to bring that police investigation to an end. One phone call, that was all it took, one anonymous phone call and Michael was in the frame. Strange how people are so willing to act on the advice of a complete stranger but they ignore the allegations of a distressed researcher, a consummate media professional with no obvious axe to grind. And, who knew then that just as I was packing up, tying up loose ends and preparing to leave the country with my three little babies, that you'd walk straight into my arms, that I'd score a hat trick. Everyone who works in the media industry deserves to die. You ruin people's lives for a living so now I'm returning the favour.'

Edward tried to speak. There was so much he wanted to know. How could this have happened? Michael was guilty. Edward had seen him, he'd walked in on him placing his hands around Tiffany's neck. And if Michael was innocent why had Liv not testified that she was with him at the time the girls were kidnapped? And Braithwaite, Braithwaite, a murderer? Edward couldn't get his head around it.

'Oh, go on then.' Braithwaite strode over to Edward and removed the duct tape. 'Ask away. We have all the time in the world. If they were going to find us, they would have by now, wouldn't you think?'

Edward gasped for breath. His lips quivered.

Braithwaite laughed. He couldn't control himself. 'Mm... Michael's brother?'

'Oh, Phillip. Good old Phillip O'Shea. He was always a stain on Michael's character. Wherever he went, however famous he got, Michael was always stuck with him. He may have pretended to care for him when the cameras were on but he treated his brother like dirt, yes, his true feelings came out when the cameras were off. Michael told me so on a regular basis and then when everything exploded, the dodgy shit Phillip had been looking up on his computer and what he'd done to that kid who lived down the road… Michael was livid. He decided not to fund his court case. A cynical move to get the press off his tail. Think about it. He threw his own disabled brother to the dogs, not for any great moral reason, not to teach him a lesson, not to try to get him to see the error of his ways, but so it didn't affect his own career. So when you and Violet came calling, trying to get yourselves off the hook, you offered Phillip a chance to get revenge and he was more than happy to get stuck in, with a little bit of anonymous coaching!'

Edward's throat was dry from both the lack of water and the sheer terror of what he was hearing. The world was spinning: everything was happening so fast.

Braithwaite seemed to sense Edward's confusion. 'An ingenious plan, don't you think? Who would ever have expected it? Not you, that's for sure. I hold you responsible, Edward. You're as bad as him, you and your precious whore.'

Braithwaite's way of talking about Violet was grating with him, but he knew that was the last of his worries…

Edward could not deny the truth of that statement.

He was too frightened to ask the next question. Braithwaite obliged.

'I know what you're thinking. Do you know why nobody ever discovered this little hideout of mine? It's because my operation, so to speak, was mobile. Yes, that's right, Edward, remember all those times I offered to give you a lift, how we went together to investigate Minnie's disappearance when all along she was there, fast asleep in the boot of my car. Whenever anyone got suspicious, when the police came to search the studios, all I had to do was gather up my little cabinet of tricks, lift up the girls and place them in the back of the car. You see, before you so rudely interrupted me, I was going to take them both far away from this place and set them up with a brand-new life. As you so tactfully tried to tell me yesterday, the party is indeed over. The show has been cancelled. And I intend to leave the country...'

But there were still questions that needed answering. Braithwaite had got his way, he'd had Michael locked up, so why had he felt the need to write a book? Start his own show? There was no need for him to come back, he'd committed the perfect crime.

Braithwaite had an answer for that as well.

'I couldn't resist the chance to right the wrongs of Michael O'Shea, giving the public the reality show they deserved. I am the one who fixed people instead of breaking them, I am the one who deserves to be remembered, to go down in history, I will...'

'Fixing people?' Edward murmured. 'And what are they? Are they fixed?' He pointed to Minnie and Jessica. Is Thomas Mallaky fixed?'

'Don't talk about something you don't understand, Edward,' Braithwaite said, curtly.

There was silence for several seconds until Braithwaite spoke once again.

'You know that no one will find you down here, don't you? You're an intelligent man, Edward, and so is your girlfriend, it's just a shame for you that I'm more intelligent. All the tracks are covered. You were a coward, you refused to stand up to Michael O'Shea before it was too late, you were like everyone else, you could have walked away but you cared only about your career prospects and now... you will pay the price.'

Edward shook his head. 'Michael is in prison, if you murder me and Violet, he'll have an alibi. You'll be prime suspect.' Sweat trickled down Edward's forehead.

'Will I though?' Braithwaite shrugged. 'I wonder where Mags is tonight? She lives alone, doesn't she? And, that's right, you went to visit her, didn't you? I can read *The Lion* copy now. In a fit of drunken rage, a crime of passion, the former producer confronted the two researchers who ruined her career and shopped her best mate, killing them with her bare hands and hiding the bodies… how tragic, how sad.'

Braithwaite cackled. 'Now…'

Edward closed his eyes and tried to imagine he was somewhere else. He did not want to hear what Braithwaite was about to say next. He knew what was coming. Everything had been explained. There could be no more stalling. Edward and Violet were about to pay the price. It was time to pray.

'Who should I kill first?'

Edward knew the answer. Of course, it was Violet. The bastard, the evil bastard.

Braithwaite strode over, rubbing his palms together in anticipation.

He stroked Violet, brushing her hair to one side and moving his way to her shoulders.

Edward could see where this was going. 'Stop!' he screamed.

'Touched a nerve, have I?'

Braithwaite was like a snake, hissing and slithering. Violet pinned herself as far as she could against the wall, a fruitless attempt to resist him. Edward could see his lips just millimetres from her neck. Then he pulled away, laughing. Braithwaite pulled on a pair of latex gloves, loaded up the syringe and started to approach Violet.

Sweat ran down Edward's face like a river. 'Don't!'

Braithwaite smirked and made a faster approach. 'Goodnight, Violet.'

Edward could only watch on in horror: he tried with all of his strength to wiggle, slither and fidget his way over, desperately shuffling all of his limbs in whatever way they would move. But it was no use.

He screamed out and Braithwaite raised the syringe, licking his lips as he struck. Violet was out cold in less than a minute. Though how 'cold' Edward could but speculate: only Braithwaite knew if she still lived.

Braithwaite approached Edward. He knew it was his turn. Minnie and Jessica were clearly not his priority, maybe he'd gotten bored of them.

Edward struggled and screamed as Braithwaite approached him.

'There are no drugs for you, I'm afraid.' He pushed Edward to the floor, directly in front of his car, his legs and his arms still tied with cable wire and duct tape. 'Now I'm going to crush you as casually and as brutally as I would a beetle.' He twisted his neck and licked his lips once again.

Edward could not take his eyes off Violet. He searched for a sign of life but he could barely see any detail through the car window. *Please be alive*, he begged, silently, *please don't be dead*.

'Lie down,' Braithwaite said, pointing to the small gap between the back of the car and the doors which led to the basement of the studios. Edward didn't want to submit but he knew it was pointless. His brief hesitation earned him a forceful shove from Braithwaite; he was far stronger than Edward had anticipated.

'You're going to have to wait until I've cleaned up, old chap,' Braithwaite said, imitating Edward's well-spoken manner, pointing to the drugs cabinet and the two girls. 'You see, we're off to the airport. There might be space for you in the boot of course, but I might have to cut you into pieces if you won't fit. Don't worry, though, your bones will be broken by this point, it shouldn't be too taxing a task.'

Edward screamed.

'Oh do shut your trap,' Braithwaite said, laughing. 'I do think we've heard quite enough from you for one day, in fact, I don't think we need to hear from you ever again!' Braithwaite taped Edward's mouth.

Next, Braithwaite scooped up the contents of the drugs cabinet into a bag. He left one syringe and dangled it in front of Edward so he could clearly see what he was doing.

'I best give them a top-up,' he said, moving first towards Jessica Butler. 'I don't want them stirring halfway through the journey.'

How could Edward have allowed this to happen? All this time he'd been so sure that Michael was behind it all and he'd pursued him doggedly, falling right into Braithwaite's trap: at that moment he didn't just feel stupid and broken, he was so fraught with guilt that he felt he deserved to die.

Then everything stopped. There was shouting, footsteps.

'Impossible,' Braithwaite whispered. There was fear in his voice.

Then again.

The voices were getting closer. Then suddenly, unmistakable loud bangs; *they couldn't be... bullets?*

Violet looked awful. The colour was slowly draining out of her skin. Edward prayed with all of his might that she wasn't yet dead. He hoped that even if *he* died now, whoever was heading this way had time to save *her*.

Braithwaite ran to the light switch and plunged them into darkness. The seconds ticked by and then somebody tried the door handle. Edward couldn't help himself. He was breathing so heavily. So was Braithwaite. Edward closed his eyes. He felt as if he was going to pass out and when a flash of light turned everything yellow he felt certain, relieved, that he was falling unconscious. It was only when he heard a familiar voice that he felt compelled to open his eyes.

'My God...'

Edward had never heard Mags lost for words before.

44

Edward was sweating. All he could see was Mags with her gun, intensely magnified from the low angle of the floor. He was facing the opposite direction to Braithwaite. He couldn't see him. He didn't know how close he was to starting up the engine.

'It's over, you sick bastard!' Mags screamed. 'I always knew there was something wrong with you but you've surpassed all my expectations. Come out now or I swear I'll do it, I'll fucking kill you.'

'Oh really?' Braithwaite laughed. Mags fired at the roof, without warning. Braithwaite flinched.

'Have you phoned the police?' Mags asked the man standing next to her. It took Edward a few moments to realise it was Mr Griffiths. He dialled straight away.

She assessed the room for a few moments.

'Is she dead?' She must have been talking about Violet.

'Who knows?' Braithwaite hissed. Edward tried to shuffle around so that he was away from the tyres. He had to avoid the firing line and see what was happening. The best he could do was to crane his neck around one of the tyres, pushing it up against the rubber.

Edward could see Braithwaite ever so slowly reaching towards his pocket but his mouth was still gagged, he had no way of telling Mags. Braithwaite pulled out another syringe and Mags screamed.

'Put it down!'

'On the contrary,' Braithwaite said, easing the syringe ever closer to Violet's neck and Edward noticed he was shaking slightly, 'you put down your gun and I don't have to give her another dose. If you take her to the hospital now, she's got a fighting chance, but another dose...'

He might have talked the talk but this time Braithwaite really was as nervous as the bumbling character he'd been playing for so long: his hands were shaking, his forehead soaked with sweat.

'Fuck off, Braithwaite!' Mags screamed. 'The boys in blue are coming, you're not going to get away with this, by fuck you're not and don't think I won't blow your brains out if I have to.'

Apart from his head – about the only movable part of his body – Edward remained still on the floor as his former colleagues drew ever close to one another.

'Drop the syringe,' Mags said.

Braithwaite held his ground.

Mags fired another warning shot at the floor, being careful to aim away from Edward, and Braithwaite flinched.

'Coward!' Mags screamed and then the faintest of noises reverberated through the room, unmistakable noises which signalled to everybody that show-time was almost over. The sirens grew louder and louder, now there were boots on the ground, in the underpass and banging on the garage door from the other side.

'POLICE, this is the police.'

'It's over!' Mags shouted.

Braithwaite didn't think so. He pushed in the syringe. Mags fired the gun. Edward screamed out and the room erupted with armed policemen...

45

Edward was supposed to be asleep. That's what the doctors had told him he needed and yet over the past few days, he'd got barely any at all. The events of the past few months played over and over in his mind even more vividly than they had in the garage. How could he have let this all happen?

Nobody had come to see him.

The police wanted a completely untainted, corroborated account of what had happened, so that meant no contact with anybody until they'd had a chance to talk to him, not even his parents...

When the officers finally attended him at his bedside, he related everything he could, his heart beating as he went, as he wondered whether he should leave out any details, soften his account; potential charges of criminal negligence had crossed his mind.

As the officers got up to leave, promising to be in touch again, a thought that sent shivers down Edward's back, he wondered where he went with his life from here. Braithwaite had died at the scene, Mags from fatal wounds several hours later. When the police entered the garage they were just in time to see her firing her gun at Braithwaite and their first reaction was to disarm her, in any way they could.

Violet had survived the ordeal, the drugs he gave her were only lethal in larger doses. If Braithwaite had been allowed to finish injecting the syringe...

A few moments later the nurse came to see him.

'You're free to go.'

'Oh?'

'Gather your things and keep taking these...' She handed him a prescription. 'To help you sleep.' she explained and pretty soon his travel bag was packed, his bed was being stripped and his name was in the process of being wiped from the board behind him.

As he left the hospital and walked down the long corridor towards the exit, he caught a momentary glimpse of two girls in adjacent beds, asleep. He lingered outside the door for a moment when he realised he wouldn't be seen. Jessica Butler and Minnie Jenkins were both still hooked up to drips with the colour drained from their faces and he couldn't help but notice the tight bandage around Minnie's knuckles where a thumb should have been. Jessica's bedside cabinet was rammed full of flowers, chocolates and get well soon cards. Minnie's table was empty...

As Edward headed to the driveway outside the hospital to wait for his parents to arrive and pick him up, he saw Violet lingering by the bus stop. He walked over.

She was heavily engrossed in a video game on her phone.

'New habit...' she said.

Edward saw his parents pull up on the kerb, on the other side of the road. There was an awkwardness as Edward, and clearly, Violet too, wondered what to do. In the end, she said, 'Goodbye, Edward.'

Edward feigned a smile. He wondered if she'd already started searching for a new job. He had decided that television was not for him. He wanted out, he might even go back to university. It seemed unlikely that he'd ever see her again. And they never had gotten together, properly.

In the distance, a hooter sounded and Edward knew it was time to go.

'Bye, Violet.'

In the end that was all that he could muster.

4 6

He had avoided newspaper headlines since he had been released. And he may have missed this one had it not been for the vendor practically shoving *The Lion* into his left hand as he climbed down the steps of the Tube station.

Handing over the twenty pence, he read:

O'SHEA: 'I'LL RUN AS MP'

Just a few weeks out of prison, tough-talking chat show host Michael O'Shea talks exclusively to The Lion *and announces a sensational new plan to bring his no-nonsense agenda into our lives, by forming his own party and running for parliament.*

'A lot of people stitched me up, good and proper, that much is clear.' Indeed, Michael was exonerated after serving time inside for child sex crimes he did not commit. 'Those people obviously thought that prison was the back of me but they are wrong. My show may have been cancelled – we're already in talks with rival channels, by the way – but prison has fuelled my fire, toughened me up. I'm going to run as an MP for my own party and the campaign starts today. We'll bring back the death penalty, no more benefits, life sentences for anyone caught dealing

drugs and we'll reform the court system. No one should have to go through what I went through. Those f***ers out to get me will pay the pr...'

Michael O'Shea smirked to himself as he necked back his cider, his third can of the day. His dark sunglasses and hoodie were clearly working miracles on the wider public; nobody had yet rumbled who he was, even though his face was plastered right in front of their very eyes. The time would indeed come when he would return, when his glorious public would once again come a-flocking and he would feel truly vindicated. But for now, at least, he had other demons to battle...

THE END

ACKNOWLEDGEMENTS

Like many debut authors, the publication of my first book has been long and arduous. I finished the first draft when I was nineteen and I will be twenty-seven at the time of publication. But as I alluded to in the dedication, this book has endured an even more unusual road than most because it was revised, published and promoted whilst I was abroad in Vietnam where the impact of COVID-19 has been minimal. This has presented me with unique challenges and opportunities and there are therefore many people to thank.

I am grateful to Lou Tompkins who gave me invaluable feedback on the early drafts when we were both students in the English and Drama Department at *Loughborough University*.

I then worked on other projects and pursued a career as a freelancer for magazines and newspapers, working as a sales assistant for a brief period in *W.H. Smith* and then completing a Masters in Early Modern History at the *University of York*.

Following the completion of my MA, I then spent eighteen months travelling. When the pandemic struck in March 2020, I found myself in Vietnam where precautionary measures had been in place for over a month. During our short lockdown of just a few weeks, I found the time and the space to attempt further revisions on the book and I am so grateful to Elka Ray and Janie Glockstein for their advice that ultimately led to me securing the deal with *Bloodhound.*

Alice and her family at Hoi An Sea Village Homestay were incredible hosts during the lockdown and the editing of the book; they cooked me breakfast every morning and helped me make sense of the unfolding situation including on one notable crazy evening explaining why a van with flashing lights and a dozen men in hazmat suits had turned up at the homestay with a government order paper! As you can imagine this was a huge distraction for several days which is now just a distant memory that I look back on with much humour.

My thanks must also go to Emily Carroll, friend-extraordinaire, who kept me sane in 2020, and the other members of the *Cosy Corner* Crew whose breakfast I also highly recommend. I must also thank Lidia, Ms Nghi and Mr Nhan of Da Nang for their friendship and for answering trivial but important questions such as 'where do you buy books in Vietnam?' and 'how do I top up my phone?'

The brilliant cover which captures so perfectly what the book is about was designed by Mel Wolfe.

And of course, I thank my publisher, Betsy Freeman-Reavley at *Bloodhound Books,* my editor Morgen Bailey and editorial manager Tara Lyons. I also thank my Mum, Ooya, Andrew, Nana and Granddad.

Finally, I am indebted to the oh-so-street-wise Ellie Stentiford, another member of the Vietnam crew, for proofreading the book before it went to print and for pointing out that the grandmother who pawned her jewellery for drugs would only be able to afford grams and not ounces of crack.

Because of the unfolding situation with the pandemic you

may well see copies of this book before I do. Whether you are reading a printed or e-book copy and wherever you are in the world, I would love to see some photos. So please do reach out to me via email: mail@harryverity.com or via Instagram: @hverityauthor.

Made in the USA
Middletown, DE
06 March 2021

34895204R00163